We Can Work It Out

ALSO BY ELIZABETH EULBERG

The Lonely Hearts Club
Prom & Prejudice
Take a Bow
Revenge of the Girl with the Great Personality
Better Off Friends

We Can Work It Out

ELIZABETH EULBERG

Point

• 10 9 8 7 6 5 4 3 2 1   15 16 17 18 19 • Printed in the U.S.A.   23 • First edition, February 2015
• Book design by Becky Terhune

For the readers who wanted this story
as much as I wanted to write it.
This book (and Author Elizabeth) wouldn't
be possible without you.

I, Penny Lane Bloom, have a boyfriend.

That's right. The girl who founded The Lonely Hearts Club and swore off boys for the remainder of her high school existence has a boyfriend.

And, no, hell hasn't frozen over.

Now I have a boyfriend I deserve. He's kind, smart, and funny. Oh, did I forget to mention he's hot?

So of course there has to be a *but* . . .

But there's just one teeny, tiny problem.

I am only one person. Believe me, there are a lot of people who think that one Penny Lane Bloom is one too many, but I could use at least three others right now.

I'm the so-called leader of The Lonely Hearts Club and want to spend as much time as possible with my fabulous friends.

But then there's Ryan. (I mentioned that he's kind, funny, smart, and hot, right?)

I so don't want to turn into one of *those* girls. You know the ones I'm talking about — the girls who dump their friends the second they get boyfriends.

I have vowed: That will never be me.

I can balance it all.

I can make the right decisions. Or at least try to.

I've totally got this.

How difficult can it possibly be?

If I Fell

"If I love you too, please don't hurt my pride."

One

It was amazing how quickly things could change.

It was only six months ago that I thought I was in love with one of my closest friends since birth.

Five months since I had my heart trounced on by the lying, cheating dirtbag.

Four months since I started The Lonely Hearts Club as its sole member.

Which means four months since everything changed.

I went from someone with a small handful of close friends to a person with nearly thirty girls who would have my back if I ever needed them (which I often did). There were some people who looked up to me because I stood up for my friends and myself. And, of course, that also meant I was openly ridiculed by other people for going against the grain.

It was all worth it.

And now it had been one month since I'd started dating Ryan. Well, technically, twenty-two days since our first date — not like I was counting or anything. (Okay, I kind of was.)

While I knew that no two relationships were ever the same, I hadn't realized, at first, how different Ryan was from every other guy I'd dated. Although in hindsight, what I had with those guys (more like immature little boys) couldn't really be called *relationships*. There were trips to the movies and pizzas eaten, but that was about it. It was more about having someone to walk down the hallways with, someone to eat lunch with, someone to kill time with after school. Insecurity blankets. None of it ever felt real.

Being with Ryan was different. I wanted to be with Ryan because of who he was, not because he was a boyfriend. And Ryan wanted to be with me for me, not because there was a vacancy for the role of Ryan Bauer's Girlfriend. We liked spending time with each other. It was mutual.

Well, maybe not *everything* was entirely mutual . . .

"Come on, Penny, it's not a big deal." Ryan reached out his hand impatiently. "All couples do it."

While I didn't have as much experience being in a relationship as Ryan, I knew I wasn't overreacting.

Ryan was wrong.

This was a big step.

One that I wasn't sure I was ready for.

Maybe other couples did it all the time, but I wasn't prepared to make such a commitment so soon. We'd only been going out for a few weeks. I didn't want to rush into anything.

There were certain things you couldn't take back.

A smile slowly crept over his face, his blue eyes sparkling with mischief. "Okay, I know how to convince you."

He stepped a few inches away from me as if he needed lots of space for whatever he was preparing to do. He cleared his throat, gave me one more crooked grin before he started clapping rhythmically. *Clap, clap. Clap. Clap, clap. Clap.*

Then in front of the entire food court at the mall, Ryan began singing at the top of his lungs, *"Oh yeah, I'll tell you something, I think you'll understand . . ."* People began to look over to where we were standing, but Ryan was undeterred. He continued to sing even though he had proven on more than one occasion that he couldn't carry a tune. Sure he was everything a girl could want in a guy — but he was also apparently incapable of being embarrassed.

I, on the other hand, wanted to hide behind the mall directory so no one could see my flaming-red face. I knew there was only one way to get him to stop.

"Fine!" I relented. I grabbed his hand and entwined our fingers. "Happy?"

He was grinning ear to ear. "Yes, very happy. Oh, how I love the Beatles."

"Yeah, they'd be so proud." I began to drag him away from the scene of the musical crime. There was no point in telling him that the Beatles hadn't gotten him his way — it was my fear of causing a scene that made me cave. It wasn't that I didn't want to hold Ryan's hand . . . but being out in the open as a couple felt too exposed.

Only a few short weeks ago, I'd been the one telling girls not to date, that all guys were lying, cheating scum of the earth. And while some of them were (hello, dirtbag Nate Taylor), Ryan was wonderful. Public embarrassments aside.

The Lonely Hearts Club had caused such a ruckus at McKinley High that I didn't want it to appear that I was backing down by being with Ryan. The Club was the best thing that had happened to me in high school, and I didn't want anything to mess that up. And I was well aware of how much a guy could mess things up.

We turned the corner to head up the escalators to the movie theater, when I spotted a few of my fellow Lonely Hearts Club members coming down.

"Pen!" Tracy waved at us, and Jen and Morgan perked up behind her.

I instinctively let go of Ryan's hand as they made their way over to us.

"Hey." Tracy hugged me, and her dirty-blond ponytail lightly brushed my cheek. She then turned to Ryan. "Bauer," she said solemnly.

"How're you doing, Tracy?" he said cheerfully, clearly wanting to get in good with my best friend. He already had her approval — she was partially responsible for us finally getting together — but with Tracy you wanted to get as far on her good side as possible.

Tracy made a show of looking him up and down. "I'm doing great, *obvs*. Got my girls, saw a movie, not dealing with *the man*. What could possibly be better?"

"Ah . . ." Ryan had no idea what to say next.

I interceded. "What are you guys up to now? Ryan and I were just . . . um, I saw him —" I stopped myself, not quite believing that I'd been about to make up a story of why Ryan and I were together. I didn't know why I felt like I had to watch what I was saying. These girls were practically my family, and I'd known Ryan for years. I should've been comfortable having us all be together, but I wasn't used to being The Girl Who Now Dates, especially with the girls I'd spent nearly every Saturday last semester with, comparing notes on the evil things guys could do.

"I'll tell you what we're up to." Jen patted her stomach. "Food. Lots of food."

Tracy could sense I was uncomfortable. She tilted her head slightly. "Well, we should get going — there's a cinnamon bun with my name on it somewhere in the vicinity. Have fun . . . but not *too much* fun."

"Oh, we won't," I promised her. Ryan poked my side in protest. "How could anybody have fun without you around?"

"Exactly!" Tracy replied. "See, Pen, you get me. You. Get. Me." She pounded her first lightly against her chest. The group started walking away, but Tracy stood her ground. "Remember, Bauer." She held up two fingers to her eyes, then turned them on Ryan. "I've got my eyes on you." She laughed maniacally while linking arms with Jen and Morgan as the three of them walked away.

"You know she's only teasing," I reminded Ryan.

He ran his fingers through his dark wavy hair. "Yeah, I know. Usually, guys have to worry about making a good impression on their girlfriends' parents, but I've also got to get the blessing of over twenty girls. No pressure."

He used the word *girlfriend* with such ease, as though it was completely clear what we were doing.

It wasn't quite as clear to me. But at the same time, I liked that he used the word without hesitation, unafraid to commit to me.

I grabbed his hand again as we got on the escalator. "Come on, the Club loves you," I assured him. "You know how happy they were when we started dating."

"Yeah, I do," he replied with a gentle squeeze of my hand. "And for your information, my mom's thrilled we're together because it means she has an automatic babysitter on Saturday."

One of the rules of the Club was that we had to have our meetings on Saturday nights, which wasn't really a big deal. Ryan and I would go out on Fridays — and sometimes we spent Sundays together if the Club wasn't up to anything. Neither of us minded.

Tracy's laugh echoed up the escalators. I looked back and saw them all giggling at something.

Ryan studied my face as I watched my friends go off without me.

"Do you want to go hang out with them?" he asked.

"No, it's fine." Although I had to admit I felt a slight sting that I hadn't been included in their girls' day out.

He wrapped his arm around me as we stepped off the escalator. "You're a horrible liar."

"I am?" I leaned into him. "Hey, Ryan?"

"Yes, Miss Penny Lane?"

I exaggeratedly batted my eyelashes at him. "You're a really good singer."

He tickled my stomach, which caused me to respond with a loud shriek. A couple walking in front of us turned around. Before I could protest further, Ryan pulled me in tight and kissed me on the forehead.

Instead of pulling away like I had before, I leaned in even closer. Despite my pangs of jealousy, I knew that I needed to focus more on the here and now. And right there and then, I knew there was nowhere else I wanted to be, and no one else I wanted to spend my Sunday with.

Two

ONE OF THE BENEFITS OF THE educational system doing everything by alphabetical order was that my school locker was only three away from my boyfriend's.

Ryan greeted me on Monday with a quick kiss on the cheek.

"Hey!" I started pulling out my books for class. "And how was your weekend?"

He closed his locker door. "It was okay."

I raised an eyebrow at him. "Just okay? That's weird — I heard that you were out with your amazing girlfriend."

"She's also extremely humble," he fired back.

Eileen Vodak, a freshman member of the Club, approached me. "Hey, Penny, do you know who the guy with Diane is? I saw them in the office — yum!"

"It's probably our new foreign exchange student from Australia," I answered. "I haven't met him yet. Is he hot?"

"I'm *right here!*" Ryan protested.

I rolled my eyes dramatically at him before turning back to Eileen.

She motioned in the direction of the hallway where Diane was now walking with a guy who *was* ridiculously good-looking. Out of respect for Ryan, I tried not to stare.

Even though Diane was no longer a cheerleader, she still walked with an extra bounce in her step and enthusiastically greeted everybody in her path. She was chatting to the guy next to her, and despite the foot difference in height, they could've been siblings: both with blond hair (hers long and wavy, his shaggy) and light blue eyes. The big difference was that his skin was about ten shades tanner than Diane's alabaster complexion.

"Penny!" Diane sang out to me. "I want you to meet Bruce Bryson." She turned toward him. "Bruce, this is my oldest friend, Penny Lane."

His expression lit up. "Like the Beatles song?" I nodded; this was always the question when my full name was used. "Bottler!"

"Ah, thanks?"

"Sorry, that means that I think that's really awesome." He spoke quickly, trying to explain himself. "I sometimes like the old Aussie slang."

"That's cool — or I guess I should say *bottler*. It's great to meet you. Welcome to Parkview, Illinois. I can't imagine you're thrilled about the weather we have for you." I noticed he was wearing about three layers of clothing.

"Yeah, I had a cozzie — er, swimsuit on at Christmas." He smiled to reveal a set of dimples.

I tried very hard not to imagine him in that *cozzie*.

Diane turned toward Ryan. "And this is Ryan, also one of my closest friends, and Penny's boyfriend." It still felt weird to hear Diane call Ryan my boyfriend, since he'd been her boyfriend for four years. She kept insisting that it wasn't uncomfortable for her, but I couldn't help thinking it had to be.

"Nice to meet you," said Ryan, offering a hand to shake. Bruce shook back — universal guy behavior.

We chatted with Bruce for a while and got all the basics. He was from Bondi Beach outside of Sydney, had never been to the US before, was a surfer (which didn't surprise me in the least), and after a semester with us, he was going to meet his family in New York City and then spend the rest of the summer traveling the US.

Diane gently took his schedule out of his hands and started to look it over. "Okay, you've got Spanish with Penny, World History with Penny and Ryan, and Chemistry with me." She continued to scan through as Tracy approached us.

"Hey, Pen, I forgot to ask you —"

Diane interrupted. "Tracy! I'm so glad you're here. I wanted you to meet the new exchange student from Australia, Bruce. You've got English with him this afternoon."

Tracy looked over at Bruce. "G'day!" she said in an exaggerated accent.

He laughed. "G'day to you, Tracy!" He scratched his head, causing his messy hair to stick up on one side.

"Welcome to Up Over, I guess." She gave him a quick smile before turning her attention back to me. "Anyways, Pen, I completely forgot to ask you about our Trig homework."

It was a little inconceivable. Tracy was standing next to a guy who was not only totally her type but who had her full attention. And she was brushing him off.

The Club had worked its magic on all of its members, especially Tracy. Six months ago, Tracy would've put Bruce at the top of her annual list of potential boyfriends, only to end up crossing him off for one petty reason or another. That list had brought her nothing but heartbreak, and now her focus was on her friends and being happy without a guy. Which was great, but still . . .

I wasn't the only one who noticed Bruce staring at Tracy as she looked over my notes. Diane raised her eyebrows at me, and I stifled a laugh. Tracy would've killed us if she'd known what we were thinking.

Once Diane realized that Tracy's attention wasn't going to come back to her guest, she moved on. "Well, I'd better get you to your first class," she told Bruce.

Bruce nodded. "It was great meeting you all."

"You, too — see you *en Español*," I replied.

Bruce leaned closer to Tracy, who was now sitting on the floor, quickly copying my notes before class. "See you around, Tracy?"

"Yep." She didn't even look up. "See you later, shrimp on the barbie, dingo ate my baby, and all that."

Even though Tracy was just being Tracy, Bruce took her jabs at Australian stereotypes as flirting. He walked off with a satisfied smile, pausing a few times to look back at her.

"Okay." Tracy closed her notebook and got up. "I'm as ready as I'll ever be."

I said good-bye to Ryan, and Tracy and I started heading to Trig. "So what do you think of Bruce?" I asked.

"He seems nice enough." She shrugged. "Do you think we're going to have a pop quiz? It's only the second week back from winter break — that'd be too cruel, right?"

Tracy's quick dismissal of a cute boy was just more proof of how much had changed in so little time.

There was never an agenda for The Lonely Hearts Club as we sat together every day at lunch. It was solely time for us to catch up. Sometimes we helped someone out if she had a problem (many times in the past, that had been me) or planned an upcoming meeting. As the group of over twenty-five members started to file into the cafeteria for lunch, we moved tables over to make room for everybody: freshmen, sophomores, juniors, and seniors.

We were all into our lunch and gossip of the day when an unexpected visitor descended on our table.

"G'day, ladies," Bruce greeted us. "Would you mind if I joined you?" While Bruce sounded relaxed, his hands were tightly clenching his lunch tray. I couldn't really blame him for his nerves. We were a little intimidating as a group.

Our table had been buzzing with voices and energy a second before, but now had gone eerily silent. We'd never had anybody from the outside join our table. Even the boyfriends didn't eat lunch with us. It wasn't an official rule, just how it was.

When no one answered, Bruce took a nervous step back. While all eyes on the table were on me to make a decision, my own eyes quickly swept the cafeteria. It was partly to see if there was a better place for him to sit and also to see if anybody else had noticed our predicament. There were a few people studying the table. At the jocks-and-cheerleaders-only table, Ryan's boorish best friend, Todd, was nudging their friend Brian, pointing out Bruce. Todd's cocky laughter sealed Bruce's fate.

"Of course." I began to make room for him. "Come sit between me and Tracy."

"Cheers," he said gratefully. "I appreciate it. Hope I'm not interrupting anything."

The group continued its silent study of our guest, which in turn made him self-conscious again. He hardly looked up as he played with his sandwich.

"So . . ." I said, racking my brain for small talk. "How was your day so far?"

"It was good." He took a bite but still refused to look up, which was wise since all eyes were on him.

I gave a warning look to the group, and a few resumed their conversations. "Well, I'll take you to Spanish after lunch, and then we have World History, so you're stuck with me for a bit."

"Sounds great." He looked to his other side. "How was your morning, Tracy?"

She took a long sip of her soda. "It was school. So do you miss your pet koala back home?"

I could see the back of his neck turning a light shade of crimson. "Um, no. Koalas are an endangered species. We have them in sanctuaries for the most part."

"Really?" Her lips turned up into a smirk. "Are you related to any hobbits, then?"

"Ah, those movies were filmed in New Zealand . . ."

I jumped in. "She's only teasing." It was unclear whether he genuinely didn't realize this, or if Tracy made him nervous because he was smitten. I was really hoping for the latter. It wasn't that I wanted Tracy to date, but it was about time someone liked her. And if that someone was the hot foreign exchange student, even better.

Tracy went back to talking with Morgan. Luckily, Diane was across from Bruce, so the three of us carried on a discussion about Australia, the US, and McKinley High, and avoided the very large elephant in the room: the Club.

Later, as we gradually began to disperse, I headed back to my locker to get my books. When I turned the corner, Ryan was shaking his head at me.

"What?" I asked, although I already knew where this was going.

"So" — he twirled a piece of my hair around his finger — "I see what it takes to get an invite to your lunch table: an accent."

I swiped his hand away. "What was I supposed to do? It was so awkward."

He laughed. "Oh, really?"

"Thanks for inviting him to sit with you guys," I replied dryly.

He folded his arms. "So you'd rather have him sit with Todd?"

He had a valid point.

Bruce was going to meet Todd in Spanish class, so I knew I had to tell him about the Club before he got some demented version of the story from Todd Chesney.

Todd and I used to get along. He was your typical playful jock who walked around like his only care in the world was scoring on and off the court. He had dated practically every girl in our class, and he'd set his sights on me right as I formed the Club. He did not take rejection well. As the Club took off, he harbored a lot of resentment toward me, which ended up in an altercation between us after what had been an otherwise insanely fun karaoke night. While he had since apologized for his drunken behavior, things hadn't been the same between us. And I doubted they ever would.

Bruce met up with me as I was walking toward class. "Hey, sorry about lunch," he said.

"There's no need to apologize." Which was the truth.

He looked around the hallway. "I felt like I was intruding. But I saw a big table of girls, and what guy wouldn't want to sit there?"

"Yeah, so there's something you should know." I figured now was the best time to tell him, but I never knew exactly what to say. *So there was this guy I'd been in love with since I was a kid and he broke my heart. I decided to form The Lonely Hearts Club and stop dating for the rest of my high school existence. Then others joined, a revolution took over the school, egos were bruised, fights were had, and in the end we decided that guys are okay to date as long as they aren't jerks.*

Maybe it was that simple?

I gave him the brief history, then said, "Originally, we sort of swore off dating; you know, boys are stupid and all that."

He nodded. "As a boy, I get it."

"But then we rethought things a bit."

"I figured, since you have a boyfriend."

"Yes." I paused before we entered class. "So we have some rules. We hang out on Saturday nights, have meetings at lunch, and do a lot of events together, basic *we are girls, hear us roar* type things." I silently cursed myself for speaking so flippantly about the Club to him. We were much more than that. I shouldn't have felt the need to downplay it.

"Sounds cool," he said. "It's for girls only, then?"

"Yeah, afraid so."

He looked thoughtful. "You know, girls aren't the only ones who've had their hearts broken."

I didn't have a response. I knew that was true, but I also wasn't prepared to open up the Club further. Adding boys to anything always brought on trouble.

I motioned for him to enter the classroom. Before I even had a chance to introduce him to our teacher, Todd came barreling in.

"Well, well." His arrogant smirk instantly infuriated me. "Are you going to introduce me to your new member, Penny? Who's the fellow lesbo?"

Standard Todd. Anytime a girl joined the Club or turned him down for a date, he automatically assumed that she was a lesbian. Because why else would a girl not want to deal with his crap? Further proof that he was a complete and total moron.

"Just ignore him," I said to Bruce.

But Bruce refused to let Todd get the better of him. "Hey, mate, I'm Bruce — the guy who managed to sit with loads of amazing ladies at lunch today. See ya around." He walked away, leaving Todd without a proper comeback. Bruce went to introduce himself to our teacher while I made my way to my seat, which was unfortunately still next to Todd. The alphabetical system could be as much a curse as a blessing.

Todd sat down and turned his back to me, which was what we did now. Still, he made no effort to keep his voice down when he said to another jock, "I guess British dudes would rather hang out with lesbians than real men. Loser."

Todd never inconvenienced himself with facts.

I knew that Ryan and Todd had been friends since they'd played in Little League. We were from a small town, and you kind of become friends with whoever was on your team or on your block. Still, listening to the crap spewing from Todd's mouth, I was thinking that maybe it was time for Ryan to be given a reminder that, unlike family, you *can* choose your friends.

Three

WHILE MY BIRTHDAY DIDN'T FALL ON Christmas or New Year's Eve, I could sympathize with people who had to share their birthday with a big holiday. Because in the Bloom household, February 7 wasn't only my birthday, it was the anniversary of the Beatles' arrival in the United States.

For years my sisters and I believed my mom refused to push so I'd be born on my parents' favorite day of the year. That might sound crazy, but my Beatles-obsessed parents *had* named their three daughters after Beatles songs: Lucy (in the Sky with Diamonds), (Lovely) Rita, and Penny Lane. (Thank goodness they stopped at three, or I might've had a poor little sister named Eleanor Rigby.)

While my parents' love of the Beatles had passed down to me, my sisters were more resistant.

"You're being so stubborn, Lucy!" Mom said into the phone, gesturing wildly to my father, who was on the other line.

"Now, Luce," Dad began, "promise us that you'll think about it."

Mom glared at him. I kept my head down while I finished washing the dishes from dinner.

Lucy's upcoming wedding was making everyone tense. This particular argument wasn't about the usual wedding-related things like seating charts, food, or flowers. No, this fight was over my parents' insistence that a Beatles song be used for Lucy and Pete's first dance. The current compromise was that Dad and Lucy would have their father-daughter dance to "In My Life," which would've satisfied most people.

My parents, however, were not most people.

"Now you're just being ridiculous," Mom groaned. "Remember who's paying for this wedding!"

I sat down at the kitchen table and flipped through the RSVPs, recognizing a mixture of family and friends. The names that didn't register were all from the East Coast, where Lucy's future husband was from.

"Well, I guess we'll talk about this when you're home next weekend," Mom said with a sigh.

I did my best to contain the amused expression surfacing on my face. At some point, my parents had to realize that while *their* wedding had included only Beatles music, posters, and groomsmen's outfits similar to the ones the Beatles wore during their famous *Ed Sullivan Show* debut performance, most other people would show some restraint.

Mom collapsed on the chair next to me after hanging up the phone. "Now, Penny Lane, you'd better not give us any fuss over your birthday. You know the drill."

I quickly agreed because I did know better. The traditional "Happy Birthday" song has never been sung in the Bloom house. I doubt my parents even know the words. No, the only

Dave-and-Becky-Bloom-endorsed song for birthday celebrations was the Beatles' "Birthday." And as much as it annoyed Rita and Lucy, I absolutely loved it.

"So what's the plan, kiddo?" Dad asked as he sat down across from me, a stack of new RSVPs in hand.

"Well, my birthday's on a Saturday this year, so the Club will be over. I figured we could do a cake. I don't really need anything special." Which was true — all I needed was the Club.

"What about Ryan?"

"He's taking me out to lunch." I'd debated asking him along that night, but I didn't want him to feel uncomfortable. Plus, I wasn't going to bend the rules for my benefit, even if it was my birthday.

"That sounds like a fun day," Dad answered. "Ryan's coming to the wedding, right?"

I looked up at my dad. I hadn't even thought about that. Ryan and I had only been dating for four weeks, and the wedding wasn't for another six.

Before I had a chance to respond, my dad lit up and said, "Ah, here's the Taylors' RSVP."

I instantly felt sick to my stomach. I had forgotten that the Taylors were invited, and I was pretty sure my parents weren't going to exclude Nate, the jackass son who'd stomped on my heart.

Mom looked down at the guest list. "They're coming, right?"

I realized I was holding my breath.

Dad looked down at their response. "Yep, two chicken and one beef."

Our dads were best friends, so I had known our paths would eventually have to cross. But I didn't want it to be at such an important family event.

Actually, I didn't want it to be under *any* circumstance.

"Ah, Dad?" I finally found my voice. "Ryan *is* coming to the wedding."

"That's great, Penny Lane!" He winked at me as Mom added his name to the list.

Yes, it was great.

I knew I could handle myself around Nate — I had proven that at Thanksgiving, when I'd finally told him off.

But it was always good to have backup.

The second I mentioned the wedding to Ryan, I realized how silly I'd been for not inviting him sooner.

He was still excited when we arrived for our double date Friday night with Morgan and Tyson.

"It's just so *public*," he teased. "Does this mean you're going to allow me to dance with you? *In front of people?*" He opened his jaw in playful exasperation.

"You are aware that I can take back that invitation at any time," I reminded him.

"You wouldn't!"

"Try me," I dared.

"Okay, I won't press my luck."

"Smart move."

"But that doesn't mean I'm going to take it easy on you tonight. Prepare to be schooled." Ryan then began doing what I could only assume was the running man, with arms and legs flailing everywhere.

It was dorky, yet totally endearing.

"Yes, well, I guess you showed me." I held up my hands and waved them exaggeratedly. "I'm *so* nervous."

Ryan stopped dancing. "Just remember this next week."

"What's next week?"

He looked at me like I should have known what he was talking about. "We're going to that indoor mini-golf place with my sister. On Wednesday."

"Oh, no." I felt horrible. "I completely forgot. I agreed to try out that new Chinese restaurant with a few of the girls."

"Okay," he said with measured understanding. "How about next weekend sometime? Clearly not on Saturday night."

"Sure." Then I realized what next weekend was. "Wait, Lucy's home next weekend. We have family stuff, and then she's meeting the Club."

"Oh," he said flatly, no longer hiding his disappointment. "Well, I'd really like to meet her, too, if there's time."

I started going over next weekend's schedule in my head, but there was something wedding- or Club-related pretty much every second.

"What about the following week?" I offered, even though I knew how lame that sounded.

"Since I'm dating such a popular girl, I'll take what I can get." He laced his fingers through mine, and we walked into the arcade, where Morgan and Tyson were already playing skee-ball.

While some people assumed that The Lonely Hearts Club allowed dating solely so I could go out with Ryan, it was actually because of Morgan and Tyson. While I was in my "all guys are evil" phase, Tyson was assigned to be my biology lab partner. At first I let his long black hair and rocker attire paint him in my mind as a shallow guy who only cared about his band. But the more I got to know him, the more I realized what a sensitive and brilliant musician he was. When he let me know that he had a crush on Morgan (who'd had a crush on him since freshman year), I realized it wasn't fair to let my bad experiences cost Morgan and Tyson their happiness.

Watching them laughing and playfully trash-talking, I knew the change to the Club had been for the best. It also didn't hurt that I got to go out with Ryan.

Morgan had one last skee-ball remaining. She stretched out her arms, put her long black hair up in a ponytail, and grabbed the ball. "And now, Two-Time Skee-Ball Champion Morgan Stephens needs only twenty points to win the game. Can she do it?"

She paused dramatically before rolling the ball up the ramp, where it landed perfectly in the fifty-point hole. Tyson groaned, while Morgan took the tickets from both of their machines. "I believe these belong to me."

Tyson's disappointment quickly faded as he pulled Morgan in close for a kiss.

"Good job!" I gave Morgan a high five. "These boys need to be shown how it's done."

"Are you willing to take on the champion?" she dared me.

"Please." I took out my quarters and slid them into the machine. "Challenge accepted."

Morgan and I played three rounds, and she kept her winning streak intact, her ticket pile growing by the minute.

"So can I talk to you for a second?" she said when we were done. Her gaze wandered over to the corner where Ryan and Tyson were shooting hoops for prizes.

"Of course." Her tone made me worried.

Morgan hesitated, nervously playing with her leather cuff bracelet. "I've been thinking a lot lately about taking the next step with Tyson — you know."

It took me a second to realize what she was taking about. In a way I did know. It was Nate's continual pressure on me to take that next step that had led to the demise of our relationship, or at least to the revelation that he was a cheating snake.

"Okay." I prodded her to continue. I didn't feel like I could contribute much since I had zero experience when it came to actual sex, but it was clear that Morgan needed to talk.

"I know we've only been dating for a few months, but he's a senior. I don't want to wait until he leaves. And I also didn't want to be a big cliché and do it after Prom. I don't know."

"Well . . ." I tried to stall since I had no idea what to say next. "I guess . . . if you're not sure, you should probably wait until you are."

She nodded thoughtfully. "You're right. I do know that I want it to be special. I don't want to make this a Club issue or anything, but I wonder if there's someone I should talk to?"

"I know that Amy has . . . experience." The fact that I couldn't say "lost her virginity" or "had sex" out loud made it clear that I was not the right person to have this important conversation with. "But if I remember correctly, it wasn't that great. I'm sure someone else has done it with better results; that information wasn't exactly on the Club's registration form."

"It wasn't? That's a shame." She laughed. "Well, I really appreciate you listening."

"Of course, anytime. You know that." Even if I was completely inadequate on the subject.

"So what about you?"

I responded with my most mature "Huh?"

"Have you and Ryan talked about . . . ?" She let the thought hang in the air.

"No!" I said with a little too much horror. The way I was handling this conversation made it painfully clear that I wasn't ready to take that next step. I tried to fight the memories of Nate's betrayal as they surfaced. I could still practically hear the echoes of Nate and that girl's cruel laughter when I caught them.

Of course this now had me wondering if *Ryan* was considering it. I knew he and Diane had planned to do it, but never went through with it.

"Hey!" Tyson came over to us, followed by Ryan, who was clutching a stack of tickets. "What are you two talking about?"

"NOTHING!" Morgan and I shrieked in unison. We were so busted.

Tyson laughed. "Okay, okay, I get it. Girl stuff."

I actually didn't think he got it at all.

Morgan looked at Tyson's empty hands. "So I take it that the game didn't go well?"

Tyson gestured in defeat toward Ryan. "I should've known better than to challenge a jock to a sports game."

"I did warn you." Ryan put his arms around me and I bristled a little at his touch. He pulled back, sensing my discomfort. "We can do a guitar game if you feel like that would even the score."

Tyson scrunched up his nose. "Playing guitar in a video game and in real life are two completely different things."

Morgan decided to up the ante. "How about the three of us play the guitar game and I'll school you both? Loser buys the pizza."

There was no way Tyson and Ryan were going to take that from Morgan.

As we headed over to their game, Ryan pulled me in close. "Everything okay? You seem a little distant."

"Yes, I'm fine," I lied.

He stopped walking and faced me. "Listen, Bloom, you forget that I know you well. You've got that look on your face that means you're either confused or worried, maybe a bit of both. So again I'll ask, is everything okay?"

I looked at Ryan and couldn't help the smile that spread across my face. I was being silly, worrying over a conversation that didn't need to happen for months, maybe even longer.

The best part of dating someone you've known practically your entire life is that you know what kind of person he is. Ryan would never force me to do anything I wasn't ready for. I was stressing for no reason.

I leaned into him. "Everything's great." Then I surprised him by planting a kiss on his lips.

"Wow!" he exclaimed once I pulled away. "That was awesome and *so public.*"

I ignored his (completely justified) teasing and dragged him by the hand to where Morgan and Tyson were waiting.

"Okay, guys, I'm in." I reached into my jeans pocket for change. "And fair warning: My parents pretty much require Beatles Rock Band family game night on a weekly basis. Get ready to hand over those tickets and buy me some pizza."

Ryan may have been the jock, Tyson the rocker, and Morgan

the gamer, but none of them had anything on me during that game.

I used my winnings to get Ryan a mini basketball with the Chicago Bulls logo. It seemed like a girlfriend thing to do . . . and I figured it was as good a time as any to start being a better girlfriend.

Four

DIANE, TRACY, AND I KEPT STARING at my computer screen on Saturday night like it was some sort of mistake. Or a cruel prank.

"Is this for real?" Diane asked.

"I think so," I replied cautiously.

Diane began to read aloud the message I'd gotten on my profile page: "'Dear Penny Lane, you don't know me, but I've heard a lot about you. The article that ran in your school paper about your club has made the rounds among my friends. You've inspired us to start our own chapter of The Lonely Hearts Club at South Lake High School. I was wondering if you could share more information about your club, like your rules. Or since we're only an hour away, maybe we could bribe you with food to talk to our club? I'm sorry if this is out of the blue, but I thought it wouldn't hurt to ask. Hope to hear from you soon and THANKS, Danielle.'"

Tracy finally spoke. "This is AWE to the SOME, guys! I mean, it's spreading for real. We totally have to share the rules, and maybe we should start a page for the Club and go global!" She leaned in to read the message again. "Yeah, we're so doing this. Send her my rules. It's my finest work, and it *totes* deserves to go viral."

I took the sheet of paper from the corkboard over my desk that contained the rules we'd implemented shortly after Thanksgiving:

The New and Improved Rules of The Lonely Hearts Club

Heretofore are thy official rules for members of "The Lonely Hearts Club." All members must agree to such terms or thy membership shall be struck from thy record.

1) Members are allowed to date, but must never, ever forget that their friends come first and foremost.

2) Members are not allowed to date jerks, tools, liars, scum of the earth, or basically anybody who doesn't treat them well.

3) Members are required to attend all Club meetings on Saturday nights. No member shall wuss out on attending due to a date with a boy. Exceptions are still for family emergencies and bad hair days only.

4) Members will attend all couple events together as a group, including, but not limited to, Homecoming, Prom, parties, and other couply events. Members may choose to bring a boy with them, but said male attends event at his own risk.

5) Members must first and foremost be supportive of their friends, no matter what choices they make. What matters most is for us to stick together.

6) And most of all, under no circumstances shall anybody take what is said in the Club and use it against someone. You all know what I'm referring to.

Violators of the rules are subject to membership disqualification, public humiliation, vicious rumors, and possible beheading.

I took the piece of paper with me as we headed to the basement (or, as my parents insisted on calling it, The Cavern). We rarely had anything on the agenda these days; mainly we ate food, watched movies, and chilled. I was thrilled to have something for us to discuss.

My parents had gotten so used to the constant ringing and knocking at our door around seven o'clock on Saturdays that they left the door open for the girls to come in and make their way down to the basement. We were usually packed by ten after, and that night was no exception.

I couldn't wait to share the news with everyone. While Diane, Tracy, and I had greeted the message with hesitant excitement, the Club was cheering before I could even get the last line out.

"Road trip!" senior Laura Jaworski called out to a round of applause.

"Really?" I replied, still feeling like it could be some sort of hoax.

"Hells, yeah!" Tracy looked at me as if I'd gone mad, then quickly took control. "Okay, let's get a page up ASAP. Who wants to be in charge of that?"

Meg Ross, the senior who'd written the article Danielle had mentioned, raised her hand. "I think once that page is up, we should all post links to it. Our group can probably reach out pretty wide in the Midwest, and we'll see what happens from there. But I think instead of us going to them, we should make people come to us."

"Yes!" Diane agreed. "We could hold an event for people interested in the Club. Remember how much fun we had planning that karaoke night? We need to do more stuff like that."

It came to me as everybody started chattering about an event. There was a night coming up that single girls everywhere dreaded. It would be the perfect time to host a Lonely Hearts Club event. And it was falling on a Saturday this year.

I raised my hand sharply and was taken aback by how quickly everybody quieted. I said only two words: "Valentine's Day."

There was so much commotion that I glanced at the door, sure that Dad was going to come down to see what all the excitement was about.

We had briefly talked about what we were going to do as a group this year for Valentine's Day — buy each member a rose, go out for a big group dinner, come back and have a Girls Rule dance party — but this topped them all.

We didn't even need to take a vote.

Work started immediately on our official page. Tracy was already drawing possible logos. One group was tasked with coming up with a list of locations for the event since, if it took off the way we all hoped it would, there was no way my basement would work. We were already tightly crammed in as it was.

Tracy brought over some designs for me to look at. "Do you realize how big this could get?" she asked. "And Valentine's Day? So perfect."

Diane nodded. "Yeah, although I thought we'd have a party or something and invite the guys. Do you think Ryan will mind not seeing you that night?"

I hadn't even thought about what he and I would do for Valentine's Day. "We can do something during the day," I said. "He'll be okay."

"But doesn't he have to do the same thing for your birthday?"

"It's fine, Diane." I tried to not get annoyed that she was more concerned about me spending time with Ryan than I was. He *knew* the Club was bigger than my relationship with him. It was bigger than any one member.

Tracy's logo designs were good, but none of them really seemed to fit. "Don't get mad," I prefaced, knowing how sensitive she could get when her artwork was critiqued, "but what about taking some inspiration from this."

I walked over to the cabinet that held my parents' records and pulled out *Sgt. Pepper's Lonely Hearts Club Band.*

Tracy took it with a shake of her head and went into the corner.

By the end of the night, we had a page up with a paragraph about the group, the *McKinley Monitor* article, the Club photo we'd taken at our Christmas party, the rules, and a save-the-date for our hopefully annual Valentine's Day celebration.

For the first time in my life, I was actually looking forward to Valentine's Day. And from the buzz that was circulating in the room, I knew I wasn't the only one.

Five

ONE OF THE REASONS I BELIEVE my parents don't mind having nearly thirty girls in their house every Saturday is because that noise is nothing compared to having all three Bloom girls at home.

You could hear the bass pulsating from our house before Tracy even pulled over to drop me off from school on Thursday. "Tell Rita I say hi," she joked.

As soon as I stepped into our house, I was greeted by the Rolling Stones blasting from upstairs.

To my parents, this was nothing short of a declaration of war. Playing the Stones in a Beatles household was like serving a bacon double cheeseburger at a vegan potluck.

"RITA!" Mom boomed from the bottom of the stairs, "YOU TURN OFF THAT RACKET RIGHT THIS INSTANT!"

"Relax, Mom," Lucy's voice came from the living room.

"Lucy!" I rushed into the living room to find my oldest sister looking over the seating chart for the wedding.

Lucy jumped up from the couch when she saw me. "My goodness, Penny Lane, you keep getting taller. Stop making me feel old!" she said as she wrapped her arms around me.

Lucy lived in Boston, and I only got to see her a few times a year. I really missed having her around.

She sat back down and patted the space next to her. "Come here and help your big sis figure out where to put everybody."

I looked over all the circles representing tables and chairs. "Where are you putting me?" I asked.

Lucy tucked her wavy, chestnut-brown hair behind her ear. "You and Ryan will be with Rita over at the wedding party table. I'm assuming you're asking because you want to make sure you're as far away from Nate as possible?"

"God, yes," I replied.

"I'm sorry that he's coming. Mom and Dad insisted. If you told them . . ." Lucy and Rita had the same refrain: Tell Mom and Dad, and Nate will permanently go away. But at this point, so much time had passed, I was convinced Mom would be so angry that I'd withheld it from her, it would be more trouble than it was worth.

Mom walked into the living room and gestured at the sound of Mick Jagger's voice. "Penny Lane, go up there and get your sister. I will not allow that *noise* in our house. Plus, your father and I need to speak to you three."

I went upstairs and knocked on Rita's door before opening it. Rita was lying on her bed with her back to the door. "Relax, Mom," she griped. Then she made a big production of turning down the volume.

I did my best impression of Mom. "For the love of Paul and Linda, I thought I raised you better!"

Rita turned around. "Hey! You're home! What are we doing this weekend besides boring wedding stuff?"

"I need you to help the Club figure out where to have our Valentine's party."

"Still no luck on the venue?" She frowned.

I shook my head. "All the places large enough are either too expensive or already booked for Valentine's Day couply stuff."

"It's discrimination!" Rita said with as much righteous indignation as she could muster.

"That's what Tracy said."

"That's why I love that girl." Rita linked her arm with mine and we headed downstairs to where Mom and Dad were waiting for us. Rita and I sat next to Lucy on the couch, with Rita in the middle. It was an automatic reflex since our parents always had us sit at large family events in chronological order. The three of us shared the same hair color, complexion, button nose, and Beatles-inspired name. It was easy enough to get us confused, especially when we were younger.

"All three of my girls home," Dad said with a wistful expression on his face. "I'm a lucky man."

Mom could hardly control herself. "We have great news!"

When Mom got this excited, it usually meant that Paul McCartney was performing in concert nearby.

"As you know, your father and I go crazy every year thinking of new ideas for our Christmas card." Her tone turned serious, as if the Bloom Christmas card was a matter of national security.

"Yes, you only go crazy about the Christmas card," Rita said dryly, before Lucy nudged her to behave. Nobody wanted Mom to fly off the handle. Her temper was especially short with the wedding approaching. "It's January — why are we even talking about next year's card?"

"Because we need to make sure we include Lucy's special day in our card."

"Please." Lucy held out her hands. "Don't let something like my wedding get in the way of a Bloom holiday tradition. And I mean it, *please*."

Our family Christmas cards always had us re-creating Beatles album covers or famous Beatles performances like the first one on *The Ed Sullivan Show* or their last concert on the roof of the Apple headquarters in London. I'd really screwed things up when I came along since my parents had to work with five people instead of four. When I was a baby, I was used as a drum set, then as a speaker. By the time I got tall enough, I could be a microphone stand or a piano. It was wonderful for my self-esteem.

With over twenty family cards, it had become more difficult each year for my parents to come up with something. We've done every album cover but one.

"Oh my God," I said, realizing what they were going to do. "You've finally figured out how to do the White Album."

"Yes!" Mom clapped her hands excitedly. "Your father came up with it last night. I called the photographer and set it all up."

Lucy groaned. "You can't be serious? It's my wedding!"

"Oh, relax," Mom said, dismissing her. "We're going to do it at home before we leave for the church. Tell them, Dave!"

Dad sat up in his chair, his voice laced with excitement. "The photographer is bringing a white backdrop. Lucy will be in her dress; the rest of us will dress in white — only for the photo, Luce — with white gloves. So the only thing that will stand out will be our heads. Then, in the corner it will simply say *The Blooms* in gray." He beamed, clearly pleased with himself.

I had to admit that it sounded pretty awesome, but I also knew that when it came to anything Beatles-related, I was in the minority of my sisters.

"Absolutely ridiculous," Rita responded. "But whatever to make the peace."

Lucy sank her shoulders in defeat. "Fine. But the life-size Beatles cutouts stay at home during the reception. *And* the ceremony." Lucy realized the importance of not giving my parents any wiggle room. "I'm serious."

"Okay," Mom relented. "Give us this picture, and John, Paul, George, and Ringo will stay home."

Rita whispered into my ear, "Remind me to elope."

While I wasn't sure whether Lucy regretted not eloping, it didn't take long to know that she was disappointed in one thing.

Her dark brown eyes swept the basement. "Why on earth did I never think of this?"

It was Lucy's first time meeting The Lonely Hearts Club. She came at a very busy time for us, three weeks away from Valentine's Day.

Diane stared at the list of crossed-out venues. "I could see if my parents would let me clear out our garage . . ."

It wasn't only that we were worried about how many people would come; we didn't necessarily want to advertise one of our homes online. We didn't really know the people who'd actually be showing up.

"There's got to be some place we aren't thinking of." Kara reached into her backpack and took out a huge book.

"What's that?" Tracy gestured at the four-inch-wide yellow book.

"It's the yellow pages," Kara replied. When Tracy returned a blank stare, she continued, "It lists companies by product or service. I figure it couldn't hurt to skim through it."

"Guys!" Meg exclaimed from where she was working on the web page with Hilary and Annette. "We already have 426 likes on our page, and someone in Mexico asked if we could live stream the event!"

"Are you serious?" I ran over to verify because I couldn't fully understand what she was saying. "What exactly do people think this is? And how did someone in a foreign country even find out about this?"

Tracy shrugged her shoulders. "Technology."

"Well, there won't even be an event if we can't figure out where we can have it," Diane reminded us.

I felt hopeless, but I didn't want to give up. If The Lonely Hearts Club could have such a positive effect on the people in this room, I couldn't imagine what would happen if it expanded.

The vibe in the basement had deteriorated to a desperate lull. I walked over to the entertainment cabinet. "I think that might be enough for tonight. Let's put on a movie."

"I don't mind working on the website more," Meg offered.

More people piped up that they wanted to continue. While I probably should've felt guilty for being the only person who wanted to call it a night, I was overwhelmed with how much everybody wanted to try until we had exhausted all possibilities.

We continued to research venues and brainstorm ideas of what to do if this party actually took place. There was an excited buzz in the room . . . until all of a sudden it went silent.

Meg stopped typing and looked up. "Ah, Penny . . ." She motioned for me to turn around.

I wasn't really sure what to expect. But the one thing I wasn't prepared to see in the middle of a Lonely Hearts Club meeting was my boyfriend.

"Sorry to interrupt." Ryan shifted uneasily as everybody in the room was staring at him. "I know I shouldn't be here, but it's just . . . I think I found a venue."

"What?" Tracy asked excitedly. "Are you *serious*?"

"Yeah, I was at park —"

Tracy cut him off. "We can't have it at a park — it's February. We'll freeze. Plus, it's so creepy to be all 'Hey, teenage girls, come to a park at night.'"

Ryan continued, "No, I mean P-A-R-C, the Parkview Area Recreation Center. I was volunteering there today when I saw that they had a flyer up for an event that they're hosting in March. So I asked if I could have the space for Valentine's Day, and it's available."

The room began chatting in approval. A lot of us had spent time there as kids, playing after-school sports, taking music lessons, or simply hanging out at their library. It had been so long since I'd been there, I'd nearly forgotten it existed.

"It's not fancy," Ryan said. "But it has a big hall. We'd need to move some of the equipment aside and put down a deposit, which would get returned if there isn't any damage. And we'd have to clean up." He paused, took a piece of paper out of his pocket, and looked it over. "There need to be some adult chaperones, but I know you were already planning to have a few parents attend. Um, and one more thing." He looked worried.

"What is it?" I asked cautiously.

"Well, since I would be the reserving member, I'd have to be there. I could work the door to make sure only people who RSVP'd got in. I wouldn't be in the way at all. I swear."

"Ryan." Tracy shook her head. "First of all, you have saved us. Second, you continue to prove that not all boys are the spawn of Satan, so good on you for that, and third, *of course you can be there*. Right, Pen?"

"Definitely." I went over to hug him. "I can't believe you did this for us."

"I knew you were worried about it, and the answer was right in front of my face." He smiled at me, and my heart leapt and soared, like in all those cheesy songs that I make fun of.

"You're the best. Seriously." I brushed my arm lightly on his shoulder, not wanting to shove my relationship in everybody's face.

"So this is Ryan?" Lucy came up to us.

"Yes!" I made the introductions.

Ryan shook Lucy's hand. "It's great to meet you. I'm excited about the wedding — thanks for inviting me."

"Of course," Lucy replied.

"Well." Ryan looked around the room. "I should probably go . . ."

I walked Ryan upstairs and stole a quick kiss before he left. When I turned around to go back to the meeting, I ran into Lucy, who'd come up to the kitchen to get a drink.

"Let me give you some advice, baby sis." She had a mischievous grin on her face. "Your boyfriend is gorgeous, thoughtful; he *volunteers*, for God sakes. Don't screw it up."

She didn't need to remind me.

Six

RYAN HAD DONE SOMETHING GREAT FOR US. Now I knew it was time to do something for him. Even if I knew it would make for a terrible, horrible, no-good, very bad evening.

"Are you mad?" he asked on Wednesday night as we walked to what I considered to be a punishment. "Because we don't have to do this."

"No, it's fine. I understand where you're coming from." And I did. But that didn't mean I had to like it.

Ryan stopped short of the restaurant door. "Listen, please try to have fun tonight. I get why you wouldn't want to do this, but it means a lot to me."

Which was the only reason I was there.

"I could remind you that I'm not invited to your birthday party or get to spend any time with you on Valentine's Day. I feel like I've been pretty understanding."

"You have," I relented. "I know you've put up with a lot, I do. But we *are* going to be together on Valentine's Day."

"Yeah, surrounded by girls who all want to ban guys. Just the kind of evening every guy dreams of!" He smirked.

"I'll make it up to you," I promised. I looked around before giving him a quick kiss.

"You don't have to make up for anything . . . after this, I promise." He opened the door. "Please remember that he's my best friend."

I took a deep breath before stepping inside to face my sentence for the evening.

A double date with Todd.

He was already at a table with a petite blonde wearing a very short shirt.

"Twenty bucks she's a cheerleader," I whispered to Ryan. I wasn't the type of person who hates on cheerleaders — there are plenty of smart cheerleaders. It was simply that Todd had a specific type. My expectations were also low because I couldn't fathom that a girl with an ounce of intelligence would agree to go on a date with him.

Ryan chuckled in response. But I could tell he was nervous. He knew that Todd and I didn't see eye to eye — and not solely because Todd preferred to stare at my chest than make eye contact.

I tried to shake those thoughts from my head, knowing I needed to make this as easy as possible on Ryan. I would play nice — if only for tonight.

"Hey, Todd," I cheerfully welcomed him. Todd returned my greeting with a suspicious look. Even though he was on a date, he hadn't strayed from his usual attire of athletic team logos, even down to his Chicago Bears sweatpants.

How romantic.

The girl looked up as we approached and gave us a warm smile. "Hi," she said.

Todd motioned his head in our direction. "This is Ryan."

"Hi, Ryan." She gave him a little wave. "I'm Nicole."

I waited for Todd to introduce me, or acknowledge my existence.

"This is Penny," Ryan said, because he was a gentleman. Nicole and I exchanged polite greetings.

I sat across from Nicole, with Ryan to my right and Todd to my left. The table was painfully silent, the awkwardness apparent even to the waiter, who saw us all studying the menu as if it contained a secret code for world peace (I'd be willing to take a stand down at our table) and walked in the opposite direction. I'd never been so jealous of a waiter in my life.

I knew this evening was too important to Ryan for me to give up. "So, Nicole, where did you meet Todd?"

She set down her menu and leaned in. "At a basketball game. I'm a cheerleader for the Winnetka junior varsity team."

"A cheerleader?" I nudged Ryan's knee. "That's *so* great!"

Ryan pinched his lips together, trying to contain a laugh. Meanwhile, Todd decided to eat the entire basket of bread sticks. I wondered what Ryan had done to get him to agree to this.

"How did you two . . . ?" Nicole gestured between Ryan and me.

Ryan reclined back in his chair and motioned for me to tell the story. Like I was going to give the full drama-filled version. "Well, we've gone to school since forever and our lockers are near each other. Ryan *Bauer* and Penny Lane *Bloom*. It really was inevitable. We probably should write the school board a thank-you note."

Something in Nicole's demeanor changed. She quickly looked at Todd. "Oh my God, I can't believe you didn't tell me!"

He answered with his mouth full. "Tell you what?"

"Are you . . . you're not *the* Penny Lane from The Lonely Hearts Club?"

Holy crap.

"Yes!" I nearly shrieked, unable to contain my excitement. I knew Winnetka was only twenty minutes away, but I was still blown away that she knew about the Club.

She leaned in. "I can't believe I'm meeting you. My friends are going to flip. We're thinking about coming to your Valentine's Day party."

Ryan looked so proud. "You should. Penny and her club know how to have a good time."

"And you're the boyfriend?" Nicole pointed at Ryan in a semi-accusatory manner. "I can't believe it. You're really okay with all of this?"

Ryan reached out and took my hand. "Of course I am. It's important to Penny, so it's important to me."

I felt a sting behind my eyes and squeezed Ryan's hand back. "Thanks, Ryan. You know, I . . ."

"Jesus Christ, Ryan." Todd groaned like he was in pain. "You're seriously going to side with Commander Blueballs?"

Ryan gave Todd a warning look. "Of course, I'm really proud of Penny."

Todd snorted. "Please. Can we all stop pretending that she's cured cancer? She formed a stupid club and now has a group of chicks to do her bidding. Whoop-dee-do! Let's all give her self-serving ass a medal."

"I don't —"

Todd cut me off. "Just shut up already. Why does everything always have to be about you?" His short, dirty-blond buzz cut revealed that his entire head was becoming red from anger.

I glared at him. "I'm not the one making this about me. Seriously, Todd, what's so stupid about the Club? Just because you aren't part of something doesn't make it stupid. The Club is many things, but stupid is not one. Amazing is more like it."

Todd threw his napkin down. "I'm so out of here." He abruptly stood up, his chair making a loud noise that echoed inside the restaurant.

"Todd —" Ryan said.

"Forget it, man." Todd started walking away from our table.

"Um, hello?" Nicole called after him. "You're forgetting your date, although it's beyond clear that this is over. Do I at least get a ride home?"

Todd turned around. "Since you seem so interested in The Lonely Losers Club, your little savior can get you home, since she's *so* wonderful." He stormed out of the restaurant, not once looking back.

Well, that went well.

I was stunned. Although I always thought Todd was more than capable of being a scumbag to his dates, I didn't think he'd make it so *obvious.* At least not in front of Ryan.

"I'm so sorry, Nicole," I said. While I knew in the long run it was best for her to get out of a relationship with Todd now, his open and harsh rejection must've stung.

Nicole was still looking at the front door, where Todd had vanished. She began to shake her head. "You didn't happen to start the Club because of him, did you? Because that would *totally* make sense."

"Not him specifically," I said. "But guys who'd done something like what he just did." I turned to Ryan, whose attention was also focused on the door. He probably thought Todd would realize his mistake and come back. His faith that his best friend would do the right thing was touching. Completely wrong and naïve, but still touching.

"Well," Nicole said, "now I *do* want to form my own club. Do you have room for me and a few friends at your party?"

Ryan answered before I could. "Of course you can. I'm really sorry about Todd — you didn't deserve that. Nobody does."

Who would've known that Todd Chesney would become one of the Club's finest recruiters?

Seven

I USUALLY COULDN'T WAIT FOR BIOLOGY to end, but on Thursday I was counting down the seconds.

Last night's disastrous double date only affirmed how lucky I was to have Ryan in my life. I wanted to do something special for him but wasn't really sure what. There was only one guy's opinion that I truly trusted.

"Tyson!" I called once the bell rang.

"What's up?"

"Can I ask you something?" I looked around the hallway. "In confidence."

His face looked serious. "Of course. Is everything okay with Morgan?"

"Yes." I was touched that his first instinct was to worry about her. "I wanted to ask your advice about Ryan."

"Oh." He seemed surprised. "I thought things were good between you guys."

"They are, but I want to do something special for him. I don't know if you heard about what he's done for Valentine's Day . . ." Tyson nodded. "I know I sometimes put him second to the Club and I want him to know that I appreciate him."

Tyson continued walking down the hallway. "Can I be blunt?"

"Of course."

"I honestly think the only thing you need to do is tell him that you care. And act like it."

"Okay." While what he said sounded easy, the expression on his face made it seem that he wasn't sure I could do it.

He shook his head. "I don't think you get what I'm talking about."

Maybe I didn't.

"When we hang out with you guys, it's clear that Ryan's crazy about you. I don't think you really see how he looks at you because you're so busy looking around like you're going to get caught. I notice it, and I'm pretty sure Ryan does, too. What I don't get is that the Club seems to support your relationship, and so do your closest friends. So what's the problem?"

"I don't know," I replied. Which was the truth. I didn't understand why I was always so self-conscious when we were in public. I wasn't so egotistical that I thought people cared about who I was hanging out with. But there was this small part of me that worried that it was all too . . . perfect. My house of cards was perfectly stacked with the Club and Ryan, and one small gust of wind could make it all come tumbling down.

"I'm sorry if I upset you, Penny." Tyson tucked his long hair behind his ear. "I don't know Ryan that well, but I think you have the capacity to break his heart. So be careful."

I could only nod in response. He paused before heading in the direction of his locker.

"Wait!" I finally found my voice. Tyson turned around cautiously. "What do you think of the Club? Honestly? As the boyfriend of a member."

Tyson didn't hesitate. "I think it's great. Honestly. Try to not mess that up, either." He laughed, but I didn't think it was funny.

Could I do both really well without messing one of them up?

My head was still cloudy by the time I reached my locker at lunchtime. I was so lost in my mind that I was ignoring the one person I was trying to be more thoughtful of.

"Earth to Penny!" Ryan was waving his hand in front of my face.

"Hey!" I exclaimed, then got on my tiptoes to kiss him. "How was your morning?"

He was caught off guard by my open affection in school. "Um, much better after that. What's gotten into you?"

"Can't a girl show her boyfriend how much she appreciates him?"

"Yes," he replied. "But why are *you* doing it?"

I pretended to be offended, but we both knew that he had me.

"Don't worry." He had a smirk on his face. "I will never subject you to another double date with Todd. I learned my lesson on that one."

"Thank God. But that wasn't it. I was thinking that since we'll both be busy on Valentine's Day, I'd like to do something special for you that Friday." I figured I had two weeks to fig-ure out what that special thing would be.

Ryan looked disappointed. "I have a game that night. What about Sunday?"

Part of me was grateful that he was the one with conflict-ing plans for once. "Sunday works."

His face lit up. "Great. Can't wait. You know, I might have something special for you as well."

I shook my head with a bit too much force. "You've already done so much, getting that venue for us."

"But I wanted to do something for *you*."

I remembered what Tyson said. "Okay, and uh, Ryan?"

He closed his locker door. "Yeah?"

"I, um, really appreciate you."

He put his arm around me as we made our way to the cafe-teria. "I know, Penny. You don't have to keep thanking me for PARC. I'm happy to help."

"No, that's not — I mean, I, uh, of course I appreciate that, but what I mean to say is that I appreciate things beyond what you do for the Club."

Ryan paused, then turned so he was facing me. "I really like it when you get flustered, so I want to have all my attention on this."

I hit his arm. "I'm trying to tell you that I really care about you, okay?"

We stared at each other. I couldn't believe I'd blurted it out like that.

I felt so foolish. I nearly looked around the hallway to see if anybody was paying attention to us, but I stopped myself. Instead, I took his hand in mine and took a step forward so there were only a couple inches between us.

"Rec center or no rec center, you really mean a lot to me. I, ah, just . . . thought, you know, you should know that." God, I was such a hopeless moron when it came to declarations of affection.

"And you mean the world to me, Penny."

There was a feeling of static electricity in the air as we both inched forward. I silenced the part of me screaming to not make a scene, to not be seen by the people making their way to lunch. Instead, I let Ryan take me into his arms, and relished having his lips on mine.

"That's enough!" a teacher boomed. "No public displays in the hallway."

Maybe I should've checked to see if there were any teachers around first. But being caught was completely worth it.

I was still floating from my lunchtime kiss by the time classes were over. It took me a second to realize that Bruce was waiting for me at my locker.

"Hey, how's it going?" I asked while I gathered my homework together.

"Good, good . . ." He kept shifting on his feet. "I was wondering if I could ask you a question."

"Of course." I stopped fighting with my history book and looked up at him.

"I don't mean to pry, but I overheard Tracy talking about this Valentine's Day party you guys are hosting, and I was wondering if people were allowed to bring dates?"

"Oh. Well, no," I replied, hoping that Bruce and I would someday have a conversation that didn't involve me excluding him from things. After his first-day blunder of sitting with us, he'd since found different people to eat lunch with. I saw him in class, but we never really got to talk that much. "It's more like a way to spread the word about the Club to other towns."

"That's really cool. Do you need any help?" he offered.

We did need a lot of help. "You know, that would be great. Ryan's going to be there, so I'm sure he'd love to have some company that isn't a parent or a girl hopped up on anti-male sentiment."

"Well, on second thought . . ." He started to back away before breaking into laughter. "Only joking. Sounds great."

Bruce's eyes lit up at the sight of something behind me. I was about to subtly brush my chin against my shoulder to see what had gotten his attention, but then I heard that familiar voice.

"Ready to go, Pen?" Tracy had her car keys in her hand.

"Yeah, just talking to Bruce here about the Valentine's Day party."

Bruce smiled warmly at Tracy. "How was your day, Tracy?"

"Standard: morning, afternoon, pretty sure evening will happen or we're all doomed." She took out her phone and began texting.

"You know," I said, "Tracy's in charge of the decorations. And you're tall, so . . ." I turned toward Tracy, who looked up from her phone. "Tracy, I'm going to put you in charge of Bruce."

"Huh?" She was beyond clueless.

"He's offered to help with the party, and I figured you'd need a tall guy for decorations."

"Okay." She nodded at him. "Fine. What to the evs."

"Awesome!" He hesitated slightly. "Do you think I could get your number, then?"

"Sure." Tracy exchanged numbers with Bruce.

I couldn't help being amused by the two of them, one completely smitten while the other was absolutely oblivious.

Then I heard that annoying, nasally voice I had hoped never to hear again. "Bruce, don't let these *things* brainwash you."

Missy Winston. Freshman. Ryan's Homecoming Date. And Public Enemy Number One of the Club. Well, maybe that honor went to Todd. It was hard to tell some days.

"G'day, Missy!" Bruce greeted. "You going to the Valentine's Day party?"

Missy's nose twitched as if she smelled something horrific (my guess was the perfume she bathed in). Then she placed her meticulously manicured hand on her hip. "No, and you really shouldn't hang out with these people, either. You don't want your reputation *ruined*."

Tracy glared at her. "Yes, because hanging with a self-absorbed freshmonster is much better."

"What to the evs," Missy replied.

"Oh, you did not just say that to me!" Tracy stepped closer to Missy, who flinched. I knew Tracy wouldn't hit her — but I'd never known anybody with the nerve to try to steal one of Tracy's sayings and use it against her.

Missy recovered quickly from her moment of cowering. Flipping her overly highlighted and newly chemically straightened hair, she said, "Bruce, you should really spend your evenings with people who know how to have a good time. Not a bunch of pathetic people who can't get a date."

Tracy took another step forward. "Remind me again, how did your stalking of Ryan turn out? Oh, yeah, right, he's with Pen. Because she's awesome and doesn't stink of desperation and cheap perfume."

Missy began walking away as quickly as her five-inch platform boots would allow. Then she called, "Are you coming, Bruce?"

"He's coming with me," Tracy replied, clearly to Bruce's delight. He didn't give Missy a second glance as he obediently followed Tracy. She didn't say where they were going, but he most likely would've followed her anywhere.

Missy watched them leave before turning her attention to me. She studied me suspiciously, probably wondering why Ryan would want someone like me when he could've had her.

"Well," I addressed Missy as I started to walk away from her, "pleasure to see you as always, Missy." I figured with people like Missy, it was best to kill them with kindness. Mostly because I hoped that it would legitimately kill them.

She continued to glare at me in disgust. "Yeah, you, too. Have fun being pathetic with your pathetic friends. I'll be spending Valentine's Day with my date, Todd."

I stopped in my tracks. "You're dating Todd now?" It didn't really faze me that Todd had moved on so quickly from Nicole. He never let anything like people's emotions get in the way of his actions.

"Yes." She smirked, clearly pleased with herself for dating an upperclassman.

"Well, good luck with that," I said before leaving her behind to find Tracy and Bruce.

She was definitely going to need it.

Carry That Weight

"And in the middle of the celebrations,
I break down."

Eight

THE BLOOMS HAD A FEW BIRTHDAY traditions I'd gotten used to in my now seventeen years on the planet. So I shouldn't have been so startled when I was woken up by my parents pulling away the curtains in my bedroom so I could be greeted by a burst of daylight and the blasting of "Good Day Sunshine."

"Wake up, birthday girl!" Mom sang in tune to the harmony.

Dad twirled her around as they began dancing in my bedroom.

Happy birthday to me.

I reluctantly kicked the covers off my feet and got out of bed. They enveloped me in a hug and tried to get me to dance with them, but since I was not fully awake, I escaped to the bathroom to splash cold water on my face.

It was going to be a long morning.

By the time I got downstairs, my parents were dancing around to the *Meet the Beatles!* album.

"Today's the day!" Mom shook her hips while flipping pancakes on the griddle.

I gave her a sheepish smile as I sat down at my usual place at the kitchen table, which had the special plate that was only used on birthdays: a photo of the Beatles eating cake with the caption HAPPY BIRTHDAY TO YOU!

I took a sip of orange juice and began opening cards. There were the standard greetings from aunts and uncles — as well as a red card with a return address that stopped my heart cold.

Nate.

I couldn't believe he thought that I'd still want to exchange birthday cards like we had since we were little. I pulled the card out and was upset to see the front had an illustration of the Beatles dressed up in their Sgt. Pepper's costumes surrounding a girl with a cake. The card read, *You Say It's Your Birthday?*

How dare *he drag the Beatles into this.*

I didn't want to open it, to read what he had to say for himself. But Mom was studying me as she stacked pancakes on a plate, and I couldn't let her know what was going on. So I opened the card and prepared myself for the worst.

> Hey Penny!
> Happy birthday! Do you like the card? I thought of you when I saw it. Anyways, I hope you have a great day. I'm excited to see you at Lucy's wedding. Surely you'll have forgiven me by then.
> Love, Nate

Forgive him? Fat chance.

I quickly placed the card back into the envelope as Dad sat

down next to me. "So, kiddo, how about we open your presents after breakfast?"

"Sounds good," I replied.

Dad picked up my cards and started looking at the return addresses. "Oh, hey, how's Nate?"

I replied by shoving a large piece of pancake in my mouth.

Mom poured herself more coffee. "Now, Penny Lane, just because you have a boyfriend, it doesn't mean you should ignore your friends."

Did she realize who she was talking to?

"I know, Mom." My voice was laced with annoyance. "Have you heard of a little thing called The Lonely Hearts Club?"

She gave me a look that made it clear that I wasn't allowed to be snippy with her, even on my birthday. "But you hardly talk to Nate anymore. You two were so close."

"Yeah, well . . ." I weighed my options. "He wasn't that great of a friend to me last summer. He's actually a big jerk, but I don't want to discuss it any further."

"But, Penny Lane —" Mom began, but Dad mercifully held his hand up to stop her.

He passed me the syrup. "So where are you and Ryan going to lunch today?"

"I don't know." He wanted to surprise me, which only put more pressure on me to figure out what to do next weekend for Valentine's Day.

"Is he coming for today's special ceremony?" Mom asked.

God, no.

"Uh, he has something this morning," I lied. "So he isn't coming until twelve thirty."

"That's too bad; he'll miss it by only a few minutes." She looked genuinely upset.

"Yeah, too bad."

The time Ryan was picking me up wasn't a coincidence. There was only so much humiliation one person could take in front of others. The Club was going to have to witness the birthday dance this evening, so Ryan could be left in the dark when it came to the "ceremony."

I figured I could give myself this one little present on my birthday.

My parents and I stared at the clock in the living room. The mood was serene and reflective (for them — I was antsy, wanting to get it over with).

To my horror, the doorbell rang shortly after twelve fifteen.

Mom jumped up. "Oh, Ryan's here in time! Fabulous!"

Yeah, fabulous.

I went after her. "Maybe he and I should go . . ."

She opened the door and took Ryan by the arm before he even had a chance to say hello. "You're here right under the wire! Quickly!" She ushered him into the living room.

I reluctantly followed, thinking, *Why can't I have a boyfriend who's always late?*

Mom glanced at the clock. "Everybody sit! We're only a couple minutes away."

Ryan sat down next to me with a questioning look.

"Just go with it," I said, aware that my cheeks were on fire from embarrassment. And the ceremony hadn't even begun yet.

Ryan looked amused. "This must be good if you're so horrified."

He had no idea.

Mom held up her hand at precisely 12:19. "I'm so glad you could be with us, Ryan, to celebrate today. This date means so much to so many. It was the start of something great. Something that changed me and Dave, this family, and the world. We are better off because of what happened this day." She began to get choked up.

Ryan smiled sweetly at my mom.

Yes, this would really be sweet if they were talking about my birthday.

She waited for the clock to hit 12:20. Both Mom and Dad were leaning forward as the second hand made its final revolution.

They began counting down, and Ryan followed their lead, caught up in the excitement. I began sinking farther into the seat cushions.

"Five, Four, Three, Two, One — Happy US Beatlesversary!" My parents chanted, right as Ryan mistakenly wished me a happy birthday.

Mom and Dad hugged, then cued up the Beatles' first number-one single in the US, "I Want to Hold Your Hand."

"Oh, I thought . . ." Ryan scratched his head, confused about what he was witnessing.

I began to explain. "The Beatles arrived in the US on this date, at this exact time, back in 1964. My parents do this every year." I glanced up at Mom and Dad, who were lost in their yearly celebration dance. "Let's go. Maybe they won't even notice."

He conspiratorially nodded as we quietly headed for the front door.

"Penny Lane!" Dad pulled me by the hand to dance with me. To my horror, Mom approached Ryan and started dancing with him.

Why oh why couldn't I have been born on February 6 or 8? Or to a sane family?

"Dad," I pleaded to the more rational of my two parents. "Please . . ."

He chuckled. *"Goo goo g'joob!"*

Or maybe not.

I pulled away but danced over to Ryan and saved him from Mom's grasp. "If you tell anybody about this . . ." I warned him.

He was laughing. "Oh, come on, this is pretty fun! They may be celebrating the Beatles, but *I'm* celebrating *you*."

"The best way to get out of this is to play along," I said.

We continued to dance but slowly made our way over to the door as "I Saw Her Standing There" began playing. I waited for the right instant to sing out, "And we are go-ing to lunch." I opened the door, and screamed to Ryan, "NOW!"

Ryan and I bolted out the door to his car. "Hurry!" I gestured at him to start the car, but he was too busy laughing. I kept looking back toward the house. "They might be coming, Ryan! Let's go!"

He was gasping for air. "You're too much. That was hysterical." He took a deep breath and finally got the key in the ignition. "Aw, man, if this is how your birthday is starting out . . ."

Yes, I was aware it was a dubious start. But having the afternoon alone with Ryan gave me hope that things were looking up.

"No, Ryan, we can't," I protested.

He kept guiding me into the restaurant. "Don't be silly, Penny. It's your birthday."

While, yes, it was my birthday, he didn't have to take me to the nicest Italian restaurant in town. The only time my parents had ever taken us to Sorrento's was when Lucy graduated high school. I immediately began doing math in my head of how much money I'd saved between babysitting and working in Dad's dental office. There was no way I was going to top this next weekend for our belated Valentine's Day lunch . . . or dinner . . . or whatever I was going to come up with.

I never thought I would regret having a boyfriend who was so generous, but it really did make it hard to compete with him.

Silly, thoughtful boyfriend.

"I should be wearing a skirt or something," I said as I placed the white linen napkin over my dark jeans.

"It's lunch. You're fine. In fact, you're gorgeous." He gently rubbed my back.

"Thanks," I said. What I wanted to do was say something self-deprecating or joking. But I was determined to be the perfect girlfriend this afternoon — one who didn't look around like somebody in the Mafia afraid of getting whacked.

"So will your mom be re-creating that little ritual for the Club this evening?" he asked, still amused by my parents. It was easy for him to laugh about it; he didn't have to live with them.

"Thankfully, no. But there are other traditions they do today. Right now they're watching the press conference from after the Beatles landed, and then they'll watch the original performance on *The Ed Sullivan Show*, even though that was two days later." I stopped myself, realizing that I was sounding more and more like them. "Anyways, tonight when I have my cake, they'll be singing along to 'Birthday' . . . with choreography."

"Please tell me someone will be taping this."

"Not if that person values her life." I should've stopped there, but he was enjoying the embarrassment of growing up Bloom so much, I decided to throw him an extra bone. "And, well, I actually kinda like it and dance along with them."

His eyes lit up. "Can I please, please renounce my fellow man for five minutes so I can witness this?"

I picked up the menu, hoping the prices would make me less hungry. Plus, it was easier for me to ignore him that way.

"Penny." He jostled my chair. "Fine, but what can a guy do to get a private performance?"

"Have a birthday," I shot back at him.

"But my birthday isn't until November!"

"Oh, well." I shrugged. "Nothing I can do about that."

A crooked smile began to settle on his face. "Or you could make up for the fact that we weren't even speaking on my last birthday. Call it restitution."

I looked at him, about to zing him in some way. But the hopeful look he had in his eyes, the fact that the scales were already tipped so far in his favor as the better half, made me relent.

"Maybe." I offered him some hope. But before he got too excited, I let him know my conditions. "But that means I'm having an appetizer. And dessert."

He laughed to himself. "I wouldn't expect anything less, Bloom."

Sadly, it was probably in his best interest to expect *much* less.

Nine

DIANE WAS THE FIRST TO ARRIVE for the party. She was helping my parents with some sort of "surprise." I had no idea what it was, but I wasn't allowed to go into the basement or look in the refrigerator.

I didn't know what the point was for all the secrecy since I knew everything was going to be Beatles themed. When I was little and going through my Disney princess phase, I once begged and pleaded for an Ariel cake. My parents reacted like I'd asked to be adopted by another family. It really wasn't fair. Rita and Lucy were allowed to have regular birthdays because they didn't share their birthday with the Fab Four.

Diane opened the refrigerator and gasped. "Have you seen your cake?"

I gave her a look that made it clear that I hadn't.

"It's something else."

"I'm sure it is."

"How was your lunch with Ryan?"

"Good." I never felt fully comfortable talking about Ryan to Diane, even though the feeling wasn't mutual.

"That's good. You don't have to feel awkward about it." She coiled a long strand of blond hair around her finger. "You know he's going to tell me anyways, and for your information, he had a wonderful time."

"Well, that's nice to hear," I said. "I think things are really good. Sometimes I struggle balancing everything, but I'm trying to make it all work."

"It's clear that you're trying. Even Ryan's aware of that," she told me, and it stung that they'd apparently discussed this as well. "Don't overthink things. Simply be with him — that's all he wants. It's that easy."

Our moment was interrupted when Tracy walked into the kitchen, holding up her phone.

"First, happy birthday." She gave me a quick hug. "Second, even though it's your birthday, it doesn't mean I can't be annoyed at you for sticking me with Bruce. He keeps texting me. How boring is life in Australia if he's this excited about putting up decorations?"

How thick was Tracy that she had no idea he liked her?

Diane decided to test the waters. "I think he's more excited about helping you."

Tracy gestured down at herself. "Well, clearly," she said, sarcasm oozing from every syllable. "But seriously, I know we let him sit with us at lunch that first day, but he doesn't really owe us anything."

"That's not it." Diane looked at Tracy with such intensity, practically willing her to figure it out on her own.

I decided to press the matter further. "Bruce seems really cool, and he's cute."

Tracy groaned at another beep on her phone. "And he likes to text. A lot."

"What do you think of him, Tracy?" I asked.

She shut off her phone. "I think he needs to get a life."

I opened my mouth to say something else but closed it instead. There was no point in trying to push her. Which was funny, because it used to take everything to get Tracy to shut up about a guy. If only Bruce had arrived last semester . . . although that would've meant that Tracy wouldn't have joined the Club.

"Tracy! Diane!" Mom called up from the basement. "Can you give us a hand?"

They went downstairs to help my parents, while I braced myself for an evening of cake, friends, and parental humiliation.

My parents had certainly outdone themselves this year. And the Club was eating it up.

A grin was plastered on my face all evening as different members of the Club posed with the Beatles cutouts that would *not* be making an appearance at Lucy's wedding. All around the basement were streamers spelling out various Beatles songs, all somewhat related to the Club: "Sgt. Pepper's Lonely Hearts Club Band," "Come Together," "With a Little Help from My Friends," "Revolution," and, of course, "Penny Lane." I already knew we'd use them next weekend for the Valentine's Day party (except "Penny Lane," of course).

The food was also properly themed: I Am the Eggman deviled eggs, Strawberry Fields salad (spinach tossed with strawberries, goat cheese, and almonds), green apples (in homage to the Beatles record label) sliced up with different dips, and Sgt. Pepperoni pizza (vegetarian pepperoni, in honor of Sir Paul).

Beatles Rock Band was set up on the TV. Erin finished singing "Something," backed by Kara, Laura, and Amy.

Even I had to admit it was pretty awesome.

"Penny Lane!" Dad gestured me to join him over at the microphone. The guitar started, and before I knew it, Dad and I were entertaining the Club with our harmonizing rendition of "Drive My Car." It was a song he always used to play at the beginning of any road trip. Or any drive longer than two and a half minutes.

The basement was filled with bodies jumping up and down to the beat. By the end of the song, everybody was joining in on the *"beep beep mm beep beep yeah"* refrain.

When we were finished, Tracy showed me some of the photos on her phone that she'd posted. There was one of me kneeling down with the microphone, singing with such over-the-top intensity, it was hilariously bad.

"You've got to text me that photo so I can send it to Ryan," I said, knowing that he'd get a kick out of seeing me be so openly dorky.

Tracy obliged, while I went over to the coffee table to get

my phone. When I went to enter my password, I saw I'd missed a few texts. One name stood out over Ryan's and Rita's.

"What's wrong, Pen?" Tracy asked.

I gestured at my phone. "Nate texted me. 'The pics look great, sorry I'm missing the party.'"

Tracy looked around suspiciously. "Who would've sent him photos?"

"I can't imagine, unless he's friends with someone who's tagged in a photo." My mind started racing. I knew that there was no way anybody in the Club would've been friends with him, or kept him as a friend after what had happened between us. "Probably my mom. Did you tag her in any photos?"

Tracy nodded. "Yeah — I thought she'd like to see them." Then her face lit up, making it clear that she had a way to fix this. "Mrs. Bloom!" Tracy called out to my mother in her most innocent voice. "Can I see your phone for a minute? I'm trying to send you some photos, but I think there's a problem with your profile settings."

Mom looked over from her Beatles Trivial Pursuit game. "I don't have one of those fancy phones, Tracy. But I'll log in on the computer and you can fix it."

The three of us headed to the laptop, which was open to the page we'd created for the Club. A week away from the event, we were at nearly one thousand "likes" from all around the world. We already had thirty-four people confirmed for the event, from eleven different cities.

Mom logged into her profile and pushed the laptop to Tracy. "Thanks for doing whatever you're doing. I'm so lost on this stuff."

As if there was ever any doubt that Mom was tech savvy, she left us with her profile up. Unattended. While I was tempted to post something on her behalf, like, "The Rolling Stones are the best band ever," we had real business to take care of.

Tracy went into Mom's friends section and pulled up Nate. I should've looked away, because seeing his profile picture with his arms around two blond girls made me cringe. But he was only on-screen for a few seconds before Tracy swiftly pressed the BLOCK button.

"Done." Tracy wiped her hands clean. "I doubt your Mom will even realize it, and if he says something to her, she can honestly plead ignorance."

"Thanks," I said. "Why can't he leave me alone? First a card, now a text . . ."

Tracy was perplexed. "He sent you a card?"

"Yeah. Didn't I tell you?" I hadn't really thought about it after I'd torn it up and put it in the trash, where anything Nate-related belonged.

"Um, let me think." Tracy was incredulous. "No, I think I'd remember it if you mentioned getting anything from that loser."

"Seriously, Tracy, I don't think it's humanly possible for

me to care any less about it." Which was one hundred percent true.

Tracy studied me. "Okay. But are you sure that you're going to be cool with seeing him in a few weeks?"

"I'll be fine." Which was one hundred percent *not* true.

Amy and Jen approached us with Diane in tow. "Hey, guys," Amy began. "We were talking about next weekend. It's been a lot of work and we thought it would be fun, and more importantly, relaxing, to do a late brunch the next day. My parents are willing to host."

"That would be great," I said.

Tracy agreed. "Yeah, especially since we're expending all this energy on Valentine's Day, a holiday that's spoon-fed to the masses solely so greeting card stores, florists, and chocolate companies can profit from desperate guys trying to get some or get out of trouble. It's *really* romantic, if you think about it."

Amy looked thoughtful. "Do you think we can fit *that* on a sign for us to hang?"

Diane had a tight smile on her face. "Ah, Pen, aren't you supposed to do something with Ryan on Sunday?"

"Yeah, but we didn't settle on a time. I'll make it later!" I tried to hide my annoyance that Diane felt the need to remind me how to be a better girlfriend. She'd said that spending time with him was enough. I was going to spend time with him.

Before I could say anything else, the lights went down. The guitar and drums started blaring over the speakers for my birthday song, compliments of my birthday compatriots. My body started instinctually reacting. My shoulders began moving to the beat, and I met my parents in the center of the living room, surrounded on all sides by the Club.

The three of us started to dance in sync. Our shoulders rolled back and forth during the guitars, and then we switched to our fists pumping to the drumbeat. When it got to the lyrics of "Birthday," my parents took over and serenaded me, complete with finger-pointing to the rhythm, and bobbing up and down on their heels. I kept dancing, getting excited for my favorite part, when Mom would sing, *"Birthday . . ."* and Dad would shake me and scream-sing, *"I would like you to dance!"* The way he did it always cracked me up as a kid; it was as if I was going to be grounded if I didn't obey his command and get down with the Fab Four.

Since the choreography wasn't that complex, most of the Club joined along in the shoulder rolling, bobbing, and fist pumping. Much to my horror, Tracy was recording the entire thing. And she was never one to respond to threats.

But I happily danced through the song. And when it was over, the cake was brought out. It was shaped like a drum with the *Sgt. Pepper's Lonely Hearts Club Band* logo on it.

"What do you think, kiddo?" Dad asked as he held up the cake for me to blow out the candles.

"Perfection," I remarked. And it was.

My parents and friends surrounded me as I blew out the candles. My wish wasn't for the Club to continue to grow; I knew that it didn't need any magical interference for that to happen.

I only had one thought, one wish that evening. And it surprised me as it popped into my head on that fun, memorable birthday.

I wish Ryan were here.

Ten

WHILE WE COULD'VE USED THE FRIDAY night before Valentine's Day to finish the party prep, we decided to take our minds off of it by going to the girls' varsity basketball game.

"Go, Jen!" Tracy screamed as Jen scored an easy layup.

"Do you think we have enough refreshments?" I asked as I looked over the growing RSVP list. Unfortunately, I wasn't allowed to completely banish tomorrow night's responsibilities from my mind.

"It's going to be great, Pen," Tracy assured me. "I don't think these girls are driving a couple hours for the soda selection."

Meg came up the bleachers and sat down next to us. "Hey, guys, did I miss anything?"

Tracy motioned to the scoreboard, where it informed Meg that the score was 6 to 2. Meg nodded and then looked at me. She opened her mouth, closed it, then went back to watching the game. Her leg was shaking nervously.

"Is everything okay?" I asked her.

"Yeah," she said, then shook her head. "No, I mean, it's okay, but I have some bad news."

"Oh, no, what's going on?"

"I got off the phone with my manager and he needs me to work tomorrow night. I know it's short notice, but at least I don't have to work until five, so I can come and help set up. I put myself in as a reserve for the dinner shift because I can make so much more in tips on Valentine's Day. I never really thought I'd get called. I'm really sorry to bail on the Club, but I had to pay for part of my tuition deposit for next year."

Meg held her breath. Did she really think I was going to yell at her?

"Don't worry about it," I said. "I think we're good. You'll be missed, but we completely understand."

Relief flooded over her face. "Thanks. I've never missed a meeting before and it's such a big one."

It was a big one, but part of me couldn't believe all these people coming to the meeting were legitimate. In my experience, when something seemed too good to be true, it was.

Meg gestured two rows behind us. "Erin's saving me a seat, so I better go. See you tomorrow!" She maneuvered herself back.

Tracy stood up abruptly. "Come on, ref! Unbelievable!" She groaned and shook her head. We were in the lead and still had three quarters to go, but Tracy liked to pretend that every game was the Super Bowl or World Series or whatever was a big deal in basketball. It probably wasn't too shocking to imagine that sports were never a big part of the Bloom household.

"Oh!" Tracy exclaimed. "I got it!" She turned to me, and I was convinced she was about to start going on and on about some play the team should be doing. Instead, I was taken aback when she asked, "How much did we raise at the karaoke thing last year?"

"I think around three grand. Jen would know for sure." I looked down in pride at the team's new uniforms, paid for by the fund raiser the Club put together. "Why?"

"Well, I'm sure the other seniors in the Club probably have similar problems. Maybe we should do a Lonely Hearts Club scholarship or something?"

"That's brilliant." It would be a lot of work, but Tracy was right. We could do something to help benefit one of the members of the Club. I put it down in the Club notebook I'd been carrying around, with all the tasks we had to do for the party.

It was something we could deal with after tomorrow night. I couldn't handle adding anything extra to my to-do list before then. I hadn't even figured out what to do with Ryan on Sunday. I'd been hoping that I'd have some divine inspiration at some point. But so far, nothing.

Diane was put in and the Club section cheered loudly for her. She was on defense when a player from the other team knocked her over.

"I'll see you outside, number twenty-four!" Tracy screamed. A few of the parents from the visitors section looked concerned.

"Maybe you should take it down a notch?" I suggested.

"What to the evs. I'm not going to stay silent when someone knocks one of my friends down."

Now, *that* was something we should use for a sign.

I found it ironic that Tracy was in charge of the decorations and signs when in fact she could not see the big sign that was in front of her.

"Is this okay?" Bruce balanced on a step stool as he put up the "Revolution" sign. "Or do you want me to put it somewhere else?"

Tracy studied the placement, then scanned the other signs posted around the rec center. "Looks good," she stated, much to Bruce's delight.

He jumped down from the stool. "Great! What else can I do to help? Anything you need! I'm also available for birthdays and bar mitzvahs. You know, I've been told that I'm a pretty good dancer ... if you need a partner." He laughed nervously.

"Uh-huh." Tracy looked down at her to-do list. "I think we're good. Pen!" she shouted even though I was only a few feet away. "What else do we need done? The Koala Kid needs something to do."

The rec center was coming together nicely. We only had two hours to move some of the equipment to the side, then set up the decorations, tables, chairs, food, and music. I went to the front where people were going to check in. We'd put a red tablecloth on the folding table, but it was still missing something.

I was staring at the table as if the answer would magically appear, when Ryan walked in the door with a vase of roses in his hands.

"That's exactly what I needed!" I exclaimed.

"Well, it's about time you realize that." He gave me a sly grin before handing me the roses and planting a quick kiss on my lips. "Happy Valentine's Day!"

I took the roses from him. "They'll look great here." I placed them on the table and stepped back. "Perfect."

"And here I thought you were showing appreciation to your boyfriend for bringing you roses."

"Huh?" I said before it sank in that those roses weren't decorations for the party, they were for me. "Oh, sorry, yes, thank you!"

He shook his head. "You're welcome." He ran his fingers through his freshly washed hair. Ryan had been working all day at the center and had stepped out to take a quick shower and freshen up. "You guys got a lot done. The place looks great."

"Really?" I was worried that the fluorescent lights and the chlorine smell from the adjacent pool weren't setting the right mood. But then again, we were going to be a bunch of dateless girls on Valentine's Day — a super-romantic vibe wouldn't have been that appropriate.

"Really. I think it makes perfect sense that you'd have the event here. I remember seeing you here at PARC when we were younger. You were a little leader even back then."

I spent a couple days a week at the rec center after middle school; the majority of our class did. But I didn't really hang out with Ryan then. He was usually outside playing on the basketball court.

"What do you mean, I was a leader? I think I may have played with you once — and that was only because it was raining outside." I tried to recall any instances when I would've been bossy to Ryan as a kid.

"You put yourself in charge of handing out the play instruments, and of course the band had to play Beatles songs. Diane used to follow you around and do whatever you said. You two were inseparable."

My heart warmed at the memory of me and Diane upstairs in the band room, pretending to be little rock stars. "We really were," I commented. So much of my childhood recollections centered around Diane. And here we were nearly ten years later, still together — thanks to The Lonely Hearts Club.

"Penny." Laura approached us with her phone in her hand. "We've had two more back out."

The RSVPs had gotten to fifty-one, but people had started dropping out the last couple days. I was worried that all of this work would be for nothing. Maybe nobody but Club members would show up.

"So how many is that, then?" I asked, afraid of the answer.

Laura began counting. "We're at forty-three guests. With the Club and our guests, we'll be at nearly eighty people."

"Paging Miss Penny Lane." Diane's voice boomed out from the microphone we'd brought in from Erin's karaoke machine. "We need you to do a sound check."

Ryan's eyebrows went up. "Sound check? I didn't realize we'd be serenaded."

I groaned. "No singing from me, thankfully. But a few of us are going to talk." I reluctantly went over to the microphone. "Testing . . . testing . . ." I tapped the microphone. "Good evening, Parkview!" My voice echoed out into the large concrete space.

I handed the mic back to Diane. "Seems to be working fine." I reached into my back pocket for the index cards that had some notes for my speech. "Do you know what you're going to say?"

Diane nodded. "Yes, so does Tracy. Don't worry, you won't be up there alone."

As I looked around the room at the Club members working in tandem with my parents, Diane's mom, Tracy's parents, and the boyfriends (including one boy hoping to be more than a friend), I knew there was no way I'd feel lonely on this Valentine's Day.

The Club changed out of our setup clothes and into our outfits for the evening. We were all wearing the matching T-shirts we'd given each other on Christmas: white T-shirts with pink three-quarter-length sleeves with THE LONELY HEARTS

CLUB on the front and our last names on the back. We figured it would help our guests identify us better.

We made one more run-through of the evening. People were supposed to start arriving at seven o'clock, we were going to mingle with refreshments and music, then Tracy, Diane, and I were going to welcome everybody around eight, tell them about the Club, and then . . . I wasn't really sure.

Everybody took their places. The parents were at the refreshment table, Diane and Kara were at the front table, other members were stationed throughout, and the guys went off to the side so they'd be there if we needed them but wouldn't make the girls feel uncomfortable.

I studied the clock and unlocked the door at seven sharp.

And so it began.

Eleven

MY PARENTS KEPT REMINDING ME THAT people usually show up to parties late. And that traffic could be bad, especially for people traveling down from Milwaukee.

But as the clock hit seven fifteen, a sinking feeling started to take over. It wasn't like I expected everybody to be lined up out the door by seven, but I thought *someone* would've shown up by then.

"It's going to be fine," Diane tried to convince me, but then she began to twirl her hair, revealing that she wasn't so sure herself. "You're used to everybody showing up on time for our usual meetings. But some people are driving a couple hours. They're going to be a few minutes late."

"I guess." I kept looking out at the cars driving past the center, willing one to pull in.

"I think it's like waiting for water to boil," Kara said. "You know, it's never going to happen if you stare."

I walked away from the door and made sure my back was to it. I resisted the urge to turn around every time I heard a car pass by. But then I could see the eyes of all the Club members nervously dart over to the front as well. I knew it wasn't my fault if nobody showed up or if this night turned out to be a huge disaster, but I did feel responsible for the Club. I was the reason they were there. I was the reason there were forty girls (hopefully) spending their Valentine's Day with us. I didn't want to let them down.

Dad came over and put his arm around me, clearly aware that I needed a pep talk. "Have I told you lately how proud we are of you, kiddo?" He gave me a tight hug. "Look at this party, it's really incredible. I can't believe how much your Beatles club has taken off."

"It's not a Beatles club," I reminded him for what seemed like the umpteenth time.

He held his hands out. "I know, I know. We're still proud of you. Imagine if it *was* a Beatles club."

Right then, I heard the door swing open. I spun around to see Diane welcoming three girls.

"Hello," one of the girls said cautiously. "I was e-mailing with Penny Lane. I'm Danielle."

"Yes!" I couldn't contain my excitement. "Hi, Danielle — I'm Penny."

She got flustered. "Oh my gosh, it's *you!*"

"Yes." I was unsure of what people expected upon meeting me. "Come on in."

Diane and Kara gave them the special name tags that Tracy had designed. Once they signed in, I brought them to a group of girls who were trying to not stare at our first guests.

Danielle introduced me to her two friends, Kim and Macallan.

I looked at the redheaded girl. "Macallan? That's an interesting name."

She smiled at me. "Yeah, my dad's a fan of . . . you know, it's a long story."

"Oh, believe me, I understand having to explain your name." I gestured to my PENNY LANE name tag. Normally, I would've had it say only Penny, but my parents got very upset when I didn't include my "proper" first name. And since they were spending their Valentine's Day with the group, I wanted to appease them the best I could.

Erin, Hilary, and Amy came over to talk to our new guests as I excused myself to meet a group of four girls who'd arrived with a mother in tow.

The mother looked around suspiciously. "Yes, I'm sorry, but are there adults present? As you can imagine, I was a little worried that they wanted to go to some event they found online."

Diane's mom approached the table. She'd been assigned to be the parental chaperone for the evening. One look at Diane's mom and you could see where Diane got her looks, although not her height. Diane's mom was nearly eight inches taller than her daughter, but everything else was the same: pale blue eyes, blond hair (her mom's in a straight bob), and a warmth that emanated from her.

"I'm Maggie Monroe. I'm so happy that you could come tonight." She shook the other mom's hand. "Why don't you come on in and I'll introduce you around and tell you how wonderful this club has been for the girls."

A steady stream of visitors soon showed up at the door. I was so busy mingling and doing my best to meet everybody that I didn't even realize it when Nicole, Todd's unfortunate date that night at the pizza place, arrived.

"You made it!" I greeted her with a hug.

"Of course, and I brought some of my friends." She introduced us, and I was very grateful that my parents had suggested name tags. There was no way I was going to remember everybody's name.

The group started chatting about ideas they had for their own Lonely Hearts Clubs. It was exciting to see the enthusiasm spreading around the room. I was listening intently when my eye caught Ryan and Bruce heading to the front door in a hurry. When I looked over to see what they were reacting to, my heart nearly stopped.

It was Todd. With Missy.

I excused myself and hurried to the door, trying to not let our guests know there was a problem. By the time I got there, Ryan already had his hand on Todd's arm.

"Don't do this," he warned.

"I'm sorry — I thought this was a party. Are you telling me that I'm not allowed?" Todd raised his voice with every word. Tracy was right behind me, helping to block our guests from the show Todd was trying to put on.

"Yes, and you're not invited," I hissed. "I guess we should've put a sign up: *No jerks allowed.*" I crossed my arms, making it clear he would have to get through me before he stepped another foot into the room.

Todd laughed. "Then what are *you* doing here?"

"Let's go outside." Ryan tugged at Todd's arm. "Come on, man, don't cause a scene. Why would you want to ruin this for her? It's a total jerk move."

"What's going on?" One of our guests asked, confused about the scene before her.

Oh, nothing, I almost said. *Todd's being his usual horror show self.*

Ryan answered instead. "Todd stopped by to say hello, but he's going now. Aren't you, Todd?" Diane escorted our guest away as Ryan stood up tall, facing his supposed best friend. He looked hard at Todd, practically daring him to defy him.

Bruce, a couple inches taller than them both, stood next to Ryan. He looked down at Todd. "I think you better get going, mate."

Todd looked up at Bruce and laughed in his face. "Wow, they've gotten to you, too." He took a step back, probably sensing that he wasn't going to win this battle. "Yeah, sure. I guess you belong here, Bauer, since your little girlfriend has taken your balls away. What a joke."

I stepped forward, but felt Tracy's hand on my wrist. "Let him go," she whispered to me. "We can't cause a scene." I knew that, but I didn't like Ryan and Bruce, or anyone else, having to fight my battles for me.

Todd looked like he was going to leave but then took the stack of name tags on the table in front and threw them up in the air as he screamed, "HAVE FUN, YOU PATHETIC DYKES!"

Ryan took Todd by the collar and pushed him out the door. I was frozen as I watched Ryan get up in Todd's face. I could only make out a few words beyond the glass door. They were pretty intense words.

I heard a voice next to me and saw that Missy was still there. "Fun party," she commented with a smug grin on her face.

"You know, Missy, you think you're so cool, but this is where Todd wanted to take you on Valentine's Day," I reminded her. "*Here.* To be a jerk. And do you even realize that he's dated half of the Club, and they would all rather be here than date him. So what exactly does that tell you? But I guess you two belong together. Now, if you'll excuse me, I've got a group of sixty amazing girls who don't need to blindly follow a guy around to make them feel better about themselves. Next time you want to call someone pathetic, take a look in the mirror."

I turned away from her and noticed that everybody had been looking in our direction. So much for not making a scene. I quickly glanced back, and was relieved to see that Missy was gone and that Ryan was again inside.

Tracy had a grin on her face. "I find it hysterical that Todd thought he could cause damage, when in fact all he managed was to reiterate to people why they need this club: loser boys."

"I'm really sorry about that." Ryan came up to me cautiously with Bruce behind him. "I don't know what he was thinking. Don't let him ruin the party."

"Are you okay?" I asked. "What happened? Did he hurt you?" I scanned Ryan for any scratches or bruises. Not that he couldn't take care of himself — Todd outsized Ryan in weight only. Ryan outsized Todd in class, smarts, looks, and pretty much every category of awesome.

"He was being Todd. I'm done." He looked beside himself. "There was no reason for him to show up, except to be a prick."

"Are you guys okay?" Bruce asked, his eyes fixated on Tracy.

She nodded. "Yes, because I'm not dating Todd. That alone makes me fan-friggin-tastic."

I tried to lighten the mood. "That was some colorful language you were using," I teased.

He looked horrified. "Oh God, you heard that? I hope your dad didn't. I was so mad —"

"It's okay," I interrupted him. "Thank you for helping with that. I really appreciate it."

We both held our gazes, and what I wanted to do right then and there was to give him the biggest, longest kiss in the history of kisses. But that probably wasn't the wisest idea in the middle of a giant Lonely Hearts Club recruitment meeting.

He cleared his throat. "Yeah, well, I better go." He gestured for Bruce to join him off to the side.

Tracy glanced at her watch. "Well, we should get ready to talk."

I'd been so preoccupied with meeting everybody that I'd forgotten we still had our speeches left.

"I guess." The nerves that had disappeared once everybody began showing up had popped up again in my stomach.

We rounded up Diane and headed toward the corner where the microphone was set up. Tracy shut off the music. We could hear the murmurs of countless conversations taking place throughout the room.

"Ah, excuse me," I said into the microphone. "Can we please have everybody's attention for a minute?" The room began to quiet down. "Thanks so much for coming. I think I've met everybody, but I'm Penny Lane Bloom." There were some cheers and I could hear a distant loud whistle that I knew was coming from Dad. "Anyways, Diane, Tracy, and I wanted to say a few words about The Lonely Hearts Club. So without further ado, Tracy Larson."

Tracy did a deep curtsy with her applause. "Thanks, everyone." She took a dramatic breath. "Hi, my name is Tracy, and I'm a former boy addict."

A few of the audience members returned with a "Hi, Tracy!"

"This is a little embarrassing to admit, but every summer I used to create a Boyfriend List. It was exactly what it sounds like: a list of guys I wanted to date, in order of hotness, *obvs*. At the beginning of every school year, I'd hold out hope that this would be the year that I'd date someone on the list. And without fail, the guys were either dating someone else or not interested. I mean, can you imagine *that*?" Tracy jokingly posed saucily to some hollers.

"But instead of me thinking, well, I guess that's okay, I would get so upset. Because I didn't look at it like the guy wanted to date someone else. I took it that I wasn't good enough." Her voice unexpectedly cracked. She paused before regaining her composure. "All I would do is beat myself up over it. I wasn't pretty enough, smart enough, thin enough. This is really embarrassing to admit, but I've never been asked out on a date. I've never been kissed. And all that would do is fill me with such sadness. Clearly, there had to be something wrong with me, right?" There were a lot of people nodding with Tracy, knowing how bad that feeling could be.

"I was obsessed with getting a date. And why? So I could date a guy for a couple months in high school and then get dumped, or move away to college and try to do the long-distance thing. That's why I'm so grateful for this club. Because none of that matters with The Lonely Hearts Club. We have friends, a sisterhood, and it has nothing to do with what guy is going to ask you to a stupid dance. We matter as individuals. We have each other, and every day I wake up so grateful that Pen over there got her heart stomped on. As much as that sucked for her, it worked out for all of us. I was resistant to the Club originally, but now I don't know what I'd do without it. Probably try to date some guy who wasn't worth it. *No, thank you.*"

There was some laughter from the audience as Tracy handed the microphone to Diane. I could see Diane's hands shake slightly. Diane was used to being in front of people — former cheerleading captain, Student Council President — so I couldn't believe that this would make her nervous.

"Hi, everybody. Thanks for coming." Her usually peppy voice was now measured. "So I'm Diane and I used to be *that girl*. You know this girl. You might have been her, or maybe it was your best friend, but I guarantee you have someone in your circle of friends who's like this. I used to dump my friends when I got a boyfriend. And, to be more specific, I dumped Penny." Her eyes were focused down. It was a history that I knew well, but didn't realize how hard it was for her to admit the truth to everybody.

I tried to nonchalantly search the room to see if Ryan was listening. But I didn't see any of the guys or parents. They knew we needed some privacy for this. The few people who'd recorded the beginning of the speeches had put their cameras down. We'd already agreed to post some photos and speeches from tonight online for people who couldn't make it, but it was clear that Diane's would be kept between those in the room.

She continued, "I had a great best friend, and what did I do the second I got a boyfriend? I ignored her. Or we'd make plans and I would cancel on her. All my focus and attention was on my boyfriend. That's all I really cared about. It got to the point that I didn't want to make any plans in case Ry — *he* would call." Diane grimaced when Ryan's name nearly slipped out.

"Well, I don't think I need to tell you what eventually happened. We broke up. While it was amicable, the damage to my friendships had already been done. It had been over four years since I'd really talked to Penny. It wasn't the easiest road back for us, but The Lonely Hearts Club not only saved our friendship, but it made me realize a few things about myself. I usually did things for other people. I spent all my time cheering for other people, so I decided to quit cheerleading last year and join the basketball team, because that's what I wanted to do. I figured it was time that I started thinking about myself. And I still have a long way to go, but for the first time in months, I'm able to look in the mirror and be happy with the person staring back at me."

The room was silent. Anybody passing Diane on the street would envy her looks, but she was talking about something deeper, about the person she was becoming.

I was so busy reflecting on everything she had said and how brave she was that I didn't register that she was trying to pass me the microphone. I finally took it in one hand and reached into my back pocket for my index cards. But when I looked down at my notes, it didn't feel right. I was planning on talking about the Club in general, what we do on Saturday nights, how we've done some philanthropic events, and so on.

Tracy and Diane's speeches had been from the heart. I felt I owed it to everybody to be real. I put the cards back in my pocket.

"Thank you so much for sharing your stories, Tracy and Diane." I looked at both of them gratefully. "It shouldn't come as a shock that this all started with a boy. And I do mean *boy*." I paused for laughter, as I was incredibly unprepared for what I had to do next.

Open old wounds.

"There was this guy I had known for forever. Our parents are best friends. We used to spend every summer together. I really thought I was in love with him. He said everything I wanted to hear and did everything I thought a guy should do, but that wasn't enough for him. He wanted more. And I felt like if I didn't give in to him, I'd be pushing him away. So . . ." I was startled at the hot stinging behind my eyes. It had been several months, I was completely over Nate, but it still hurt.

"So I went down to our basement to surprise him. I was going to . . . you know." I looked around the room, hoping that I wouldn't have to be even more humiliated by detailing this private moment. "Well, it seemed that the jackass couldn't wait any longer. I found him with another girl in a very compromising position, naked." I waited to see how much this would upset me, but instead, I was practically empty inside. It felt like it had happened in another life.

"So I was hurt, I was upset, and I started to think about all the crap my friends and I went through for guys. Or the lengths we went through to get them to give us the time of day. I didn't want to deal with it anymore — what was the point? And being the child of Beatles fanatics, The Lonely Hearts Club came to me. I originally thought it would only be me, but then I told Diane about the Club, and it sort of took off. Which I guess is an understatement, given that I'm up here speaking to all of you.

"And while the Club was originally a nondating club, it has become something much more: a community of amazing women who support each other. We have study groups, we help out with fund-raisers, and we're even considering doing a scholarship. While, yes, members can now date if the guy or girl is worth it, we have always been about, and will continue to be about, being there for each other. The Lonely Hearts Club has already surpassed any expectations I could've ever had. If this can grow beyond McKinley High, then . . . then I think that would be awesome.

"So, ah, we're going to hand out the rules that we made, although your clubs can make your own. And a few other members are going to talk a little about the Club and the things that we do."

I quickly passed the mic to Teresa so she, Kara, and Jen could take over. Out of the spotlight, I breathed a sigh of relief.

After the three of them went through the rules and answered some questions, we turned the music back on.

As soon as Kelly Clarkson was blaring, I felt a tap on my shoulder.

"Penny Lane." Mom looked concerned. "I need to speak with you. Alone."

"What's wrong?" I glanced around, expecting to see a fire or a riot, by the look on her face.

"I think we need to talk about Nate."

Holy crap.

She'd heard everything.

Twelve

I BEGAN PACING THE SMALL KITCHEN in the rec center as Mom closed the door. I hadn't realized she was there during the speeches. I hadn't seen her. Now she knew I'd been planning to lose my virginity to Nate. Which seemed so insignificant compared to the life I was about to lose.

She silently studied me for a few seconds before talking in an even voice. "I want you to explain what happened."

"I think you heard what happened," I said in an accusatory tone. "I didn't know you were listening."

She looked guilty. "We all agreed to go to the back, but I wanted to hear the speeches, so I snuck away from your father. I certainly wasn't expecting to hear *that*. Why didn't you tell me? Your father is going to lose his mind."

A laugh escaped my throat. Dad was the last person in my family who'd ever "lose his mind." But then again, his best friend's son had cruelly played his baby girl.

"I was embarrassed," I confessed. "And hurt and foolish. I didn't want you to know what I was going to do. How desperate I was being. I thought I would disappoint you."

Mom pursed her lips. "Well, I can't say I'm *proud* of that behavior, Penny Lane. But what you did does *not* in any way compare to what *he* did." Then a realization came. "You had to see him at Thanksgiving. And he's invited to Lucy's wedding!"

"I dealt with him on Thanksgiving. He's aware that he needs to stay away from me. I don't want this to ruin Dad's relationship with Mr. Taylor. Do you have to tell him?"

She paused a second. "I'll think about it. I don't know how we can uninvite Nate to the wedding at the last minute, but I can't believe he acted with such disregard for you and your feelings. I thought he was such a *nice* boy."

Yeah, so did I.

There was a knock on the door. Diane stuck her head in. "There you are. A few of the girls from other towns want to talk to you."

"Thanks, I'll be right out."

After Diane closed the door, Mom finally looked me in the eye. "I'm not sure how to handle this — it's a lot to process."

"I know," I said. "I'm sorry you had to find out this way."

Mom placed her hand gently on my face. "Well, I'm sorry this happened to you. And that you felt you couldn't come to me. But I guess you had plenty of people you could confide in. I've always liked the Club, but I don't think it's until now that I understand how much you really needed it."

"Thanks, Mom." I gestured toward the door. "I should go. Do you want to join us?"

Mom shook her head. "I need a few more minutes."

"I understand."

I did. I had months to process what had happened. I left her to her thoughts as I continued to process the only way I knew how — surrounded by supportive friends and, now, supportive strangers.

There was part of me that felt uneasy that Mom knew the whole story.

But there was a growing part that felt relief that she finally knew the truth.

"To the Club!" The group held up our drinks on Sunday morning at Amy's house.

We were all in sweatpants, hair up, and exhausted from yesterday's preparation, party, and cleanup. Everybody was in good spirits over how well the night had gone. The number of new friends we'd made was apparent from the constant buzzing of phones with friend requests, texts, and messages.

Meg started working on a map of the areas in Illinois, Wisconsin, and Indiana where people had come from, putting dots up to represent all the new clubs.

"I'll start working on an American and world map, too, because we'll obviously need it," she said as she showed us the eleven dots on her map already.

"So crazy," I said as I took another bagel and sank back down on the couch. While I was emotionally and physically exhausted, I was also grateful to have an excuse to go somewhere this morning so I wouldn't have to deal with Mom, who was still anguished about what to do with what she now knew. I was sure I was only putting off the inevitable, but I preferred to do that as long as humanly possible.

I looked at the clock, trying to figure out when I'd need to leave to make myself presentable for my date with Ryan.

My eyes were getting heavy by the time a movie was put on. I placed my head against a pillow and rested my eyes. I was going to close them only for a few minutes. Then I would leave and prepare for my date with Ryan.

Yes, that was the plan.

Just a few minutes.

I was startled awake by Diane's voice. "Penny, wake up!"

My eyes opened groggily. "What's going on?" I asked.

She held out her phone. "Ryan called me, worried about where you were."

"Where I —" I glanced over at the clock. I had slept for over two hours, and from the confused members aroused from sleep, I wasn't the only one who'd crashed. "Crap."

"I told him we all passed out and that you'd call him right away." Diane looked worried.

I reached for my phone, which I'd left on the counter. There were four texts and two missed calls. The texts showed the deterioration of Ryan's tolerance.

Hope brunch is going well. Can't wait to have you
all to myself. :)

You said 3 right? Or do you need more time?

Everything OK? I'm getting worried.

Why aren't you picking up?

I waved good-bye to the group as I called Ryan, shoving my feet into my fleece boots.

"Hey," he said in a short tone I hadn't heard since our pre-couple cold front last semester.

"I'm so sorry. I over-napped. I'll be right over," I explained as I grabbed the keys to my mom's car. Then I caught a glimpse of myself in the mirror — my hair was in a messy ponytail with flyaway hair everywhere and my right cheek had an imprint from the couch on it. I was wearing baggy sweats and no bra. "Actually, do you mind if I run home first and change? I don't think you want to see me like this. I'll be a half hour, I swear."

"Well, I guess if it doesn't interfere with your plans." His voice was too controlled. It was clear he was losing his patience with me. And it was completely warranted.

"My plans?" I said before I realized what he meant. I was supposed to come up with something fabulous. And I hadn't done a single thing. "Yes, of course, my plans. No, no . . . it'll be fine. I'm really sorry. I'd better run so I don't keep you waiting any longer."

I did my best to not break too many traffic laws on my way

back home. I burst through our front door and took the steps two at a time. If there was a record for showering, changing, and getting ready — I certainly didn't break it. The thirty minutes that I'd promised Ryan quickly turned into forty-five when I couldn't figure out what to wear since I really didn't know what we were going to do. After settling on dark jeans, a charcoal gray ruched top, and black knee-high boots, I ran back downstairs. I yelled something to my parents about running late but stopped when I saw I only had thirteen dollars in my wallet.

"Dad." I ran into the living room. He looked up from his book. "I'm really sorry, I messed things up, I'm running late, and I don't have enough money. Can I borrow forty dollars, please? You can take it out of my next paycheck."

Thankfully, Dad didn't ask any questions and handed over the money. Now I only had to figure out what to do with it.

I pulled up to Ryan's house an hour after I'd promised him he'd see me in thirty minutes. He was out of the door before I even had a chance to pull into the driveway.

"Hey!" I said as cheerfully as possible when he got into the car. I leaned over and gave him a kiss on the cheek. I'd planned on kissing him on the lips, but he refused to face me. "I'm so, so, so sorry. This is all my fault, I was really tired from last night, I completely passed out, and my phone was on vibrate — it's like a Greek tragedy!"

His eyes continued to look forward. "What's your big surprise?"

"Yes, well . . ." There was no more stalling. I was a seventeen-year-old girl with limited funds, and there really wasn't much I could do to top Ryan's birthday lunch. "I was thinking that we could go . . . bowling and . . . then get dinner."

Lame.

"How long have you been planning that?" Ryan's clear hurt and frustration were starting to freak me out.

"Look, I'm really —"

He cut me off. "Sorry. Yes, you've mentioned that. You know, Penny, I wasn't expecting a private concert or anything. Actually, we could've just gone to the mall. But the fact that you've put zero thought into it really hurts."

"You're right," I conceded. "But it's really hard to top what you did. I mean, how do you out-wonderful Ryan Bauer?"

I meant it as a compliment, but Ryan didn't see it that way.

"Are you kidding me? *It's not a competition.* I did what I did because I *wanted* to do something nice for you. Because I *care* about you."

"Then why the hell do you always have to go running to Diane?" I was startled at that coming out of my mouth. While it was slightly annoying that they talked about our relationship, that Diane was the first person he called when I didn't pick up my phone, I didn't realize how much it truly bothered me until now. "I'm sorry I'm not the perfect girl-friend that she was."

Ryan looked shocked. "I'm *so* sorry that I was concerned about my girlfriend who I hadn't heard from all morning even after I repeatedly texted and called. At least Diane picks up her phone."

We sat in silence for a few minutes, the only noise coming from the running engine of the car.

Ryan mercifully broke the silence. "You know, Penny, I try. I really do. I try to be okay when you book yourself far in advance to do things with the Club. I try to not get offended that you're happier when you're with your friends than with me. I try to not notice how uncomfortable you are when I touch you in public. I try to understand that you've been very busy with everything and maybe haven't had a lot of time to think of anything. And truthfully, bowling and dinner sounds great. But it was very clear that you figured that out the second those words came out of your mouth. It really sucks to always feel like an afterthought." He reached for the car door handle.

"Ryan, please don't." I put my hand on his shoulder, willing him not to leave.

My mind raced at what I could say or do to reverse everything he had said. But I couldn't shake the fact that he was right. He had understood all my Club craziness. He had helped pull off last night.

And what had I done to show my appreciation?

Absolutely nothing.

"Let me make it up to you now," I said, desperation seeping into my voice. "We can go to the arcade. I'll get a ton of quarters. Or we can see some movie or watch a sports game. Whatever you want."

He opened the car door. "Forget about it. Let's call this day a wash and I'll see you in school tomorrow." He got out of the car.

"Ryan, I am truly very —" He slammed the car door shut.

I sat in the car a little while longer, stunned over how much I'd screwed things up. I knew I had to get out of his driveway before the cops were called. I started driving around aimlessly, not ready to go home and deal with my parents, who'd certainly know something was going on.

I turned onto Tracy's street. I tried to steady my breath as I slowly made my way up to her front door.

Her brother, Mike, answered the door. "Hey, Penny, what's up?" He turned his back to me. "Tracy! Penny's here!"

Tracy emerged from her bedroom upstairs. "What are you doing here? What happened with Ryan?"

I decided to stop pretending that I could handle it all. Because it was clear that I couldn't. I let everything go.

The pressure of being the leader of The Lonely Hearts Club.

My inability to balance having a relationship with the one guy who was worth it.

There, in Tracy's foyer, I collapsed on the floor in tears.

Something

"You're asking me, will my love grow?
I don't know . . ."

Thirteen

I SHOULD'VE ASKED FOR THE ABILITY to turn back time for my birthday.

Ryan didn't return any of my texts on Sunday night. He didn't answer his phone when I called. And as I walked to our lockers that Monday morning, I dreaded the welcome I would receive.

"Do you want me to go with you?" Tracy asked when we reached the section of the hallway where she had to turn toward her locker.

"No, I'll be fine." Which we both knew was a lie.

I had mixed feelings of relief and anxiety when I saw that Ryan was at his locker, putting his coat away.

"Hey . . ." I said cautiously. "How are things?"

He closed his locker. "Fine. I've got to go talk to Ms. Cowan." He turned to walk away.

"Look, Ryan." I stepped around in front of him. "I know I screwed up. Really. I don't know how many times you want me to apologize, but I'll stay here all day if that's what it'll take."

"I need some time," he said before sidestepping me and continuing down the hallway.

I walked to my first class in a haze. I heard my name being called out, but I couldn't focus.

"Penny!" Diane nudged me lightly. "You look like you're in a different world."

"I don't want to talk about it," I snapped at her.

"Um, okay."

"Although maybe I should ask *you* since he tells *you* everything."

She furrowed her brow. "What are you talking about? Is everything all right?"

I stopped cold and studied her. "Do you seriously not know?"

She shook her head. "Know what? I have no idea what you're talking about."

"I think Ryan and I are breaking up." I didn't want to admit it, it hurt to even say it, but that was the only outcome I could imagine from what had happened.

"*What?* What happened yesterday? He couldn't be *that* upset because you were late."

"No . . ." I admitted. "It was that I was late, and hadn't planned anything, and keep putting him second to everything else in my life. I don't blame him for being upset with me. I can't be the girlfriend that you were."

"You know better than to compare yourself to others."

"Clearly." I gestured at Diane's perfect hair, body, and clothes.

"That's not what I meant. Comparing yourself to others will only drive you insane. You know that I wasn't the perfect girlfriend. I was needy. I'd freak out if I didn't hear from him every morning, afternoon, and evening. Give him some time to cool down." Diane linked her elbow with mine. "You know he's crazy about you. It'll all blow over before you know it."

Diane was one of the smartest people in our class. She was used to being right about pretty much everything. Usually, I would trust her opinion.

But I'd been there. I'd seen how upset he was. I knew what I did (or, more accurately, what I *didn't* do). I didn't think this was going to blow over.

There are certain things in high school that you get used to seeing on a daily basis: your locker, the front office, the bathrooms, the teacher with the bad comb-over, the trophy cases that line the hallway.

So when I walked into the cafeteria, I immediately knew something was off. Something had shifted.

And then I spotted it.

Ryan wasn't sitting with Todd and his other friends at their table. He was with Bruce at a smaller table in the corner.

"What's going on?" I asked Tracy as I sat down.

Tracy, always on the forefront of McKinley High gossip, dished. "Ryan went up to the table like usual, although he wisely went to the opposite side from where Todd was. But Todd was all 'no way man, you made your choice' and basically evicted him."

Just add that to the list of horrible things I had done to Ryan. I knew that Todd's only issue with Ryan was that he was with me. And the fact that Ryan had stood up to Todd on Saturday. For those petty crimes, he'd been exiled from his group of friends.

The entire cafeteria could sense the tension. The room was filled with whispers and curious glances. For his part, Ryan pretended to be really into whatever story Bruce was telling him.

Of course Todd would handle Ryan's defiance like a spoiled toddler, but I couldn't believe that the other people, like Ryan's friends Don and Brian, wouldn't stand up to Todd.

Why did Ryan have to suffer for my sins? Well, not really my *sins*, since I'd done nothing wrong.

Maybe Ryan shouldn't have to be the only one to put Todd in his place. Maybe I needed to remind Todd of what was what. I hadn't had to do it yet . . . this week.

"Pen," Tracy said, "I know that look, and it's a bad idea."

"What look?" I asked innocently.

She smirked at me. "Oh, come on. The look that says that you want to go over there and take Todd down a notch."

"And you would have a problem with that *why*?"

Tracy lowered her voice. "Because things aren't that great between you and Ryan right now. So he probably wouldn't appreciate you causing a big scene on his behalf."

"But I feel like I have to do something. Maybe this will show that I actually do care about him?" I reasoned as I pushed my lunch aside.

"I think what you need to do is be there for him, especially now."

"But I've tried." My voice sounded as exhausted as I felt.

"Give him some time. He feels burned. He'll come around." She reached out and patted my hand. "Here, have my brownie."

Tracy loved dessert and would never give up a brownie unless I was in big trouble.

I spent the rest of lunch listening to everybody talk about their morning classes and ignored the ticking time bomb sitting at a small table in the corner of the room.

I decided it would be best for me to spend the rest of the day with my head down. If Ryan was going to ignore me, then I would do my best to ignore the panic that was starting to spread throughout my body.

It wasn't like I hadn't been dumped before, but the thought of Ryan breaking up with me was almost too much to handle.

As I turned the corner for Spanish class, Bruce caught up to me. "Hey, Penny! ¿Cómo estás?"

"Fine." I didn't have the energy to translate anything into Spanish. I was still having trouble deciphering English. "How was lunch?"

"It was good. Ryan's a cool guy," he said, either unaware of the problems Ryan and I were having or an excellent actor. "I actually had a question for you."

"Shoot." I went to enter the classroom, but Bruce paused outside the door.

"Yeah, so I was wondering if you think Tracy would go on a date with me?" His eyes filled with hope.

I hated that I had to crush his spirit.

"Tracy's not into dating right now." That was putting it lightly. "She's really into the Club, so I don't think she's open to anybody asking her out."

He nodded slowly. "Do you think you could talk to her for me? See if she'd be willing to go to dinner? I think she's fantastic — funny, cute, and, you know, a bit of a spitfire." He laughed.

I was very aware of that.

I didn't think there was any changing Tracy's mind, although I was a little concerned that the Club had turned her away from ever wanting to go on a date. She'd gone from constantly obsessing and fantasizing about going out with a guy to pretty much ridiculing the entire concept of dating. Maybe it would be nice for her to go on a date with a good guy like Bruce.

He'd been so supportive with Ryan and the Club, so I decided to throw him a bone. "Sure, why not?"

I figured that among the three closest people to me — Tracy, Diane, and Ryan — Tracy was the only one I hadn't gotten mad at or into a fight with in the past twenty-four hours. Trying to see if she would go on a date was the best odds of me going for the trifecta.

Best to go big or go home.

Oh, how I wanted to go home.

Fourteen

I WASN'T THAT EXCITED WHEN I woke up the following morning. But then, I figured it would be pretty hard to top the awfulness of yesterday.

While I waited for Tracy to come pick me up for school, I contemplated the different ways to bring up a possible date with Bruce. I figured her driving with her baby brother in the backseat would make it less likely for her to attempt any bodily harm.

After exchanging our usual morning greetings, I decided to go for it.

"Hey, Tracy, Bruce is really interested in you."

"Well, I *do* have a great personality," she deadpanned.

Mike snickered. "Wow, a boy likes Tracy. Clearly, the world is about to end."

Tracy shot him a look in the rearview mirror. "No, but your life will end if you keep that up."

Mike wisely decided to put his headphones on.

I continued to plead Bruce's case. "Would you ever think of going on a date with him? He's pretty smitten."

Her face turned into a scowl. "Not really. I mean, yes, he's hot and charming and has an accent and apparently is the first guy to come to his senses about my feminine wiles, but what's the point?"

"What do you mean, what's the point?"

The point, it would seem, was to have fun with a cute boy. Did she need any other reasons beyond that?

"He's going back Down Under in a few months, so what's the point of going on a date with him? It won't go anywhere. I mean, let's look at any relationships in high school — they aren't going to go beyond high school, for the most part. Bruce won't be the love of my life, so I'd rather not waste my time." She said it so matter-of-factly. I almost missed the old Tracy, who used to overreact to anything boy-related.

"I hear what you're saying, but with that logic, why should I even date Ryan?" I gestured back to Mike. "Or Mike and Michelle?"

Tracy kept her eyes fixed on the road. "Yeah, like I'm touching that with a ten-foot pole. Sure, you guys could get married and live a happy life, but all I'm saying is there's a reason why all those romance books end with the guy and girl getting together. Because if you show what happens after the first date, it will be filled with disappointments. In the real world, most of those relationships would end in a few weeks. Well, except Elizabeth Bennet and Mr. Darcy. I may have a heart made out of coal, but even I can't deny Jane Austen."

"How romantic of you," I teased, but what she'd said hurt. I hadn't really thought about my future with Ryan beyond Prom. I didn't even know if we had a future past last weekend.

I had no idea if we were even still dating since there was a general understanding that people who were dating actually acknowledged one another.

"I think the word you're looking for is *realistic*," she stated before glancing over at me. I don't know what I looked like that made her quickly reverse her feelings, but she rushed to add, "But, Pen, Ryan is really great. He makes you happy, which makes me happy. I'm simply saying that dating isn't what I want right now. We are two different people. So don't give up on him."

But what she said before was sticking with me. I thought that maybe I *should* stop, knowing that we probably wouldn't have a fairy-tale happily-ever-after. We'd been dating for less than two months and we'd already had more drama than all my past relationships combined.

Well, except for Nate. But I didn't count Nate as a relationship anymore.

That hadn't been real.

But what Ryan and I had was.

Or maybe it wasn't.

After all, there was a time I'd thought what I had with Nate *was* real.

How could I tell?

There wasn't any way to tell if Ryan's cold front was still hovering. Because you have to be around someone to know if he's still mad at you. The fact that he hadn't been at his locker much was all the answer I really needed.

I was dragging my feet to get to lunch, when Bruce spotted me. He waved me down. "Hey, Penny!"

"Hey, Bruce."

"So did you talk to Tracy?" He looked so hopeful.

I guess it was better to rip the bandage off. "Well —"

"Bruce!" Brian Reed approached us. "Hey, man, I was wondering if you could help me out with geography. Maybe we could eat lunch by my locker and go over it?"

Bruce glanced at me expectantly, but I wasn't going to look a gift horse in the mouth. "I'll leave you guys to it. Talk to you later!" Then I hightailed it out of there.

When I entered the cafeteria to sit with the Club, I realized how stupid I was. Brian was one of Todd's minions. And with Bruce away at lunch, Ryan was sitting at that small corner table by himself. This was a sight I didn't think anybody had ever expected. One of the most popular people in school was sitting by himself. I couldn't tell if people were intimidated to join him or were afraid of Todd's wrath if they did.

I glanced over at the Club's table and met eyes with Diane. She quickly turned to see what I was gesturing to. She got up, but I began to shake my head. This was something I needed to do. She nodded, and I headed over to the only other table besides Todd's that I was positive wouldn't greet me with open arms.

"Mind if I join you?" I asked with an apologetic grin.

Ryan looked up, a flash of relief registering on his face. "Sure."

It was the most he had said to me in two days. So there, in front of the entire cafeteria, I had my first school lunch with my boyfriend.

"Bruce had to help someone study," I explained. But Ryan's glance darted over to where Todd was. He wasn't stupid. Ryan knew the game Todd was playing. "So . . ." I let the word hang out there for a beat too long. I was going to apologize, but I had used that phrase so much in the last forty-eight hours (and, if I was being honest, the last few months) that the sentiment had lost its meaning. *Sorry* was only a word.

Ryan looked at me. "So . . . my dad called me on Sunday and requested my presence this week. It was right before you were supposed to pick me up, so I wasn't in a good place. I'd like to say it's better now, but I don't know what he wants. And with my dad, he always wants something: validation, to get under Mom's skin, bragging rights, someone to talk down to."

I'd never met Ryan's dad. He was like an urban legend, although he was rarely spoken of. I knew better than to bring him up to Ryan. His parents had divorced over ten years ago. His dad was some bigwig lawyer in downtown Chicago who never showed up to Ryan's games when he said he would.

"That has to be rough," I said, suddenly grateful for my parents. "Do you want to talk about it?"

He picked at his sandwich. "Actually, I was hoping that you could go with me. It's at some ridiculously expensive restaurant in Chicago on Thursday. I figure we can have a nice meal on dear old Dad, *if* he shows up."

I was both surprised and honored. "Of course. Whatever you need."

"Thanks." He gave me a weak smile. "And I think it's time that I apologize for how cold I've been. It was the one-two punch of him calling me and demanding I come see him. There was no 'How are you, son?' It was 'You need to come see me.' Then you were late and I felt a little taken for granted."

"Don't apologize. I was a total jerk. I mean, not as big of a jerk as Todd. But still."

A laugh escaped Ryan's throat. "I think it would be pretty hard for anybody to achieve that level of . . ."

"Loserdom?" I graciously finished for him.

"Yeah." He seemed to relax considerably. "I like how he thinks ignoring me is going to make me think that I'm the one who did something wrong. The only thing I find upsetting is that he's tainted all these people who I thought were my friends. Who asks someone to pick sides? That's what he asked the basketball team to do yesterday. Everybody pretty much ignored him, but they're also not quick to stand up to him in the cafeteria. At least this way I get to eat my entire lunch without him pawing over everything I packed."

Of course Ryan said this right as I was eyeing his bag of chocolate chip cookies. "Yeah, but, you know, it's polite to share."

Ryan, at first confused that I was defending Todd, then saw what I was looking at. He slid the bag across the table. As I grabbed it, he reached out and held my hand. We stayed there for a few minutes, his hand entwined with mine, grateful that we had seemed to get over our speed bump relatively intact.

He leaned forward and, like a magnet, I was drawn toward him. "I appreciate your breach in protocol to come sit with me," he said, rubbing his thumb against the side of my hand.

"Of course. Although I should warn you that this breach might make you the target of the full wrath of The Lonely Hearts Club now. I can try to see if they'll call off their plan for revenge, but there are some lines that can't be uncrossed."

"Oh, really?" He had an amused expression on his face. He quickly looked over at the Club's table. "And what do you think the Club would do if I kissed you right now, in front of the cafeteria, the school, and those who wish to do harm to me solely for wanting to spend some time with my girlfriend?"

I silenced all those voices in my head screaming that we were going to get caught, that I was going to be taunted. "I would say that would be a bold move. Are you prepared to be a wanted man?"

He continued to inch forward. "Yes, especially if you're referring to yourself as the person who wants me."

I did. I closed my eyes and kissed Ryan. I ignored the murmuring and pulled away right as Tracy screamed, "GO, PEN!"

And she claimed she didn't believe in high school romance.

A few teachers looked over at me, but by that time Ryan and I, faces fully flushed, were enjoying his mom's homemade cookies.

Reconciliation had never tasted so sweet.

Fifteen

I REALIZED THAT IN ORDER FOR me to stay with Ryan and be in the Club, some sacrifices had to be made.

Nothing in the rules stated that a member had to have lunch every day with the Club. So I discussed it with the group and they understood that until order was restored to McKinley High, I would eat lunch every other day with Ryan and Bruce.

Although I didn't know how much I wanted order to be restored if it meant that Ryan and Todd would be besties again.

By Thursday, there were more people at Ryan's table. Not only because Diane and Tracy decided to join us, but two of Ryan's basketball friends also came over. Bruce was delighted that Tracy was there, although I feared he took it as a sign that she liked him. Fortunately, it also meant that he stopped prodding me about my conversation with her.

Things became more relaxed at school, but as Ryan and I made our way to Chicago to see his father, his nerves were very apparent. As were mine. Every time the traffic stalled on the interstate, I was relieved to be given a few more seconds before having to meet the man, the myth, the deadbeat dad. We were going to some fancy Italian restaurant and I wore my black Homecoming dress since nothing else in my closet was appropriate. I couldn't help but laugh when Ryan pulled up wearing *his* Homecoming outfit. Getting into the car gave me a glimpse of what could've been last year, and what our future could be.

Ryan tapped the steering wheel impatiently. "I probably shouldn't be dragging you into my family problems."

I placed my hand on his neck. "It's okay. I want to be there for you. Plus, I'm so ready to carbo load."

"Be sure to order a lot of food. Daddy Dearest has a lot of grievances he needs to pay for, and since money is the only thing that he cares about . . ."

The Chicago skyline began lighting up in the distance. The tall buildings glistened against the darkening night sky. As a kid, I always got chills when we drove along North Lake Shore Drive, with Lake Michigan to our left and downtown Chicago in front of us.

Although we'd budgeted time for Chicago's notorious traffic, we were a couple minutes late as we made our way up to Spiaggia. As soon as the restaurant doors opened, I knew I was out of my depth: high windows overlooking Lake Michigan; intricate, oversize chandeliers; marble columns. Pretty much the opposite of any dining experience I've ever had with my family. Or anyone. Ever.

As we approached the hostess, I tried to stand up a little straighter. Which was a challenge, since walking in heels wasn't a particularly strong suit of mine.

The hostess looked up the name, and then gave Ryan a warm smile. "Yes, I've been informed that one of the members of your party is running late. You can take a seat in the bar until he arrives."

"Figures," Ryan said under his breath as we made our way to the bar.

I scanned the small area for two seats when I spotted this tall, tanned, bottle blonde staring at us. I, in turn, was trying to not stare at her ginormous chest, but I figured if you spend that amount of money on something and wear a dress low-cut and open, you wouldn't mind eyes straying in that direction.

Right as I looked away, she started waving. I glanced behind us to find no one there.

"Do you know her?" I asked.

"No." Ryan looked very confused by the woman's attempt to get our attention.

She kept waving. Then she called, "Ryan! Over here!"

"Ah, well, she apparently knows you."

Clearly fed up by us ignoring her, she came over and, to my horror, gave Ryan a huge hug. "Ryan! Finally! We meet!" Everything she said was punctuated with a bounce of her heels.

"I'm sorry, do I . . . ?" Ryan was clearly perplexed.

I started looking around for hidden cameras, wondering if we were on some sort of prank show. Or if Ryan's dad had decided to hire his son a stripper for the evening.

The girl — she had to be only a few years older than us — grasped his arm tightly. "Oh. My. God. Did your dad keep me as a surprise?"

So it *was* a stripper, then.

"You know my dad?" Ryan asked.

"Duh!" She then held out her left hand, where a diamond the size of a tennis ball sat on her ring finger.

Oh. My. Trophy. Wife.

After reading Ryan's expression, she put her hand up against her mouth. "Oh! No! I guess that's what he wanted to tell you tonight. He's going to be so mad."

Ryan shook his head. "Let me make sure I'm getting this straight. You" — he pointed at her with open disgust — "are engaged *to my dad*?"

She hugged him again, her silicone smashing against Ryan's chest. "Isn't it great! I'm going to be your new mom!" She then giggled. And with yet another shock, I realized it wasn't the giggle of some thoughtless ditz. It was the giggle of some-one who was very, very nervous. Scared, even. She hadn't planned for this any more than we had. Plus, if I knew anything about Ryan's dad, it was that he liked to be in control of the situa-tion, so she was most likely going to get in trouble for telling Ryan. Even though she had also been conveniently left in the dark.

Ryan opened his mouth before taking a few stunned steps back. He mumbled something as he headed toward the eleva-tor and pressed the DOWN button angrily.

"But . . ." The girl's shoulders slouched as she helplessly watched Ryan leave.

This was clearly a disaster, and the girl now looked as shipwrecked as the rest of us. I reminded myself that she wasn't the person to be mad at. The person to be mad at hadn't bothered to show up on time.

She looked at me for an answer. I didn't know what to tell her.

"Sorry," I mumbled. Then I followed Ryan out of the restaurant.

Once we got in the elevator, I touched his arm, and he pulled it away. "I need a second," he said. His jaw was clenched tightly.

We silently made our way back to his car. Ryan sat in the driver's seat for a couple of minutes without making a movement or a sound. I knew there was nothing I could say to make him feel better, so I remained quiet.

The ringer on his cell phone broke the silence. Ryan didn't move to pick it up or even look at who was calling. I guessed by the "Imperial March" ringtone from *Star Wars*, he knew exactly who it was.

"Do you want me to drive?" I offered, trying to get him to react to something.

And then he finally responded. He reacted in a way that shocked, scared, and impressed me. Because in that parking garage on the Magnificent Mile, Ryan Bauer absolutely lost it.

He started hitting the steering wheel repeatedly, then shook it so violently I almost got out of the car. "Asshole! Asshole! Asshole!" he screamed. Then he let go and collapsed back like a rag doll. Tears started rolling down his cheeks. "I'm sorry, Penny, but I can't deal with his complete and utter bullshit anymore. I can't wait to turn eighteen so neither of us is legally obligated to pretend that we're family." He began to laugh bitterly. "Some father. How long do you think he's known her? Do you think she has *any idea* what she's getting into?"

His phone rang again. He shut it off and threw it into the backseat. "And I'm sure the only purpose of tonight was so that he could pretend to be this great dad to impress her. He's such a fraud."

He leaned forward and rested his head on the steering wheel. "And I'm going to have to be the one to tell Mom."

I placed my hand on his cheek. "Do you want me to be there when you do?"

He shook his head.

"Ryan, you know how I always joke that I hope I'm not like my parents. Well, I know I am. But you are nothing, *nothing* like your father. I don't have to meet him to know that."

He didn't reply.

"I mean, we both know how attracted you are to au naturel." I playfully gestured at my chest, which wasn't tiny, but it was nowhere near the watermelons we'd just encountered. "Oh, and you're the opposite of an asshole, so that right there should count for something."

He finally sat up, wiped away the tears on his cheeks, and nodded to himself. It was something I'd seen him do when he was getting ready for a big play on the court. "Okay, moving on." He turned the key in the ignition, then looked at me. "Can you drive? I'm afraid I'd break some NASCAR record right now."

As we got out of the car to switch places, I pulled him into me and hugged him tightly. Everything that Diane and Tyson had said to me came flooding back. All Ryan wanted was for me to be there, be present, for him. I may have failed at that in the past, but I knew that now all he needed was for me to hold him and to help him through this.

It was something I wasn't going to screw up.

Sixteen

Up until that point, I approached everything with an either-or mentality. It was always Ryan or the Club. And while I couldn't let my relationship with Ryan interfere with the Club (and vice versa), I *could* influence the Club's social calendar.

Saturday night the Club would attend the last home game for the guys' varsity basketball team. Then afterward we'd go out for cupcakes and milk shakes.

No either. No or. Total harmony.

Plus, there would be cupcakes, so win-win all around.

First, though, came Friday night. Morgan and I were on our way to hear Tyson's band play at a tiny coffee shop the next town over. Ryan was going to meet us there after practice.

I loved it when a plan came together.

"Do you think you can help me run an errand first?" Morgan asked as she pulled into a parking spot in bustling downtown Parkview.

"Of course," I said as we got out of the car.

Morgan was nervously biting her fingernails. "Thanks, I think I need some backup for this."

We walked into a drugstore that I was more than familiar with. Morgan grabbed a cart and started filling it seemingly at random — a bottle of soda, cotton swabs, lip balm — as she made her way down the aisle. Her eyes swept the store in a nervous manner.

My immediate reaction to her suspicious behavior was that she was thinking of shoplifting. Nothing else made sense.

"Do you need help finding anything?" I asked.

She shook her head. "I know where I'm going." She picked up a can of hair spray and studied it intently. As soon as a woman pushing a stroller passed us, Morgan quickly walked down to the feminine hygiene section.

Was this what all the fuss was about? Buying some tampons?

"Um, do you want me to do this?" I offered.

Morgan haphazardly picked up a box, then turned her back to the display. "No, it's okay."

I followed her eye line and realized we were standing right next to the condom display. Morgan quickly picked up a box and put it behind the tampon one so she could read it more discreetly.

"Morgan!" I hissed. "You do realize that *my mom* works here."

She gasped. "Oh, God, I forgot. I wanted to have someone here with me so I didn't have to do this by myself."

Just as I was walking out of the aisle and away from any evidence that could sentence me to the guillotine, I heard my mom's voice. I froze with fear.

"Penny Lane, why, isn't this a nice treat!" Mom approached me in her white pharmacist's coat. "Sue thought she saw you walk in. Hi, Morgan!"

Morgan gave Mom a weak smile, the blood draining from her face. She was clenching her boxes as if her life depended on it.

"I thought you guys were going to Tyson's concert." She looked between us.

"Yeah." I tried to remain calm. "We wanted to pick up some stuff, soda, and the like . . ."

Morgan looked down at her hands, trying desperately to not show what was behind the tampon box. "Yeah, that time of the month and everything." She gestured toward the box and then went to place it in her cart. As she did her best to hide the proof of what we were really doing there, the boxes separated.

It was like watching a bomb slowly descend. In reality, it probably took only two seconds, but in the middle of the store with my mother as a witness, it felt like eighteen hours of torture. When the box of condoms finally landed on the floor, it was like an explosion had gone off in my chest.

There, between our three sets of feet, lay the evidence in all its "for her pleasure" glory.

It took Mom a few seconds to process what she was seeing. Once she did, her head jolted up and she grabbed me by the elbow. "In the back. Now."

Morgan stepped forward. "Please, Mrs. Bloom, this isn't Penny's fault. She didn't know what I wanted to do here. It's not her, it —" She finally took a breath. "Please don't tell my parents."

Mom studied us with pursed lips. "Penny Lane, we need to have a talk when you get home tonight. And you need to be back by nine, not ten."

I didn't even bother trying to protest. There was no point.

Morgan looked at the basket, not sure what to do next.

Mom held out her hand. "I'll take that."

We exited the store quickly in a flurry of apologies. Once we got outside and into the safety of Morgan's car, I finally exhaled.

"I'm so sorry." Morgan put her hands over her face. "I didn't know what to do, and I thought if I walked in with someone and didn't make it a big deal, it *wouldn't* be a big deal." And then she said the understatement of the millennium. "That was a disaster."

"Why didn't you tell me that you decided to finally do it?" I asked.

She slumped even farther down in her seat. "I wasn't sure. Then I thought if I could handle the responsibility of getting some condoms, then maybe I was ready. I guess I have my answer." Morgan started slapping her forehead, as if trying to rid herself of the memory. She groaned, "I think I'm going to die from embarrassment."

Yeah, I was going to actually die from being murdered. By my mother. For a crime I wasn't committing.

"Listen, I understand if you don't want to go tonight," Morgan said. The color that had drained from her face had returned, and then some.

I thought for a moment. "No, we should go. It's probably the last time I'll be let out of the house until I'm thirty."

Plus, I figured it would be best to warn Ryan that he should probably go into the witness protection program.

Music had always helped me escape from my troubles. I'd had to lean on John, Paul, George, and Ringo more times than I could remember.

But there was a cloud of insecurity, worry, and genuine fear that no music could help me through that evening. Even though Tyson's band was good, the cloud kept hanging over me all night. As much as Morgan and I tried to joke about it once we got to the coffee shop, I knew what this meant.

I kept thinking about what my mom had seen. What she must've thought of me. First, she had to overhear that I was dating Nate behind her back, that I had planned to sleep with him, and that instead I'd caught him sleeping with someone else. Now she'd caught me in the condom aisle.

Was she ever going to trust me again?

I walked slowly up our driveway at a quarter to nine. After I'd confided in Ryan about what had happened, he'd insisted that I get home even before my newly imposed nine o'clock curfew.

When I walked through the front door, I saw Mom sitting at the kitchen table, sipping tea. There wasn't any TV or music on. She wasn't reading. She was simply sitting there patiently.

Waiting for me.

She pushed out the chair across from her as I walked into the kitchen, and I sat down. She tapped her fingernail against the ceramic mug with artwork from the *Revolver* album.

"I don't think I need to tell you how proud I am of what you've done with The Lonely Hearts Club, Penny Lane."

I nodded.

She continued in a measured voice. "The initiative and strength it took to start it and lead by example is truly amazing."

I remained silent, waiting for the inevitable "but" that was to come.

"Your father and I have really come to enjoy these Saturdays with the girls. And that party on Valentine's Day was extraordinary. You truly have started, in the words of John Lennon, a revolution. But . . ."

And there it was.

She pinched the bridge of her nose, as if the thoughts swirling in her head were causing her pain. "But truthfully, I don't know how much I can trust you anymore. You lied to me about Nate, you lied to me when you said that you and Ryan weren't even thinking about taking a bigger step, and then I had to find you in my store, of all places, buying condoms."

After a few seconds of silence, I realized it was time to plead my case.

"I never lied about Nate," I stated. "Yes, I didn't tell you what was going on, because he wanted to keep it a secret. He told me a lot of things I shouldn't have believed. Believe me, Mom, I wish every day that I never fell for Nate. That I didn't get duped by his lies. But I did. And I've moved on. I'd prefer to never see him again, but I don't think I could stand Dad looking at me" — my voice cracked — "the way that you're looking at me now. I betrayed your trust. I know that. I thought I was in love." I couldn't help but laugh at my own naïveté. "And then when everything went badly, I wanted to pretend it hadn't happened."

Mom nodded solemnly. "I wish you felt you could've told me all this after it happened."

"I know, and I'm sorry. If it makes you feel any better, I did tell Rita and she threatened his life."

"Oddly enough, that does." Mom reached for my hand across the table.

I felt we had a truce on the Nate situation, but I knew this conversation was far from over.

"And I swear, Mom, Ryan and I are not even talking about next steps." Our relationship was in a delicate enough position without adding that to it. "I didn't know why we were in your store." Then I decided to reason with her rationally. "I mean, do you think I'd be stupid enough to do that where you work?" I would've hoped she had more faith in me than that.

"So you've already put some thought into it?"

"What? No!" I exclaimed.

Maybe I should join Ryan in witness protection.

"Well, let's talk about it, then." From the chair next to her, Mom pulled out the dreaded props for "the talk." She immediately opened to a flagged page of the female reproductive system.

She began her epic speech. "When a man and a woman, not a bunch of teenagers, fall in love, true love . . ."

I didn't protest. I sat there and took my punishment. Given the circumstances, it could've been much, much worse.

Seventeen

ONE PERSON'S HUMILIATION WAS ANOTHER'S SOURCE of pure joy.

Tracy wiped away a tear. "That is seriously the greatest thing I've ever heard. I wonder if I can get the security tapes from the store so I can see the look on your mom's face."

I ignored her as we made our way up the bleachers to where The Lonely Hearts Club was sitting at the game on Saturday. Diane, Jen, and Jessica were meeting us later, since they'd had an away game that afternoon.

Tracy continued, oblivious to my annoyance. "As I said before, these high school relationships simply aren't worth it."

"Thanks for reminding me. Yet again."

The smile on Tracy's face vanished. "You know I'm only talking about myself. The story is hilarious, but you're right, high school romances can be fun — for some people. Or at least that's what I've been told."

I ignored her passive-aggressive comment and spotted Ryan's mom and eight-year-old stepsister seated a section over from us. "I'm going to say hi to Ryan's family, since, you know, I'm only a pawn in the high school romance hierarchy. Gee," I raised my voice into a fake coo, "I hope I'll be able to make it over there all by myself without my boyfriend to escort me."

"You know that's not what I meant."

Which was true, but what was also true was that Tracy's negative opinion on dating guys in high school came from me.

Katie, Ryan's stepsister, waved happily when she saw me approaching. "Hi, Penny!" she called out. She had on an over-size McKinley sweatshirt.

I gave her a quick hug as Ryan's mom moved over to make room for me.

"Great to see you, Penny." Her eyes went over to the Club. "I see you convinced the girls to come out tonight. That's great. I can't believe how big the group has gotten. And you've broken out beyond Parkview — you must be so excited."

That familiar sense of pride arose in me. "Thanks, I really can't believe . . ." My voice trailed off as Ryan's mom put her hand up to her mouth like she was about to be sick.

"Is everything okay?" I asked.

She nodded in disbelief. "Yeah, it's . . ."

I looked over to the entrance where an older guy had walked in. He looked familiar, but I couldn't quite place him. He had on dark jeans and a seemingly expensive black leather jacket. He was tall, lean, with black wavy hair with some gray around the temples, and blue eyes.

"Is that Ryan's dad?" I asked, almost scared for the reply.

Ryan's mom nodded her head slowly. "Yeah. I guess if the mountain won't come to Mohammad . . ."

It was clear that she'd had no idea he was coming, so I had

a feeling Ryan was also clueless. His reaction, though, would be much more furious than shock.

"I, ah, should go," I excused myself. It looked like he was going to come over, and I didn't want to be there when he did. I didn't want to meet Ryan's dad, especially after what he'd put Ryan through. I didn't want to betray Ryan by being polite to his father when his father couldn't extend the same courtesy to his only child.

Once I got back to my seat, I studied Ryan during their warm-up to see when the realization would kick in that his father was there. I couldn't figure out a way to warn him. Maybe he already knew and was doing an excellent job of ignoring him. I knew he was a very focused athlete, but there was no way this wouldn't affect him.

After the national anthem, the starting players were announced. The Club cheered loudly for McKinley, although we were significantly more subdued when Todd was introduced. When Ryan's name was called, he ran out to the middle of the court and high-fived his fellow teammates. He looked over briefly to where his mother was sitting, then froze.

He saw his dad.

Anybody else seeing Ryan probably wouldn't have noticed anything, since he quickly returned to shaking out his arms and legs. The team went back into a huddle. Todd said something to Ryan, which resulted in Ryan pushing him away. I couldn't tell if it was typical teammate teasing or Todd being his general loser self.

From the tip-off, it was clear that Ryan was not in the zone. He missed his first basket, lost control of the ball, and failed to stop a simple layup when he was on defense. And that was only the first two minutes of the game.

Ryan Bauer didn't miss shots. He didn't let the other team score. And he certainly didn't lose his composure.

But this was not his day.

After Ryan missed another shot, he ran down the court, his cheeks flush from frustration, his jaw tightly clenched.

"COME ON, RYAN! FOCUS!" his dad screamed.

Todd looked up in the stands and a smirk crept onto his face when he realized who was there.

As they ran down the court, Todd bumped into Ryan and said something that caused Ryan to push Todd again, with more force than last time.

One of the opposing players dribbled down the court, and as he went to shoot, Ryan jumped up and blocked the shot. But he was too aggressive and was called for a foul.

Ryan backed away from the free throw line as the other player scored a basket. Todd came over to him, and I hoped with all my might that Todd would do the right thing and try to calm Ryan down. They had no chance of winning if he didn't.

Todd lightly tapped Ryan's head. And since they were only about forty feet from us, we were able to catch part of the conversation, especially one word that stood out.

"Wait." Tracy sat up a little straighter. "Did Todd just say something about you?"

I, unfortunately, wasn't hearing things. There was no reason for my name to be brought up during a basketball game.

Ryan walked away from Todd. But I'd never seen him this upset. Not when I blew him off the day after Valentine's Day, not when his friends chose Todd over him, not when his dad kept his engagement a secret. All of which had happened in less than a week.

Although I'd never craved the attention of being center court, at that instant I wanted to rush onto the court and give him a hug. But I knew there was nothing I could do. Ryan was on his own. With the majority of the school watching. With his father watching. And with Todd kicking a guy when he was down.

For the next few minutes, the banter and bumping between Todd and Ryan escalated — so much so that the coach finally called a time-out. I ignored the cheerleaders as they took to the court, and watched the coach get in both Todd's and Ryan's faces.

"Ah, what's going on?" Tracy asked.

"Yeah," Kara called out next to her. "Why are Ryan and Todd fighting during the game? Isn't their aggression supposed to be saved for the other team?"

I looked at both of them and noticed that the majority of the Club was leaning forward to hear what I had to say. So it was apparent to everybody, not only me. I looked over and saw Ryan's mom pleading with his dad, probably asking him to leave.

The whistle blew and they returned to the court. I felt I had to do something to let Ryan know there were people there who cared for him.

I stood up and screamed, "GO, RYAN!"

A lame attempt, yes, but little did I realize the ripple effect such a short, and anemic, attempt at support would have.

Todd started laughing right there in the middle of the game. He pointed at me and said something to Ryan.

And then something happened that I never in a million years thought I would see.

Ryan Bauer, Golden Boy and Straight-A Student, punched Todd Chesney in the face and tackled him to the floor.

There was a flurry of whistles being blown and teammates pulling the two off of each other. Gasps of disbelief, as well as a few boos, emanated from the stands. Todd and Ryan were being restrained, each by two other players, but they were both still trying to attack.

I sat there helpless and horrified as the referees came over and ejected both Ryan and Todd from the game. Todd broke away from his captors and got in the face of the ref, gesturing accusatorily toward Ryan.

Yes, it had been Ryan who'd started the fight, but Todd hadn't helped matters. Ryan would never have acted that way unless he was pushed too far. The kind of week he had would've been too much for anybody.

Although it was about time someone punched Todd in the face. I only wished it had been me.

The commotion on the court finally quieted down as Ryan and Todd were escorted to the locker room by the assistant coach. They were followed by Todd's dad and, much to my horror, Ryan's dad.

I stood there unable to move. I knew there was nothing I could do at that moment to make the situation any better, but I also thought I needed to be there for Ryan. I mumbled something to Tracy before I slowly made my way out of the gym and around the corner to the locker room exit.

The fluorescent lightbulbs buzzing overhead kept me company, as I'd occasionally hear noise drift from the gym. And then I'd hear yelling in the locker room.

"What the hell were you thinking? What kind of behavior was that?" A voice I didn't recognize was booming loudly. "I thought you knew better. But I guess not. I'm embarrassed to call you my son."

I moved a few feet from the door so I wouldn't have to be subjected to what was a very private, very demoralizing, very rough conversation. One that I was positive was aimed at Ryan.

The door swung open suddenly, which caused me to jump back.

I was face-to-face with Ryan's dad. He didn't even give me a glance before he stormed away. The door opened again with much less force and it was Ryan's mom, looking visibly upset.

She stopped when she noticed me. "Oh, Penny. Good, you're here. A friend's watching Katie because I need to . . ." She looked toward her ex-husband.

"It's okay, go," I said, knowing that someone had to have the unfortunate task of trying to reason with Ryan's dad.

She bolted after him. "Get back here! How dare you talk to . . ." Her voice faded as she went around the corner.

I heard some more voices behind the door and found myself holding my breath.

Todd and his dad both walked out. His father was going on and on about how unfair this all was. Todd was looking down at the floor but then saw my feet and looked up. A bruise had started to sprout from his right eye.

"Oh, great, come to rub my face in it?" he asked, his face hard.

"I didn't, I'm not . . ." I stumbled over my words.

He laughed coldly. "Yeah, whatever. You can do whatever you want and not care about what happens, huh?"

I had no idea what he was talking about.

"It's funny." He gestured to his dad. "She forms this stupid club all about not changing when you get a boyfriend or whatever crap she's brainwashing chicks with, but it's *her boyfriend* who's changed the most. What's that called? Irony?"

I was impressed that Todd was able to accurately define the word *irony*. He must've been studying for the SATs.

Todd's dad had his arms folded, clearly not interested in whatever it was his son was going on about. "Come on, let's go."

They both turned their backs on me, but I was startled when I called out, "Wait!"

Todd turned around and his father told him to meet him at the car.

"What do you want?" Todd took two steps forward. I glanced at the doors, willing Ryan to appear.

"I, I . . ." I suddenly felt exhausted. I was so sick of fighting. "What's your problem, Todd? Really? So you don't like the Club. Get over it. We're not going anywhere. You don't like Ryan dating me. Well, that's not your call. Why do you keep having to *poke, poke, poke* at people until they snap?" I jabbed him with my finger to emphasize my point. "*Poke, poke, poke.* Do you really get so much pleasure in making people miserable? Does it make you feel like a bigger person?"

"Yeah, this is my doing." He narrowed his eyes. "Let's look at Bauer's life since he started dating you. He's lost most of his friends. He's had his ass handed to him by his dad, which isn't anything new, but I've never seen him so mad. And there was something else." He dramatically tapped his finger to his lips. "Oh yeah, he's been thrown off the basketball team for the rest of the season. So who's really the one taking everything away from him? Not me." Todd gave me one last disgusted look before he walked away. Leaving me alone with his accusations swirling in my head.

I couldn't believe Ryan had gotten kicked off the team. They had only a couple games left in the season, but still. Ryan didn't get kicked off teams. He also didn't get into physical fights. Or into any trouble.

I was trying to make sense of what had happened, when the door opened slowly. Ryan walked out with his head down, his hoodie covering his face.

"Hey," I said lightly, not knowing what I could say to make any of this better.

"Hey," Ryan replied. He lifted his head slightly to reveal a bruise forming under his left eye.

I approached him cautiously and wrapped my arms around him. His arms stayed limp at his sides for a few beats before he reached around me, his grasp tightening. I felt him exhale sharply. I held on to him. He didn't need me to question him or try to make him think that everything was going to be okay.

Because, truthfully, I had no idea what was going to happen next. So much had already changed for him as it was. And not for the best.

After a few minutes, we heard the final buzzer echo from the gym. Ryan broke away from me. "I guess we should get going. I don't know if I can handle an audience right now."

We quickly walked to his car, but once we were safely inside, he didn't move to turn on the engine. He let out a forced laugh.

"What's so funny?" I asked.

"Oh, nothing. I'm simply trying to figure out what the hell happened to my life."

"Ryan . . ." I started to reason with him, but he shook his head.

"I know that this is for the best." I don't think even he believed what he was saying. "I used to love going to practice and playing with the guys, but it hasn't been the same in a really long time. It isn't fun anymore."

"Well, that's because of Todd."

"I guess." He finally turned the ignition key and pulled out of the parking lot.

He *guessed*? This was all Todd's fault. Ryan would never have punched him if he hadn't been antagonized. Yes, this was all one hundred percent Todd Chesney's fault. How dare Todd try to lay the blame on me.

But it really shouldn't have surprised me, because passing the buck is what cowards do.

Ryan was driving aimlessly around town. "Do you want me to drop you off at the diner? Isn't that where you guys are meeting tonight?"

"Oh, yeah." I glanced at the clock; the Club would be arriving shortly. "But I don't need to go."

"No — you should go. I need to get home and talk to my mom."

"Are you sure?"

"I'm sure."

I felt bad leaving him, but I didn't really know what else I could say. "Do you want to hang out tomorrow?" I offered.

"If I'm not grounded," he stated matter-of-factly.

"Oh." I hadn't really thought the repercussions of the game would filter outside the basketball team.

"But your mom will understand that Todd was being Todd, right?"

"I don't know. I've never been grounded before, but getting into a fight, in public, seems like something that would warrant it."

"You've *never been grounded*?"

"No. Have you?" He gave me a sideways glance, his lips curling into a grin.

"I plead the Fifth." *Of course* I'd been grounded. I lived in a house where not cleaning my room, "sassing" mom, and referring to "Revolution 9" as "noise" would get me grounded. Either my parents' tolerance for teenage shenanigans was low or Ryan really was that perfect.

It was a toss-up.

Ryan pulled over in front of the diner. "Here you go. Try not to get in too much trouble, Groundy McJuvie."

"Okay, Grounded at Seventeen. Hey, maybe that should be the name of your memoir?"

"Not *Down and Out by Seventeen*?" he said. Then his face fell.

"Are you sure you're okay?"

"No," he answered. "But I'm sure it's not going to be solved tonight. You better go in there and defend my honor."

I tried to play it off lightly. "You punched Todd in the face, so I pretty much think the entire school envies you right now."

"Right." His face was blank. I had no idea what he was thinking. Maybe it was best that I didn't know.

"Well . . ." I tried to think of something to say to ease his tension, but then remembered that sometimes actions speak louder than words. I leaned in and kissed him. Hard.

He pulled away. "Have a good night."

Okay, maybe trying to make out with my boyfriend right after he was suspended from his basketball team wasn't my smoothest move.

I quickly exited the car and entered the diner. The Club was sitting at a few tables in the back. Tracy caught my eye and stood up. "What are you doing here?"

I pulled over a chair and ignored her quizzical stare. "Ah, this is The Lonely Hearts Club meeting, right? You may have heard of me, Penny Lane Bloom? I kinda started it."

The Club's attention turned toward me. There were murmurs of shock that I was there.

"Guys," I said, trying to not feel offended that they, for the first time, looked unhappy to see me. "It's a Saturday night. Why wouldn't I be here?"

"But Ryan . . ." Tracy was shaking her head back and forth like it was about to explode. "You left him?"

"No, I didn't *leave* him. He said it was fine."

But now I was wondering if it really was fine.

The whole time at the diner, I was there physically, but my mind was with Ryan. He said that he didn't need me, but maybe he did.

I couldn't protect Ryan from his dad or Todd. I could, however, control my actions.

And I chose to leave when I should've insisted on staying.

Be there for him. It was supposed to be as simple as that.

But I wasn't there for him.

All I could do was second-guess.

Eighteen

IT'S FINE.

That's what I kept hearing from Ryan anytime I brought up Saturday night or anything else, really.

But it wasn't fine. Nothing about what was going on was fine.

Ryan did throw the first punch, but everybody at school on Monday was acting like he was a stone-cold criminal. And I was certain these were the same people who, if given the chance, wouldn't have minded taking Todd down a peg or fourteen.

I'd gotten used to stares and whispers of accusation long ago, but this was new territory for Ryan. Sure, there was plenty of gossip when he and Diane first broke up, but it was mostly people placing bets on who'd be his next girlfriend.

The odds had never been in my favor on that one.

All day I kept looking around whenever we were together. Ryan kept saying, "Penny, it's fine. It's not as big of a deal as you're making it."

But it was.

Was he not paying attention, or did he really not care?

I was pacing around our lockers at the end of school, waiting for him so we could go back to my house to study since he didn't have basketball practice anymore. But he was late.

Ryan was never late.

My head began to pound. Todd's voice kept repeating in my head, saying that Ryan had changed since we'd started dating.

Had he?

It was time to examine the facts. Since Ryan and I had started dating, he and Todd were no longer friends (a plus as far as I was concerned). He no longer sat at his regular lunch table. His other friends had been keeping their distance. He wasn't speaking to his father. He'd gotten into a fight. He'd been kicked off the basketball team.

Yikes.

Well, at least he hadn't been grounded. His mom felt that given the "extenuating circumstances" of his dad being there, his actions, while not condoned, were understandable.

But that still didn't explain where he was.

Hilary Jacobs walked past and probably noticed me staring at Ryan's locker. "Hey, Penny. Ryan's in the principal's office."

My stomach sank. "He is?"

"Yeah, he was called there at the end of class."

I ran off toward the office but saw Ryan as soon as I turned the corner.

"Hey!" I said with relief. "I was getting worried."

"Sorry, I had to talk to Braddock." He kept up his pace.

"Oh, is everything okay?" But I could tell by his stoic look that it wasn't.

"Yeah, I mean, no. He took me off the Student Advisory Committee."

"He *what?*" I practically screamed, causing people who hadn't been staring to do so now. But of course it made sense. I was naïve to think that what happened on the court would've stayed on the court. Ryan probably should've been suspended. This was the first time I was grateful Principal Braddock notoriously favored, and often turned a blind eye to the behavior of, the male athletes at the school.

Oh God, I thought. *Is this going to affect Ryan's college applications?*

"He said that he felt my actions on Saturday didn't give him a choice. Then, of course, he wanted to discuss what chances I think they'll have in the play-offs."

"Is Todd still on his kiss-ass committee?"

"I don't know." Ryan opened his locker. "I'm trying to not keep tabs on what Todd's up to."

"I bet he is," I groaned.

Ryan sighed. "It's fine."

I almost screamed when he said that.

"Seriously, Penny," he continued. "It's for the best."

I couldn't contain myself any more. "Is it? Is it *really?*"

How could he think that losing two important parts of his student life was a good thing?

He threw his hands up in the air. "What am I going to do? Nothing. I don't have a time machine. I've made my choice. I have to live with the consequences." He zipped up his jacket and started walking toward the exit.

I followed slowly behind him.

Yes, he had made a choice, hadn't he?

He'd chosen me.

And look at the price he's had to pay for it.

Tuesday.

"How are your grades?" I asked Ryan cautiously during lunch, hoping his stellar academic record hadn't been jeopardized as well.

Ryan shrugged his shoulders indifferently. "They're good."

"Good, like normal people good or like Ryan Bauer good?" I wanted clarification, since my grades, which were decent, wouldn't be considered good to Ryan, who thought an A-minus was average.

"Penny, they're fine."

Fine.

Wednesday.

I'd become hyperaware of every minute I spent with Ryan. On the outside he looked the same (except for the bruise on his face and small cut on his lip from the fight). But everything else had changed so much. I had to find one thing that was still going well for him. I had to convince myself that I hadn't ruined his life.

"So . . ." I tapped on Ryan's notebook. He looked up at me. "I've been thinking a lot about choices lately. You know? Like the decisions that we make."

"Okay." He pushed his history book aside with a sigh, like he was annoyed with me. "Go ahead."

"Do you ever have any regrets? About anything?"

There. I threw out my line to see if he would take the bait.

"Of course — don't we all?" He went back to writing in his notebook. "We have to live with our mistakes. There's no point in torturing yourself over it."

No point torturing yourself.

Thursday.

Decisions.

I kept going over and over in my head how to make things right with Ryan.

You'd think with everything that had happened, we'd be closer than ever, but something was wrong.

He wouldn't talk to me. Sometimes he wouldn't even look at me.

He kept insisting that he was "fine," but being around him made it clear how miserable he truly was.

The damage had been done with Ryan's dad, Todd, and the basketball team. There was nothing I could do about that. But there was someone else who had also hurt him the last couple of weeks.

Me.

I tried to talk to him, but there was no use. At times it felt like there was this wall growing between us. A wall that was being built brick by brick because of the consequences Ryan had to suffer because he chose me.

We were stuck. And the only answer that kept appearing in my head was the hardest one.

Freedom.

His freedom.

I kept thinking about what Tracy had said, *"What's the point?"*

What was the point of Ryan being with me if it was only causing him misery? What was the point if we'd only end up hurting each other? Hadn't I hurt him enough as it was?

I didn't want to let Ryan go, but I was being selfish keeping him in my life. We didn't need to break *up*, but what if we took a break? A little sabbatical, so he could get everything back to where it was. So he could get to a place where he was happy, where he wasn't regretting any decisions he had made.

"Everything okay?" Ryan asked as he pulled into the driveway at my house. "You've been a little off all week. Is it wedding stress?"

I'd been a little off this week? Yes, there was a lot going on with the major family event that was happening in less than two days, but *I* wasn't the one in denial. I wasn't the one brushing off everything that had been going on as being "fine."

Because despite what Ryan kept repeating, it wasn't fine. It was the opposite of fine.

"No, I've been thinking . . . what do you think about taking a vacation?"

Ryan's eyes lit up. "I think a vacation sounds awesome. What kind of vacation?"

The words were caught in my throat, but I knew I had to do this for him. "A vacation from me."

He slouched back in his seat. "What do you mean? A vacation from you?"

"With everything going on, I thought that maybe it's best for us to take a little break. Maybe hit the reset button." I felt a hot sting behind my eyes, a heaviness weighing on my heart.

"You mean get everything back to where it was before you had to balance me and the Club?"

"No. This has nothing to do with the Club." Although a part of me wondered if deep down inside it did. Emancipating Ryan would mean that I would no longer be forced to choose between the two. He'd no longer have to feel the hurt of being an afterthought. "Wouldn't it be nice for you to have everything back to normal?"

"Normal? You think my life would be normal without you in it?" Ryan's voice started to rise. "Is that what this week was all about? All the questions? With everything happening, you want to add *breaking up with me* to the list?"

"No, no," I protested. But wasn't that what I was doing? "It's not a breakup. Don't you think your life would be better without me in it? All I've done is cause you pain."

His mouth fell open in disbelief. "And *this* wouldn't cause me pain? Do you honestly believe that my life would be better without you in it?"

I had to look away. "Yes," I said so softly I wasn't sure he heard me. "But we aren't breaking up."

"Then what are we doing?"

"Do I really need to go over everything that's happened to you since you've been with me?"

"None of that stuff had anything to do with you."

"Can you honestly say that?"

"Penny, look at me." He placed his hand gently on my knee.

I couldn't. I kept my gaze to my hands clenched in my lap.

"Is this what you really want?" he asked.

No.

But how could I keep doing this to him? And how could he not see that things *would* be better if he wasn't with me?

"Penny" — Ryan's tone became increasingly impatient — "I asked you a simple question. What do *you* want?"

"I . . ." Hot tears ran down my face. *I want you, but I don't want to hurt you anymore.* "Please don't make this more difficult for me."

"Difficult for *you*? What about *me*? This is all *your* doing. *You're* the one who wants a break." His voice was hard. "Okay, so let's make this easy on *you*: Are you in or are you out?"

There it was. I already knew what I had to do, but I didn't want to do it.

I let Ryan's words give me strength to do what needed to be done.

I'm simply trying to figure out what the hell happened to my life.

I've made my choice. I have to live with the consequences.

No point torturing yourself.

"I'm out," I said meekly before running out of his car.

I kept replaying another thing Ryan had said.

It's for the best.

But that was one statement I couldn't believe.

Friday.

Pure hell.

I kept my head down all day in school. I refused to acknowledge the whispers from everybody, including The Lonely Hearts Club. All I needed to do was get through the school day. I avoided Ryan. I avoided everybody. I stayed numb.

I had made *my* choice. And I had to live with the consequences.

Let It Be

"There will be an answer, let it be."

Nineteen

IF THERE WAS EVER A GOOD time to break up with a guy because you were ruining his life, I guess right before your sister's wedding would be it.

We were so busy Thursday night entertaining Lucy's fiancé's family, I didn't get a chance to tell my family about Ryan. But it was only a matter of time before they found out, especially when he was supposed to be my date at the wedding. As difficult as it was to get through the school day on Friday, I knew as soon as I walked into our house, there'd be so much to do. I hoped I wouldn't have enough time to be miserable.

"Penny Lane, you're finally home!" I heard feet quickly coming down the stairs. Lucy rounded the corner and scooped me up in her arms. "It's so quiet around here with everybody off running errands. Can you believe it? I'm getting married tomorrow!" She laughed and seemed so happy.

I managed something that resembled a smile.

Lucy studied me. "Is everything okay? You were so quiet last night. Not like anybody can get a word in edgewise around Rita."

"Yes, everything's great," I lied.

"Oh, and I forgot to tell you that I was organizing the gifts last week. You wouldn't believe how many boxes came to our apartment. I don't think we're going to have room for anything else. Why on earth did we insist on getting a rice cooker?"

"Especially since you don't cook," I reminded her.

She took my hand and led me to the couch. "True. Anyways, we got Ryan's gift before we left. That was so sweet of him — he didn't need to get us anything."

I felt my bottom lip start to quiver. Of course Ryan had been thoughtful enough to get them something off their registry.

"Penny, I'm your big sister, I know there's something wrong. Please tell me." Lucy put her arm around me, and that simple act of comfort broke apart the numbness that had taken over my body. I was able to find some solace that I was in private as the sobbing curtain fell.

I told Lucy everything about the last couple weeks, about how much I'd been struggling with balancing the Club and Ryan. About everything Ryan had been through because of me.

"So" — I wiped away my tears — "he's not coming to the wedding. It happened yesterday, and I haven't had the strength to tell Mom."

"Don't worry about the wedding." Lucy hugged me. "That should be the least of your concerns. So we'll have an extra chicken — who cares! What I do want to know is how you're doing. Truly."

That was such a tough question to answer. It was one I'd been avoiding for the past twenty-four hours. "I'm okay.

Actually, I'm not. I'm confused, I'm angry, I'm sad, I feel sick, and then sometimes I feel like I don't know what I am."

"Oh, Penny." Lucy tenderly brushed my hair out of my face. "You're in love. It can be great, and sometimes it can suck. Believe me. You wouldn't have all those emotions if you didn't care. Is there any way you can make it work?"

I thought about it. I really did. I already had regret about what I'd done. Could I make it work? But it hadn't been working. What would make me think things would be different? They wouldn't. There had already been too much collateral damage.

"I can't, believe me," I said with finality.

We heard the garage door open. I ran to the bathroom to make sure any evidence of my breakdown was gone.

Dry eyes, closed heart, can't lose.

I heard Mom talking Lucy's ear off about some hotel snafu with her cousins. By the time I got to the kitchen, Mom was in full wedding dictator mode.

"Okay. I've been going over the car situation going from the ceremony to the reception." She took out the binder she'd been filling since the day Lucy got engaged. "Penny Lane, do you think it would be okay if Ryan didn't come in the limo with the wedding party but rode with your uncle Dan instead? I don't think there'll be enough room. Unless he wants to drive there himself. Whatever he wants."

"Um," I stalled. I knew that it was now or never. Maybe she'd be grateful to not have to deal with another body. "Well, see . . ."

Mom looked up at me, annoyed. "I know you want him in the limo, but there isn't room. And I really want the entire wedding party to be together. Less chance of there being any issues getting to the reception."

"Mom," Lucy started, but I stopped her.

"It's not a problem. Ryan isn't going."

"What?" Mom started shaking her head. "But he RSVP'd!"

"I'm sorry. We . . ." I reminded myself to stay strong and took a deep breath. "We broke up."

I kept hoping the pain would lessen every time I had to say those two words, but it didn't. It got worse.

"Oh, Penny Lane." Mom moved forward in an attempt to embrace her baby girl, but I backed away.

"It's okay, Mom. Really. I'm fine. It wasn't working."

Telling everybody that I was "fine" when I was the opposite, just like Ryan did, only confirmed my suspicions that he was truly miserable with me.

Mom turned to Lucy for a better explanation, since she wisely didn't believe mine. Lucy simply returned her look with a tight smile and pretended to pore over the itinerary for the big day.

"All right." Mom nodded. "Do you want to talk about it?"

"Not really," I said, grateful for being able to tell the truth for once.

"You'd let me know if you wanted to talk about it, or if you needed anything, right?" she gently prodded.

"Yes, I'll be fine." Then a thought occurred to me. "Is it okay if I bring someone else?"

"Of course," Mom replied. "As long as they like chicken."

The thought of being at Lucy's wedding by myself, even if I was surrounded by family and friends, made me uneasy. I wanted to have someone there with me. A partner. A confidant.

And I already knew the perfect wedding date.

Twenty

"YOU BETTER NOT EXPECT ME TO put out," Tracy said as she put the finishing touches on her makeup. "I don't know what you've read in the bathroom stalls, but it's all false. Well, except about me being a good time."

"Yeah, right," I said as I carefully buttoned up the white shirt I was wearing for our family Christmas photo. Ever since my hair and makeup had been done, I'd been afraid to touch my face or my head. It probably wasn't the wisest move to have us do an all-white photo shoot when there was a good chance something was going to get smudged before the wedding.

Tracy and I went downstairs to where the photographer had the white background up. I put on my white gloves and stood on my mark. There were a few test shots for lighting. We were ready, except for one thing: The bride was still getting her hair done.

Mom looked at her watch. She called upstairs to see when Lucy would be finished. And then she gasped. Dad, Rita, and I moved to the bottom of the stairs . . . and there at the top was the blushing bride. She was absolutely stunning.

"Oh. My. Sir Paul," Mom said in a near whisper. "Lucy, you . . ." She quickly ran to get tissues as the sight of Lucy in her white princess dress, her hair in long ringlets with half of it pinned up with flowers, made us all weepy.

Lucy cautiously made her way down, with her two other bridesmaids, Sarah and Joy, holding the back of her train.

I dotted the corner of my eyes with tissues to try to not ruin the makeup that had been expertly applied only an hour before.

The five Blooms stood in a circle, beaming. I took a step forward to give Lucy a hug, but Mom wasn't going to let an emotional moment potentially ruin a photo she'd been waiting for decades to accomplish. "We need everything to stay white!" she commanded before we let something like running mascara or lipstick destroy everything. Hadn't she ever heard of Photoshop?

We fell into line and got what was sure to be *the* benchmark Bloom family Christmas photo taken. Once our parents were satisfied, which for a simple photo took a surprisingly long time, we got to pretend we were a family that took standard wedding photos. But first, four of us had to get out of our white ensembles.

Rita and I put on our bridesmaid dresses, deep purple chiffon knee-length creations with fabric motif flowers on one shoulder. Both of us had our hair curled and pinned up with the same flowers as Lucy's.

Watching our family pose for photos, one would assume we were a regular family.

"Now, Lucy, can you please humor us with one more shot?" Mom asked as Dad brought out the Beatles cutouts from The Cavern.

Or maybe not.

Once we got to the church, there was a flurry of activity: more photos, last-minute alterations and instructions. The only calm thirty minutes we had was during the actual ceremony. But as soon as Lucy and Pete were pronounced husband and wife, and walked down the aisle to an instrumental version of "All You Need Is Love," it was nonstop chaos. We had more photos in the church and then outside the church, followed by a nearby park and a beach overlooking Lake Michigan. It probably would've been fun if it hadn't been forty degrees out.

By the time we got to the reception, I didn't think I could smile anymore. My cheeks hurt, but every time I saw Lucy and Pete, I couldn't help but grin. Lucy and her *husband*, Pete. It was such a foreign concept to me. *Lucy's married.*

The reception ballroom was decorated in deep purple, white, and silver streamers, flowers, and candles. I looked around to find Tracy, but with every turn I ran into an extended family member or friend. After nearly thirty minutes of saying hello, taking more pictures, and trying desperately to get some food and take off my high heels, I finally found her.

She was in a corner, charming my aunts and cousins from my dad's side. "Pen!" She pulled out the seat next to her. "You look like you need a seat and a drink."

I collapsed into the chair. "And food." I'd been enviously eyeing all the passed hors d'oeuvres.

"Hey, squirts!" Tracy snapped her fingers, and two of my younger cousins came running over to her. "I need you to get a soda and some cheese, those little quiche things, pretty much everything. But I don't want you filling up the plate with veggies. Only the good stuff. And tell them it's for the bride's sister. Hurry it up!"

They both laughed and went off running.

"I see that you've got them properly trained," I remarked.

"This is what I've learned from years of babysitting: You've got to keep them occupied. And show them who's boss."

"Isn't being the boss your theory on pretty much everything?"

"True." She laughed. "It's worked out pretty good for me so far."

I couldn't argue with that. Tracy was one of the most in-demand babysitters in our area. The kids loved her and they knew better than to cross her. Most people did.

It took the kids only a couple minutes to bring me sustenance.

"Good job." Tracy high-fived them. "I may even let you boogie down with me later. Now go bother your parents — we've got girl talk to do."

They both hugged her before running off obediently. I gratefully began devouring my plate.

"We're seated over there." Tracy pointed to a table to the

left of where Lucy and Pete would be sitting with the parents and grandparents. "I put our place cards down next to the guy you walked down the aisle with. He seems nice."

I called her bluff. "You mean he seems *cute*."

"Cute, nice, what to the evs. It's a wedding. That doesn't mean that I can't practice my flirting skills. I don't want them to be rusty by the time I get to college."

"Speaking of Brent the groomsman." I took a big bit of cheese. "He has a fifteen-year-old sister outside of Boston who we need to recruit."

"Pen." She put her hand on my shoulder. "I personally take it upon myself to talk to Brent about the Club."

"How noble of you," I replied with my mouth full.

"The sacrifices that I make for you," she said. Then she lowered her voice. "How are you doing?"

The jumbo shrimp I'd been eating got caught in my throat. As long as I was busy with the wedding and my family, I didn't have time to really think about how I was doing. "Okay, I guess."

She placed her hand on my shoulder. "We don't have to talk about it. I didn't want you to think that I'm not worried about you. You said that you were fine, but . . ."

I nodded. I knew Tracy could see past my brave facade. I felt I had no choice but to keep it up for at least the next few hours. And I knew it wouldn't be hard during such a truly happy occasion.

A voice boomed over the speakers, asking us to find our seats. Tracy and I got up and moved over to our table. We weaved among so many different people who had so much influence in my life: aunts, uncles, cousins — I couldn't help feeling the love pouring from everybody.

I was in such a blissful state by the time we reached our table that I was nearly knocked over when I saw the one person I hadn't been expecting. I knew he was going to be at the wedding, although I figured he'd be seated several tables away. He wasn't. He was four seats away, directly across from me at our round table.

He grinned as I approached, and I did my best to ignore his gaze.

Tracy, though, wasn't going to let him off that easily.

"What the hell?" She went right over and picked up his place card. "There's no way you're sitting here." She stormed off to find someone to fix the problem.

I sat down and greeted everybody at the table except him.

He stood up and leaned over the table. "Hey, Penny."

I had no choice but to acknowledge him.

In my most indifferent voice, I replied, "Nate."

Twenty-one

I SHOULD HAVE KNOWN THAT NATE wouldn't be able to resist making my life miserable. It was what he excelled at.

But while there would always be the Nates of the world, I fortunately had the Tracys of the world on my side. She came barreling toward the table with my mom and someone from the catering staff right on her heels.

"There seems to be some mistake," Mom explained to the woman, who was shuffling papers in her hands.

The woman walked around the table, comparing the place cards with the seating arrangements. "Oh, yes, you see, we had a last-minute cancellation and moved a couple things around to make sure all the tables were full. We did get approval from the bride on the changes."

Mom glared over in Lucy's direction. I couldn't really find fault with Lucy — she'd been so busy getting everything ready, she probably didn't realize it had been Nate who'd been moved to my table.

"It's fine." I waved my hand dismissively over to where Nate sat. Then I grabbed a warm dinner roll and started talking with Brent, hoping that between the food and the conversation, I wouldn't have to look across the table for the remainder of the meal.

And it worked, for the most part. Sure, I felt self-conscious the entire time. I tried to be super focused on my conversations with the people directly to my left and right while also trying to ignore his incessant attempts to join in. I'd nearly forgotten that he was there by the time we finished our entrées. But then Tracy got up to use the restroom.

Nate plopped down in her seat. "So you're really going to ignore me all night?"

It was difficult to meet his eyes — and not because they had any power over me anymore. I was distracted by the oil slick on his forehead. "It seems that I'm not going to be that lucky." I picked at the remainder of my chicken.

"How long are you going to hold a grudge against me?" He reached out to touch my arm, but I pulled it away.

"How long have you got?" I looked around the room, hoping someone would save me. My mom's back was to us, Rita was engrossed in a conversation across the room, and Tracy was nowhere to be found.

I sighed. "Look, Nate, I'm not interested in being friends with you. I want nothing to do with you. I've moved on and I wish you would, too."

He laughed and a piece of food flew out of his mouth. "Yeah, if you truly moved on, you wouldn't have a problem being in the same room as me."

"It's just that I don't like being stuck in confined places with jackasses."

His right lip curled up. "Yeah, right. Tell me, where's this boyfriend of yours? Actually, let me guess: He wasn't perfect enough for you, so you dumped him. Seems to be a pattern with you."

"What?" I shot him a go-to-hell look that Tracy would've been proud of. "Let me tell you something about Ryan Bauer. I didn't catch him trying to screw someone in my parents' basement. Don't you dare think you can compare yourself to him. You don't deserve to even *think* his name — or mine for that matter." I stood up.

"Yeah, it's always the guy's fault." Nate snorted. "Take some responsibility, will ya, Pen? Sure I wasn't perfect, but your victim mentality is getting old."

I opened my mouth to say something, but before I had a chance, one of my younger cousins came running by and spilled an entire glass of soda on Nate's head. Nate shrieked like a little girl. He started cursing as he grabbed a napkin to wipe the sugary concoction running down his suit.

It was one of the greatest sights I'd ever seen.

"Oops," seven-year-old Jason said. "I'm so sorry, mister. My mom told me not to run. You won't tell on me, will you?" He gave Nate his best puppy-dog eyes.

Nate walked away, cursing under his breath.

Jason looked over to the side of the room where Tracy was standing, a broad smile on her face. After she gave Jason a thumbs-up, he skipped away happily.

It was a nice reminder that the Tracys of the world would always win.

The fate of the Penny Lanes had yet to be determined.

♥ ♥ ♥

Once the dance floor opened and the music started playing, my mood quickly changed. There on the floor, I was dancing with the young and old. Family and strangers. Old friends and new friends.

Music was the ultimate equalizer.

The DJ was playing a mix from so many decades — classic Motown, the Beatles (*duh*), the Village People, Madonna, Beyoncé, Teenage Kicks — that everybody was having a blast.

There, on the dance floor, I was truly happy. Everything I was stressed about melted away. All around me were smiling faces celebrating with their feet.

Dad was twirling Tracy around while Buddy Holly blasted on the speakers. Mom grabbed her side and motioned that she was going to sit down for a few minutes. I happily kept swaying my hips and shimmying all over the floor as I sang along loudly.

Tracy danced her way over to me. "You can't be stopped, Pen. You're a dancing machine."

I wiped the sweat from my brow and kept up with the rhythm as the music switched to Lucy's favorite boy band from when she was a teen. Tracy and I joined her friends as they sang along with very specific dance moves that were probably from some music video. I'd never gone through that boy-band phase — probably since I had the ultimate boy band in my life from the very start.

"We've got to start dancing more," Tracy commented as she bumped her hip into mine. "I'm pretty sure I've earned another piece of wedding cake." She motioned for me to join her as she made her way through the crowded dance floor to the table with extra slices of cake.

I searched the table for a corner slice, and dug my fork into the vanilla frosting. "I love how music just lets you go. We really do need to dance more often."

"Penny!" Nate's mom walked up to me with her arms extended. "I haven't had a chance to talk to you tonight. How are you? You look gorgeous!"

I embraced Mrs. Taylor, not wanting to hold her responsible for her son's behavior. "I'm great, thanks. How are you?"

"Good. Missing you." She rubbed my arm. "Listen, sweetie, can you do me a favor? Nate looks bored. Can you dance with him? You two used to be so close." She gave me a hopeful (and completely oblivious) smile.

I gave Tracy a little nod to not get involved. She happily shoved more cake into her mouth.

I contemplated my options of how to handle this. The easy way out would be to dance one song with him so Mrs. Taylor could continue to live in ignorance. Or I could end this silly charade once and for all. I hardly had enough energy to be happy, let alone to deal with his crap.

"Actually, Mrs. Taylor, I'm busy having fun. Your son has been a lying jerk to me the last few months, so I really don't want to waste any more time on him. Sorry that I can't help you out, but if I have to spend any more time looking at his smug face, I might punch it in." I threw up my hands like it wasn't my decision.

She stood there flabbergasted. "But . . . what . . ."

"I'm really sorry, truly. Things aren't the same between Nate and me. But that doesn't mean anything has to change with your relationship to my parents. Now, if you'll excuse me, I have some more dancing to do." I gave her a polite smile before heading back to the dance floor.

"Have I told you lately that you're my hero?" Tracy asked.

"Not enough. But you know what they say, Tracy — the truth will set you free."

While I hated being so blunt, and admittedly a little rude, to Mrs. Taylor, I felt a weight lift from my shoulders. It was all pretty much out there. There was no reason I had to keep up appearances anymore as far as the Taylors were concerned. Nothing was going to get in my way of enjoying my sister's wedding. Other than being utterly heartbroken.

Tracy and I got back on the dance floor. The plan was to do a little dance, make a little love (to the cameras), and get down.

But someone else had other plans.

Tracy and Jason were doing the robot in the middle of a circle that had formed, when my arm was yanked forcefully.

"We need to talk," Nate said angrily as he dragged me to the side of the room. "What the hell is your problem? What did you say to my mom?" His face was blotchy, and a bead of sweat was making its way down his temple.

"I told her I wasn't interested in babysitting you." I pulled my arm away from his grasp.

"You've got some serious issues." His hands were in tight fists.

"Well, we both know that my taste in past crushes is seriously suspect. Thank God I got over that." I narrowed my eyes. "I was tired of pretending that you and I are *just swell*. My mom knows. And now your mom knows that you're an ass. Although I'm sure she would've found out eventually by the simple fact that you live and breathe around her. She was bound to get wise to your ways."

"God, you need to get over yourself," he practically spat at me. "Do you think I wanted to come to this wedding? Maybe I should thank you. Now I won't be forced to grovel at your feet any time our parents demand we hang out."

"Oh, is that what you've been doing?" I volleyed back. "Because if this is your idea of groveling, you need some work. Believe me, I'd be happy to never have to see your face again."

He laughed exaggeratedly. "But what are you going to do, then? Guess you'll need to find someone else to blame all your problems on. How fortunate for Ryan or whoever the next guy is that you decide to torture."

I took a step forward so I was only inches away from his face. I hadn't been that close since the last time we kissed. The memory alone was enough to make me want to hurl chunks. "I love how you keep telling me that I blame others, yet you never once have taken responsibility for what you did. Tell me, did that naked girl simply fall on your lap? What a horrible thing to happen to you!" I dramatically rolled my eyes.

"You're such a bitch."

"And you're a lying ass," I stated. "Tell me this, Nate. If you think so poorly of me, then why are you so desperate to get me to forgive you? The texts, e-mails, cards . . . Why do you even care? I can't imagine that you're so deluded that you think there'd ever be a chance that we would get back together." I looked him directly in the eye, making sure he would understand what I had to say next. "Because that will never, ever happen. *Like ever.*"

He clenched his jaw. "Why can't things be like they were? I'm not talking about us dating. I'm talking about how we used to be friends, *real friends*, Penny."

I paused for a moment. "Yes, we were friends. But then I saw the true you. I don't want to date you, I don't want to be friends with you." Then a thought hit me — why had I never realized this before? "You know what, I used to idolize you, and you took advantage of that. Honestly, the only reason I think you can't let go is because you're not in control of me anymore. I have my own opinions, my own life outside of you. That's what the cheating was all about, wasn't it? You like to collect things. You like to be the one in charge, but I'm not someone who can be forced on a pedestal, then be expected to do what I'm told."

"Oh, I think you like being put on a pedestal just fine."

I opened my mouth to reply, but then I thought better. Why was I bothering? I didn't want anything more to do with

Nate. I wanted to go dance with Tracy and my family. I wanted to finally move on. Sure, I wasn't a perfect girlfriend. I could be rash and make things messy and complicated . . . but wasn't that the point of relationships? To find someone who would love you, flaws and all?

"Nate, I'm done with this."

I turned my back on him. I was tempted to say one last passing zing, but I decided I'd rather spend my energy on being with the people I really care about.

Mom approached me cautiously as I maneuvered back to the dance floor. "I saw you were talking to Nate. Is everything okay? I was going to go over there, but it seemed that you were doing a fine job handling it."

I gave her a big hug. "Yep. Everything's fantastic. Although Mrs. Taylor might want to have a word with you. I couldn't contain myself any longer around her."

"Of course you couldn't." She put her arm around me. "You are my daughter, after all."

Yes, I was. We Bloom women did not put up with crap very well and could only hold so much in. And for that I would always be grateful to my mother, mood swings and all.

As if the DJ could sense what I needed, "Twist and Shout" came on. My family got into the center of the room and started singing along loudly. Even Rita couldn't resist.

Dad sang the lead to Mom, who twisted away while Lucy, Rita, and I popped up from behind my dad to sing the background voices. And during the crescendos of "aahhs," we each took a turn, spreading our arms out — with Dad dropping to his knees and screaming the last part. It would be a miracle if any of us had voices left by the end of the night.

As we finished, with Dad collapsed dramatically on the floor, the crowd around us cheered. Mom motioned for us to take a bow. We did the deep bow the Beatles always did after a performance.

Tracy was smiling as she held up her phone. "Blackmail material." She started to play the video she'd recorded.

"I wouldn't put it past you," I said.

The music started up again and we danced. And then we danced some more.

"Tracy!" I practically screamed. "I got it!"

She looked confused. "You got what?"

"This!" I gestured around. "For the scholarship. We hold a dance. With music from all these decades. Get the community involved. I know it'll be a lot of work, but imagine how fun it could be."

Tracy's eyes lit up. "Like a dance-a-thon. We could do one with teams, and have contests, and prizes." She got out her phone and started vigorously typing.

Yes, a dance would be perfect to help raise money for our scholarship program.

And it would keep me busy for months. Because as much as I'd let go of Nate, getting over Ryan was going to be a whole other monster.

Twenty-two

EVERYBODY AGREED THAT THE DANCE-A-THON WAS a brilliant idea.

Or at least that was what it seemed like, from the countless texts Tracy and I received on Sunday as we sat around my bedroom, exhausted from the wedding.

By Monday morning, I was still running on fumes from very little sleep. I hardly had a voice from all the singing and talking over the music, and was pretty sure I still had remnants from the gallon of hair spray that had been used to keep my hair in place.

I yawned as I opened my locker. I heard someone call my name and replied in a very raspy voice.

I heard a familiar chuckle next to me. I was so sleepy, it took me a few beats to realize it was Ryan. I hadn't seen him since the breakup.

Breakup. That word still didn't sit well with me. Not like *boyfriend* and *girlfriend* ever had.

I snuck a quick glance over at him and noticed him studying me. "I take it you had a good weekend?" he asked.

"Yeah," I replied, my voice sounding like it had been sanded down.

"So . . ." He played with the corner of his textbook. "How was the wedding? Were you able to handle being around Jackass?"

I appreciated Ryan referring to Nate by his proper name.

"Yeah." I grabbed a throat lozenge out of my bag, as every word was painful to speak. "I . . . I . . ." I didn't really know what to say. "It was really nice of you to get them a present. I'm sorry . . ." I stopped, tired of always apologizing. I should've considered getting an *I'm sorry* tattoo on my forehead; it would've saved us both so much time. And misery.

"Hey, Bauer!" Todd's voice boomed down the hallway. He was followed by his pack of dudes and their girlfriends: Brian and Pam, Don and Audrey, with Missy trailing behind him. The former Elite Eight minus Ryan and Diane.

Now they were the Sucktastic Six.

Todd strutted over to Ryan and put his arm around him. "I've decided that you've been in prerogative long enough."

"Wow, Todd, I guess you really showed me with your witticism." I started to back away, much to Todd's delight. But there was one thing I wasn't going to let him get away with. "But what exactly did you mean by *prerogative*? Don't you mean *purgatory*?"

Brian snickered and Todd snapped his fingers at him, which made Brian quickly shut up.

I'd never understand why people fell over themselves to please Todd. As he had often proven, he wasn't that smart or even good-looking. So he was a slightly above average athlete. That was it.

The only thing he ever really excelled at was bullying, but I had had enough of that.

And it seemed that I wasn't the only one.

Ryan maneuvered himself away from Todd and began walking down the hallway alone. As much as I wanted Ryan to rejoin his former friends, I was secretly happy he'd turned his back on them, even with me out of the picture.

"Seriously, Bauer?" Todd called after him. "I have my limits. You should be grateful."

"Yeah, you're so generous." I covered my remark with sarcasm. But like so many things, it was lost on Todd.

I also turned my back on him and started walking to class. Todd called me a bitch under his breath as I left.

Yeah, so I'd been told.

While that word could sting, the only two people who had ever called me that were Todd and Nate. Two guys who felt they were better than me. That I should've felt honored to be in their presence. That I should've allowed them to get away with cheating, lying, and bullying.

But I didn't.

Because I stood up for myself and my friends. Because I had enough of them making other people feel like they weren't enough. Because my life would be so much better without them in it. Because they were so not worth it.

So if being a strong, independent woman made me a bitch, then I was a total bitch.

And proud of it.

Our house hadn't fully recovered from the wedding — torn wrapping paper on the floor, guest booklet on the counter, empty gift bags and envelopes scattered throughout the living room — so I didn't feel too guilty that I made a mess with plastering schedules, venue possibilities, and other brainstorming ideas on every surface of the kitchen.

Even though the wedding had been over a week ago, my throat still hurt. I sipped on some hot tea as I looked at the calendar. Everybody thought I was crazy suggesting we do the dance-a-thon a week before junior Prom, but I also knew that I wouldn't have to worry about Prom. Sure, the Club would all go together, but it was more the who I didn't want to think about.

My phone rang. "Hey, Diane," I said. Then I glanced at the clock — she was running a few minutes late, which wasn't like her.

"Okay, I'm here, but I want you to brace yourself," she said with a quiver in her voice.

Immediately my mind went to Ryan. She hadn't said much about him since the breakup. I pretty much pretended our relationship hadn't happened. It was the only way I was going to be able to get through this. Plus, Diane knew she would be the last person I'd want to talk to about it. I didn't like shutting out one of my closest friends, but I needed to keep moving forward. If I opened up to her, I was afraid of what would happen. I was barely hanging on as it was. I was grateful to have the dance-a-thon to throw myself into. I'd been reluctant to delegate any of the tasks because I wanted to do it all myself. That way I'd have no free time to think about the decisions that *I* had made.

Diane, however, insisted on coming over to help.

"What's going on?" I ran to the door and opened it.

I hadn't fully braced myself for what would be on the other side.

It was Diane. With short hair. Like, boy short, with a light pink streak in her bangs, which were swept over to the side.

"So?" She nervously fiddled with the same silver Tiffany's bracelet that I also wore on my wrist. Matching bracelets had been her gift to Tracy and me that Christmas.

"Oh my God." I reached out and touched her hair. I'd known Diane practically my entire life, and she had always had her gorgeous, flowing locks. They were such a part of who she was.

It probably shouldn't come as a shock that she still looked absolutely stunning. Her hair was no longer hiding the perfect angles of her face. Her blue eyes stood out even more.

I was mesmerized.

"Please say something — you're freaking me out." She wrapped her arms around her petite frame like she was cold.

"You look amazing!" I brought her inside the house and started circling her, studying the New Diane from every angle. "What made you decide to cut it?"

"I think I had a midsemester crisis when basketball finished last week. I usually had cheerleading to keep me busy in the spring, and, you know, other things."

Yes, I did. Like being a full-time girlfriend.

"I should've done it earlier." She reached up and touched the back of her neck. "All season long, I kept having to put my hair up in ponytail after ponytail. It would never stay in place. Then I had to use a headband to keep the flyaways off my face. But I guess I didn't have guts to do it until now."

"And the pink?" I asked.

She smiled knowingly at me. "I might have short hair, but I'm still that girly girl you've come to love to tease."

We sat down at the kitchen and started going through the list of things we needed to do before Saturday's meeting.

"You do realize that we have to find another venue. Did you want me to see if . . ." She let the thought hang in the air. It was the closest she had come to talking to me about it.

"No," I replied. It wasn't my pride preventing me from asking Ryan if he'd get PARC for us — it was logistics. What we really needed was the high school gym. But Principal Braddock hadn't even let us have the fund-raiser we did for the basketball team in the high school because the Club was involved. He wasn't a fan of the Club . . . or of me personally.

I had such a way with the male species.

The doorbell rang and I got up to answer it. If I'd been shocked by opening that door to Diane's short 'do a few minutes before, I was nearly knocked over when I saw what was waiting for me this time.

It was the last person I'd have ever expected to visit me at home.

And she was crying.

Missy.

"Is everything okay?" Diane asked, coming over to see who it was.

Missy shook her head and began speaking through tears. "Todd . . . he . . . how could he . . . dumped . . ." And then she began to wail.

Diane pushed me aside and escorted Missy inside. As she sat down at our kitchen table, Diane handed her a tissue.

"Thanks," Missy sniffled. "What happened to your hair?"

Of course Missy wouldn't let something like heartbreak stop her from criticizing Diane's hair.

While Diane explained her new look, I continued to study Missy. Diane was too polite to question her motives in showing up at my doorstep, but something seemed off. Missy regarded me as her mortal enemy (the feeling was mutual), yet here she was.

"What's going on, Missy?" I asked flatly.

A tear, tinted black from her mascara, ran down her face. "I didn't know where to go, and I know we've had our differences, but Todd was being so horrible."

So far her story checked out. "Go on," I prodded, keeping my guard up.

"I thought that if I hung out with Todd that, like, I'd be super popular. I don't know . . ."

Yes, I also didn't know why people thought that.

She looked down at the table, as if that magically explained everything.

"Are you for real right now?" I asked. Diane seemed a little taken back at my bluntness, but did she really think I would open my arms, and the Club, to Missy? Did Missy really think that? "You've done nothing but make fun of the Club and its members. So Todd allegedly broke your heart and you want me to let bygones be bygones? And what? You want to be in The Lonely Hearts Club now?"

Missy started crying again. *And the Oscar goes to . . .*

"You don't believe me?" She jutted out her bottom lip.

"Why should I?" I replied. I wouldn't have put it past Todd to ask Missy to go undercover and sabotage the group. Granted, it was a little ambitious for Todd, since it would require a brain and some planning, but it was possible.

"But I thought . . ." Missy looked lost. "I thought that you were someone people could go to when they needed help. I'm really upset right now, and I don't think my friends will understand."

"I'm sorry that you don't have friends who would understand," I said. And I truly meant it. But I also knew the kind of person Missy was, and that people have a tendency to attract friends who are like them. So if Missy was around people who weren't good friends, what did that say about the kind of friend she was?

I went on, "But you can't treat me and my friends like crap and then think that we'd be there for you when you need us. Because I feel that if Todd called you right now, you'd go crawling back. The Lonely Hearts Club isn't something you use when it's convenient to you. It's a family. A family that we have chosen for ourselves. And I don't see you being a part of it."

I hated kicking someone when they were down, even if that person was Missy. But I couldn't shake the feeling that she wasn't here for the right reasons. Ever since we'd met on her first day of school, she'd been nothing but dismissive and vindictive.

Missy stayed silent for a few beats, then turned to Diane. "What do you think?"

Diane touched her shoulder. "I think that you need to figure out what you really want out of high school. You've been blindly following guys around all year. What do *you* want to do? What are your interests? I think that Missy needs to spend some time with Missy. Alone."

Missy nodded slowly and then got up from her chair. "Thanks." Her voice was so small, it almost made me feel bad for her. Almost.

It wasn't like I was suffering from amnesia.

Despite what Nate had suggested, it was possible for me to forgive people. I'd forgiven Diane for ignoring me for four years. Her friendship was worth putting the past behind us.

But forgiving and forgetting were two very different things.

Diane and I watched Missy walk down the sidewalk. "Do you think that was real?" I asked.

Diane reached up automatically to twirl her hair, then studied her hand when she realized her reflexive gesture was now impossible. "I don't know. I feel bad for her, but you did the right thing. I can't believe she thought you'd be willing to even talk to her. Either she's faking it or she's really that desperate."

I knew more than most what heartbreak could cause a person to do. Maybe Missy was telling the truth. Maybe this was an elaborate scam. I didn't know what to believe anymore. What I did know was that time would eventually reveal what was real.

Twenty-three

I SEQUESTERED MYSELF IN THE LIBRARY for nearly an hour after school on Friday to get as much homework done as possible before I spent the weekend working on the dance-a-thon. I'd also been avoiding my locker so I wouldn't have to face the consequences of what my decision had cost me. Since the hallways were practically deserted, I didn't even glance before rounding the corner to my locker. I thought I was safe. Why on earth would he have been there?

But there Ryan was. At his locker, getting his books together. I stood still, debating an escape in the opposite direction. But then he turned around and our eyes locked. There was no other choice but to go to my locker.

We hadn't really spoken since my first day back after the wedding. Sure, I'd seen him in class, but I made certain to be around a Club member to help distract me.

"Hi," I said cautiously.

"Hey," he replied. "You're here late."

"I've been in the library. You?"

"Student Council meeting."

"Student Council!" I hit him on the arm before I could stop myself. Ryan was still on Student Council. So there *was* one thing I hadn't completely destroyed for him.

He looked confused. "Yeah, I've been on it since we were freshmen. Well, I should get going. Sorry to ruin your streak of avoiding me."

"I'm not —" I stopped myself from lying to him. He knew better. "How are things?"

"Things are just great," he said with a hint of sarcasm.

"I see that you're sitting with most of your friends at lunch again."

"Yep."

Ryan was back with all of them — except Todd. I don't think Ryan had any desire to repair that relationship. But all the other guys seemed less concerned about pissing Todd off, so they sat with Ryan when they wanted to.

"So things are . . . better?" I needed validation that the breakup had been worth it.

He sighed. "What do you want me to say?"

Honestly, there wasn't an answer he could've given me to make me feel better. If he was doing great, then it proved that I had ruined his life. If he was miserable, then it confirmed that I had made a horrible mistake.

"I want to know the truth," I told him. Even though I wasn't sure that was the case.

"Fine, here's truth: I'm glad Todd's out of my life. That guy was toxic and it was only a matter of time before I realized that. My dad always has been, and will continue to be, an ass. I missed all of two basketball games. Braddock's advisory committee was a joke, and I'm happy to not have to waste any more time on it. So my life isn't that different from a few months ago save for one *big* thing. The thing that hurt me the most. I don't know what else you want to hear. I'm not going to stand here and make you feel better about what you did." Ryan turned on his heel and walked away from me.

I was the one who'd hurt him the most. There were no guarantees that I wouldn't hurt him again. I'd tried to make it work, but I failed. I'd hurt him. I didn't want to hurt him again, so I needed to stay as far away from him as possible.

I tried to find solace in the fact that his life seemed to be getting back to normal. That he was better without me. He had every right to hate me.

But as much as I searched to find comfort in that, all I felt was my heart tearing further and further apart.

There was only one solution I had to being in this much pain: The Lonely Hearts Club. Fortunately, it was as strong and busy as ever. We had five weeks to pull off the impossible.

If it were any other group of people, I would've had my doubts. But I had faith in us.

The basement resembled a war room: to-do lists, venues, and ideas were plastered on the walls.

"Okay." Diane took charge at our meeting that Saturday. "We've got to go over the rules."

Tracy stood up. "Rules? Rules? We don't need no stinkin' rules!"

Diane continued without missing a beat. "Actually, we do.

The dance-a-thon will last twelve hours. People will register in teams of four to six members. A member of the team must be on the dance floor at all times. Each team is required to have sponsorship of at least four hundred dollars to participate. There will be prizes for the team that raises the most money and the team with the best costumes. We'll also have a raffle and door prizes. Which means we need to get prizes." She started distributing a spreadsheet. "I've broken down a list of businesses downtown for us to approach. Let me know if you or your family has any connections at these stores."

So many hands went up in the air, there were only a few places we'd be forced to cold-call.

Diane looked over her list before turning her attention to me. "Do you want to talk about music?"

When didn't *I want to talk about music?*

"Yes, so we're going to start the dance off with music from the fifties and then work our way up to current music at the end. Tyson's band's going to play an hour set with music from all the decades."

Morgan interrupted, "He promised to do some Beatles, Penny."

"Oh, he doesn't have to." I glanced up at the ceiling, knowing full well how my parents felt about anybody but John, Paul, George, and Ringo playing their music. "We're also going to work with a vendor to get a percentage of food and beverage sales. The website is being updated so we can handle ticket sales and sign-ups, although we'll also see if we can get businesses to sell tickets as well. We're in really good shape, except . . ."

It always seemed to come down to location, location, location.

The hotels we looked into would cut into our profits, even though Hilary's dad was working on getting us registered for something like tax-exempt status since all the profits would be donated. Every day, another issue would pop up. Our little dance was becoming more and more complicated.

But that only intensified my drive. I felt like we had to do this. *I* needed to do this. Every second that I wasn't at school, studying, or working, I dedicated to the dance-a-thon. It was becoming an obsession. I kept telling myself that it was all for the Club. I hoped I was right.

Jessica stood up. "My mom's working on getting the elementary school. She seems to think if the community really got involved, they'd be more open to it than if it was only a Club thing."

There was some rumbling in a corner. Meg stood up and said, "Actually, the seniors have been talking. We can't begin to tell you how much doing this for one of us means. But we also think that it would give the Club a boost if we split the profits with another organization. So half would go to the scholarship student, the rest to another worthy cause. Like PARC. The people there have been really supportive of us and, well, it has seen better days."

Murmurs of agreement began sprouting up in the room.

"I think that's a great idea," Diane said, then put it up to a group vote.

It was unanimous.

At the end of the meeting, Michelle approached me and asked if I had a second to talk.

"Of course," I said, rubbing my forehead. A dull ache had begun to throb in my temples. "What's up?"

She hesitated. "I talked to Missy Winston the other day. She's really upset about Todd breaking up with her, which is so unlike her. She's had a lot of boyfriends but always moved on quickly. She's really torn up."

I'd been paying attention to Missy that week, and she hadn't been anywhere near Todd or his crowd. She sat with her friends and looked really depressed. She had on only about half the makeup she usually applied, and her hair was mostly up in a ponytail. You could even see her roots. It gave me the slightest sense that she wasn't trying to hide her real self anymore.

"Anyways," Michelle continued, "I understand that you're hesitant to have her join the Club and all, and even I've had issues with her in the past. But Missy's bark is way worse than her bite. Her parents got divorced last year and she's sort of used that to pretend to be this tough, confident person. I'm not asking you to invite her to join us, but all I'm saying is that she wants to prove herself to you and the Club. So maybe we could give her a task for the dance-a-thon? Nothing major, but something to see how she handles it. I think it would mean a lot to her."

"I'll think about it," I replied, still not fully able to conceive of Missy as Club material. Although Michelle had a point — maybe we *could* give her some task. We certainly needed the help. But it had to be something that wasn't too important, in case she was really trying to sabotage us.

"Thanks." Michelle started to walk away, then paused. "For the record, she didn't ask me to speak to you. I did it because I felt it was the right thing to do."

I nodded. I wanted to do the right thing as well. Problem was, that was sometimes easier said than done.

It wasn't difficult for someone who openly detested me to be civil to me in the privacy of my own home, but I decided to test Missy's sincerity in the most public place of all: the McKinley High School cafeteria.

"Hey, Missy!" I said enthusiastically as she walked in with her two clones behind her.

"Hi, Penny," she said in a quiet voice. I hadn't even realized she was capable of a quiet voice.

"Can I talk to you?" I asked. Her shadows gave me the familiar look of disgust that Missy used to share with them.

But this time Missy didn't share it back.

"Of course," she said, halfheartedly turning to her friends to say she'd be right back.

They both stared at her with their mouths open, as if they didn't know how to find their lunch table without her.

We walked over to the side of the cafeteria, several inquisitive eyes on us, including Ryan's. He knew as much as anybody how I felt about Missy.

"Look," Missy started, "I get it. I do. I understand how you can question my motives. To be honest, if you'd come to me a month ago asking for something, I would've treated you the same way. Or worse."

At least she was being honest.

She gave me a shy, quickly fading smile. Her attention was behind me for a second. Then she glanced down at the floor and began to nervously shake her leg.

I turned around to see Todd approaching us, a victorious smirk on his face. I had a feeling I was going to get busted. I knew I shouldn't have believed anything Missy said. Now Todd was going to reveal his prank on me and enjoy every second of it.

Todd glared at Missy but put his arm around me. "I see you're picking up my trash again, Bloom. Maybe you should rename that club of yours The Todd Chesney Has Broken My Loser Heart Club."

Missy burst into tears and ran out of the cafeteria. Her two friends got up from their table and chased after her.

Todd laughed — until I jerked my elbow sharply into the side of his stomach. He bent over, clutching his side. "What the hell? That's assault."

"No," I pushed him away from me, "that's called *just desserts*."

Twenty-four

THE LONELY HEARTS CLUB WAS NOT a dictatorship. So I put the quandary about Missy to a vote.

"We'll decide this Saturday," I said on Wednesday, two days after the cafeteria run-in. Missy had been absent from lunch the day before, and something about that had unsettled me. So we presented the facts to the Club. They'd have a couple days to think it over and we'd make a decision together. As a team.

We then shifted our focus back to the important matter of the dance-a-thon. The elementary school had agreed to let us have the event there, so we were finally able to move forward on getting sponsors and, more important, people to the event.

It all was coming together. Even people outside the Club were interested in getting involved.

"Penny!" Bruce caught up to me on the way to Spanish. "Do you need help with your party?"

"That'd be great. Thanks, Bruce." He'd been nothing but nice and helpful since he'd arrived. I really wished I could do something for him, but there was no way I was going to be able to change Tracy's mind. I was suddenly overcome with a coughing fit.

"Are you okay?" Bruce asked.

I could only nod as I continued to cough. I'd been feeling run-down the last few days, but I thought that, as long as I kept busy, it would go away.

"Here." Bruce grabbed my bag. "Whoa," he commented as he felt the weight. "What do you have in here? Bricks?"

I'd been putting all of my afternoon books into my bag so I would only have to go to my locker twice a day. The less Ryan had to see me, the better. For us both.

"Sorry about that," I finally said once my coughing stopped. "Anyways, we'd really appreciate the help. All of us."

"Don't worry." His dimples deepened. "I won't bother you about Tracy anymore. A guy can take a hint."

"I personally think she's nuts for not giving you a try. But the Club has meant so much to her, I think she's worried about doing anything to ruin it."

Or maybe I was talking about myself.

Bruce's usual cheerful demeanor turned reflective. "Do you know why I wanted to help out with the Club so much? It wasn't solely because of Tracy, although that played a huge part."

I shook my head.

"I had my heart broken before I left to come here. I was a wreck when I arrived, and at first I thought having distance between her and me would help. But it wasn't that simple. When you told me about the Club, that's what I thought I needed. To be reminded about what's important. But it's hard to do when your heart's torn apart and you're thousands of miles away from home."

I could only understand the heart part. There was no way I'd be able to handle what was happening to me if I was on a different continent, away from my friends and family.

"I'm so sorry, Bruce." I looked around the hallway to make sure we didn't have any eavesdroppers close by. "Do you want to talk about it?"

At first I didn't think he was going to say anything; he appeared to be almost lost in a memory. "There was this girl, Zara." He winced slightly when he said her name. "I had a crush on her for years but never thought anything would happen. I submitted the application to study abroad, and since I have the worst luck ever, I found out I got accepted the day after our first date. At first she was supportive about me leaving. We were going to make it work. It was only five months. And then . . .

"I thought everything was great with us. I almost didn't want to come here, but my parents thought I was foolish for even thinking about turning down the opportunity. Then she broke up with me at my going-away party by walking in on the arm of another guy."

He looked exhausted. "I know the Club has some pretty negative opinions of guys, but the hurt can go both ways. It's not a guy or girl issue — it's a people issue."

I'd never really thought about a relationship from a guy's perspective. It was always from the point of view that I had experienced: the girl who lost her best friend because of a guy, the girl who got cheated on, the girl who was afraid to trust again.

It was nearly revolutionary to think that a guy could get as hurt as a girl.

I couldn't handle thinking about what I had done to Ryan. He'd made it very clear how much I'd hurt him, but the only thing I could do was rationalize that it was for the best.

"So I'm slowly getting by. Every day it's easier."

I nodded in agreement with Bruce, although it hadn't gotten easier for me.

"And honestly, my crush on Tracy has helped. I thought I'd never be able to get over Zara — and then I walked into school that first day and saw Tracy. She's unlike anybody I've ever met. A true original."

Yes, she was. I hated that the first guy to understand her had to be from thousands of miles away and had come at a time when being with her wasn't a possibility.

"So, in a way, your Club has reminded me that I'll be okay. So I guess I should thank you for that." Bruce paused before heading into class. "You know, you should really think about letting guys in."

I laughed. True, guys could also get broken hearts, but I wasn't about to open that can of worms. Although there was no reason to ever worry about something like that happening. New members have one major obstacle they have to face. No guy in his right mind would ever challenge it.

Tracy.

❤ ❤ ❤

Tyson was a nervous wreck.

"Every day, I want to vomit when I check the mail," he said the following day as we were getting ready for biology to start. He was waiting to hear back from his top college, Juilliard.

"They'd be insane to not take you." I didn't say that only because he was a friend — he was truly a gifted musician. I knew that in a few years I'd be able to say that I knew him when.

"From your lips . . ." He drew on his notebook, the black ballpoint pen digging into the paper with more aggression than he reserved for his lyrics.

I hit his arm lightly. "You know you nailed your audition —"

"Penny Lane Bloom," our teacher interrupted. I looked at the clock, knowing that I hadn't missed the bell. "Please report to the principal's office. He'd like to have a word with you."

I gathered my books and kept thinking about what I could possibly have done to warrant a word with Principal Braddock. Once I arrived, I felt immediate relief that my parents hadn't been dragged in again. But then, they wouldn't be here to have my back.

"Miss Bloom," Braddock called through his opened door.

I walked in cautiously, assuming the worst. His eyes were on his computer, but he gestured at the chair in front of his desk. I obediently sat down.

"Hi, Principal Braddock," I tried to say with an ounce of respect. It was extremely difficult.

"Let me get right to the point." He finally stopped typing and looked at me. "I've heard about your dance-a-thon."

Oh, crap.

Of course he had to stick his nose into it. He was going to find a way to make the elementary school take back their offer.

"You're having it at the elementary school?" He rubbed his bald head. It was reflecting the fluorescent lights from the ceiling.

I nodded weakly, dreading where this was going.

"And part of the proceeds will be going to a scholarship for a senior member of your club and the other to PARC?"

"Half and half," I replied.

He leaned back in his chair and placed his hands on his stomach. "You know that I used to go to PARC when I was little. That's where I learned how to play football." He looked over at the wall in his office that was a shrine to Braddock's former athletic glory at McKinley and at college.

I stayed silent. I figured it was the best way for me to avoid trouble.

He looked back at me, like he was weighing his options in his mind. "I'm still not one hundred percent on board with this little club of yours. But I do appreciate your support of PARC and the Club's understanding of the importance of continuing education through your scholarship."

My silence was now due to utter disbelief.

"So . . ." He continued to study me. "I figured that if you wanted, we could let you have your event here."

"What?" I blurted out, completely flabbergasted that he would offer the school to us.

His demeanor didn't crack. "You're a student at this school. Part of the profits for the event would go to a student at this school. So it would only make sense that your event take place at this school."

I picked my jaw off the floor. "That would be great. I . . . I really . . ."

He waved his hand dismissively at me. "Yes, I'm sure. I'll have Mrs. Hutnick give you the requirements. They're from the Board of Education, so they'll be very similar to the elementary school's."

I nodded slowly, the realization that we would get to have our event here sinking in. And then I said something I never thought I would ever say.

"Thank you so much, Principal Braddock."

The corners of his mouth turned up. "My pleasure."

I got up to leave, but thought better of it. He had no problem pulling the karaoke event from the school only days before. I remembered something my mom once said about trust: *While someone's word is great, there is one thing that's even better.*

"Principal Braddock?"

He looked up from his computer. "Yes?"

"I hope you won't find this rude, but do you think I could get all of this in writing?"

Twenty-five

I'D BEEN SO FRAZZLED WITH THE dance-a-thon planning, it was only a matter of time before something slipped through the cracks.

I quickly glanced around the corner to my locker the next afternoon to find that the coast was clear between classes. I walked as fast as I could without drawing too much attention to myself. I was about to extract my forgotten biology note-book in record time, when a sneezing fit took over my body.

My overweight bag fell to the ground as my body began to convulse with every sneeze.

"Are you okay?" a voice asked next to me.

"I'm fine." I began to wave off the person when I realized it was Ryan. I turned my back to blow my nose in semiprivacy while I cursed my plugged ears for the fact I hadn't been able to recognize his voice. "Sorry, allergies. Or a cold. I don't know." I popped another lozenge in my mouth.

"You don't look well," Ryan said with a softer voice. He was clearly concerned, which made me feel much, much worse. He shook his head. "I know it's none of my business, but you've got way too much on your plate. You can't do it all." He grimaced, as he was more than aware of my inability to juggle too many things at once.

"I've got it under control," I assured him, although I didn't need to. Ryan didn't have to worry about me. Yes, I'd been under the weather and I'd been having trouble sleeping, but that was solely because I had so many details of the dance-a-thon to stress over.

At least that was what I'd been telling myself.

"Okay, fine." He opened up his locker. "Sorry I said anything."

I hauled my bag to my shoulder and felt the weight of four classes' worth of books and notebooks weighing me down. It wasn't a weight that I liked to carry, but I had no choice.

I could handle a lot of things — but more interactions like that was not one of them.

In addition to avoiding my locker like the plague, I spent the next three weeks focusing every waking minute on the dance-a-thon. I quickly learned that I functioned much better when I was busy.

Now that we'd secured the high school, we quickly moved forward on getting sponsors, raffle prizes, and, of course, people to participate. We already had over fifty teams registered — from high school students to senior citizens. And while the dance-a-thon's main goal was to help get scholarship money for a senior Club member, it also had made the community and surrounding areas more aware of The Lonely Hearts Club's existence. Our website traffic had gone up significantly and we added more clubs closer to Parkview.

"Okay," I said, calling our lunchtime meeting to order. "Where are we with all the raffle prizes?"

Missy spoke up first. "I've gotten commitments for baskets from both the spa and hair salon downtown as well as a gourmet food basket." She reveled in the positive response from the group.

We'd decided to give her a chance. She technically wasn't an official member yet, but she was sitting with us at lunch and making an effort. Missy had approached every task we'd given her with steadfast determination. She was even willing to go to the businesses we didn't have any connections with to ask for a donation. Michelle went with her to make sure the Club was being represented properly, but Missy took the lead.

While she and I were never going to be best friends, I'd gotten to know her a little better. Behind her tough facade, she was a sensitive person with a biting sense of humor. She and I had even exchanged a few pleasant greetings in the hallway between classes.

Crazier things have happened.

"Great! Thanks, Missy." I started to sneeze. After almost a month of coughing and sneezing, I finally admitted that I had a nasty cold. Mom had given me really strong cold medicine, but nothing was helping. I felt like crap, but didn't really have any time to focus on that since there was too much to do. "So I think on Saturday we'll get the music ready and the posters done." I looked down at the list of things we had to do.

"Hey, Penny." Diane looked around at the group. "I know we've been so busy with the dance-a-thon and all, but we can't forget the *other* dance that's happening. So a few of us were planning on going to the mall on Saturday to look for Prom dresses, if anybody's interested in joining us."

The dance-a-thon was one week away, Prom was two. I figured I would run to the mall the day after the dance-a-thon for my dress. Or I'd wear what I'd worn to Homecoming. It really wasn't a priority.

"That sounds like fun." I started to cough uncontrollably as the unfortunate people sitting next to me scooted away.

"Maybe you should go home?" Tracy looked at me with concern.

"I'm okay." I picked at my turkey sandwich. I didn't have much of an appetite but tried to take a couple bites. It tasted dry, even when I chased the bite with water. I pushed my food away. "Diane, do you want to take over?" I asked as I searched my bag for my afternoon cold pills.

"Of course." Diane started talking about other things that needed to be done while I desperately tried to drink the water in front of me. I probably should've stayed home. Usually, I wouldn't have minded missing a few days of school, but there was exciting news about the dance-a-thon or new clubs every day. I didn't want to miss a minute of it. A horrible cold wasn't going to drag me away.

I felt sluggish as everybody got up from the lunch table. I

was making my way to my locker when Hilary ran up to me. "Hey, Pen, I was hoping I could talk to you for a minute."

"Of course," I said, even though every word hurt my throat.

"I didn't know when a good time would be to talk about this, but I've met somebody." She looked down at the floor. "And, I don't know, I thought I should tell you that I really like him and want to ask him to come with us to Prom."

I blew my nose loudly. "That's great. Who's the lucky guy?"

Hilary's face glowed at the thought. "His name is Glen. We met at work. He goes to school in . . ." I tried my best to concentrate on what she was saying, but there was a buzzing noise in my ears. I slowed down my pace as a warm sensation made its way through my body.

I tried to steady myself by placing a hand on the wall.

Then I blacked out.

Twenty-six

"WAKE UP, PENNY!" A VOICE CALLED out to me.

My eyes tried to open, but they felt so heavy. I snuck a quick peek and saw the school nurse standing over me. Tracy and Diane were behind her, looking really worried.

"Wh-wha-wha . . ." I tried to talk, but my mouth was dry.

The nurse held up a glass of water with a straw. I drank greedily from it.

"Small sips," she said. "I think you're dehydrated, so you need to take small sips so your body has a chance to properly absorb the liquid."

I ignored her and kept drinking. I was taking in the room and tried to remember how I'd gotten there.

"You fainted," the nurse started to explain.

"And you scared the crap out of us," Tracy continued. "I told you to go home. You look horrible, Pen. You've been running yourself ragged and it's caught up with you."

Diane nudged Tracy. "That's enough."

"Sorry." Tracy gave me a weak smile. "I'm really worried about you, but I know that you'll be getting an earful from your mom."

And at the mention of her name, Mom burst through the door of the nurse's office. "What on earth happened?" She listened patiently to the nurse but began checking my vital signs, wanting to give the second opinion.

Dad came running in a few minutes later. There was a lot of discussion among my parents and the nurse. I heard the words *exhaustion*, *dehydration*, and *rest*. I also heard Mom repeatedly say that she'd told me to take it easy.

Tracy came over to my bedside as the grown-ups continued their conference together in the corner.

"What happened?" I asked, still trying to piece it all together.

"You were talking to Hilary, and she said that all of a sudden you turned white and just collapsed. I was a few feet behind you and saw you go down, but assumed that you'd tripped or something." Tracy took my cold hand in her warm one. "Bruce was with me and he bolted over — that's when I knew something was really wrong. Bruce, Hilary, and I all tried to get you to wake up, but you weren't responding, besides some incoherent mumbling — you know, typical you." Tracy tried to play it off lightly, for which I was grateful. "Bruce picked you up and took you to the nurse's office."

"He did?" I was grateful to Bruce but also embarrassed that I'd been carried through the hallway in front of everybody.

Tracy nodded, looking impressed. "Yeah, and pretty much the entire Club followed him. Everybody's outside right now, wanting to know how you are. The office isn't happy to have so many of us skipping class, but we kind of took a stand.

Braddock seems annoyed, but he didn't force us to go back to class. We all want to make sure you're okay."

"The Club's outside waiting?" I was touched by their unwavering support for me.

Diane came over to the bed. "Of course they are. Bruce as well." She exchanged a glance with Tracy. "And Ryan."

Why was I so surprised that Ryan would be outside? I'd fainted in front of practically the entire school.

I groaned at the thought, but my reaction caused everybody in the room to panic.

"What's wrong? What's the matter?" Mom came over and grabbed my wrist to check my pulse.

"I have a headache," I responded, which was partly true.

Mom reached in her purse and pulled out some aspirin and more cold medicine. It looked like she'd raided the pharmacy before she'd left. I obediently took the pills as Mom instructed. Tracy left to get my books.

"You're going home and staying there for the rest of the week," Mom commanded. I was so tired that all I could do was agree with her. I was only going to miss a couple days of school, and that would give me some extra time to work on the dance-a-thon.

As if she could read my mind, Mom shot me a warning look. "And you are to *rest*, Penny Lane. You can do homework, but that's it. And, Diane, I think the Club needs to meet somewhere else this weekend. Penny Lane needs her rest. Period."

Diane nodded her head vigorously. She knew when the only choice you had was to agree with my mom and agree quickly.

My head began to pulsate when I sat up. I had to steady myself. Dad came over to help me up. "Be careful, kiddo. Do you want me to pick you up?"

I shook my head, not wanting to appear even weaker to everybody. I waited a few seconds for the pulsing to subside, and then tried to sit up again. I had to drink some juice before I was allowed to leave.

The nurse glanced at the door. "You have quite the adoring public waiting for you." She touched my shoulder gently, as if I was a breakable china doll.

"Thanks." I finally stood up, and Dad steadied me with his arm wrapped around my waist. "I think I'm okay, Dad. Only tired. I'll go to sleep as soon as we get home," I promised.

Once the door was opened, the quiet whispers on the other side suddenly stopped. I felt immense pressure to appear to be completely fine, although by the concerned looks everybody in the room had been giving me, I was sure there was little I could do to fake the appearance of being well.

I plastered a smile on my face as I turned the corner and saw the worried looks coming from the Club. A few members of the office staff looked annoyed as they started filling out late slips.

"Hey, everyone. Sorry for the scare," I said. "I'm going home to sleep for about four days, but then I'll be back in fighting form." I scanned each of their faces, this family that I had built up over the last six months. I gingerly made my way to the office exit, trying to make eye contact with each of them so they knew I was really okay. I was also searching for Ryan, but he wasn't there.

My eyes settled on Bruce. "Thanks so much. I hope I didn't hurt your back."

He shook his head. "No worries. I'm glad to see you're feeling better."

"Yeah, thanks. I hope nobody gets in trouble for skipping class."

"Please," Tracy said. She held out her hands like she was balancing the options. "Go to class or be there for you — like there was a choice."

At that comment, the office secretary cleared her throat and started handing out slips for people to finally go back to class.

Dad put all my stuff into Mom's car, and I went home with her. I rested my eyes during the drive and couldn't wait to collapse in the privacy of my own bedroom. I felt so heavy as I walked up the stairs. I didn't even bother taking off my jeans before I got under the covers.

Mom knocked lightly on the door. "I brought you some juice and crackers." She sat at the edge of my bed. "Are you okay? And I mean with everything that's been going on lately. You've seemed so distracted and driven by this dance-a-thon, I don't know if you've really had time to deal with . . ." Mom studied my face, wondering how far she should push me.

I curled up onto my side just as a well-timed yawn took control of me. "It's this stupid cold, and yes, I've been pushing myself a little too much. But I'll . . . get . . . some . . ."

And then I let sleep overtake me. I drifted off to a place where I didn't have any responsibilities, where I didn't have to pretend to be happy when I didn't feel like it, where I wasn't heartbroken.

Usually, if anybody slept past nine in our house, even on the weekend, Mom would wake them up. Her attitude had always been that if you sleep in, you're wasting the day away.

Who knew that all it would take to let you sleep in was to pass out at school. So she let me be and I slept, and slept, and then slept some more. It was amazing how much better twenty hours of sleep could make me feel. And I took Mom's advice and didn't do any work besides the occasional home-work assignment the following day.

I was watching TV in the basement when I heard the door-bell ring Thursday afternoon. I was able to convince Mom and Dad that I could be left alone, so I slogged up the stairs and opened the door before looking to see who it was. Had I known the identity of the person on the other side, I would've at least tried to fix my messy ponytail, or run upstairs to try to not look like the homeless person I was presently impersonating.

"Hey," Ryan said sheepishly.

"Hey," I replied. "What are you . . ." My immediate reaction was that I was seeing things.

He held up a bag. "I brought you some stuff."

I glanced at the clock in the living room — it was a little before two. "Shouldn't you be in history right now?"

"I'm at a doctor's appointment." He winked at me.

"You're skipping class?" I asked. "And your downward trajectory continues . . ."

He frowned slightly at my comment. "Do you want me to give you the bag or are you going to let me in?"

I stood there staring at him. I couldn't believe he was here.

"I thought you hated me," I blurted out before I could stop myself. I blamed the exhaustion.

Ryan shook his head. "I don't hate you, Penny. I'm mad at you, yes, but I don't hate you."

"Fair enough." I maneuvered so he could come inside. Ryan had every right to be mad at me for hurting him. He also should've hated me for everything that I'd done to him, but he didn't. That thought alone made me feel significantly better.

Ryan walked over to the kitchen and began unloading the bag. "So there's Gatorade to help rehydrate, ice cream to help with your sore throat, and" — he unwrapped a plastic bag, and as soon as the smell hit my nose, my stomach automatically began to growl — "cheese fries . . . because they're cheese fries."

I nearly lunged at the fries, but instead took out two forks and began diving in with mine. "Do you want any?" I said with a full mouth.

"I already ate. Plus, you need it more than me."

"Thank you," I said before pulling an extra cheesy fry from the plate.

"Oh, I almost forgot." He reached into his messenger bag and handed me Abbey the Walrus, my childhood stuffed animal that I'd given to his stepsister. "From Katie. She wants you to get better soon."

I hugged my old stuffed friend, not the least bit embarrassed for Ryan to witness my affection toward an inanimate object. I set Abbey on my lap as I continued to eat my fries. It should've been awkward to be so close to Ryan, especially since it had been tense between us. However, it felt comforting to have him here.

It took only a few minutes to clean the plate and drink a glass of Gatorade.

"How are you feeling?" Ryan asked while he nervously ran his fingers through his hair.

"Better. I really appreciate this. Obviously." I gestured at my empty plate.

"You gave everybody a scare yesterday." He paused. "Especially me. So I guess I was right."

"You were right?" What wasn't Ryan right about? Except his obliviousness to the many ways I'd destroyed his life.

"You were doing too much."

"I know, it's so silly, I think I was . . ." I tried to find the right words to make everybody else feel better about what had happened to me. In the past twenty-four hours, most of my energy had been spent answering texts and IMs about my health.

Ryan reached over and held my hand. I stared at our hands in shock. It was something I had gotten used to when we were still together, but now . . .

He leaned forward. "This doesn't let you off the hook for what you did, but all I want is for you to get better. I can't help but feel a little guilty, since I've been so cold to you lately."

"Are you kidding me? The only person responsible for my fainting spell is me. As for us . . ." It was so weird to think of Ryan and I in terms of *us*. "I've been the one staying away from our lockers. I've been the one who's been avoiding you. It's been all my doing and all my fault," I said, hoping he realized I wasn't only talking about the past month. "Even you have to admit, I kind of deserved a little coldness."

"Yes, you did." He laughed before giving my hand a squeeze. "I've really missed you, Penny."

He was so close to me that I felt woozy again, but not from exhaustion. Even though I'd been the one who ended it, I wasn't ready for either of us to move on. I desperately wanted to tell him everything, beg him to take me back, but it didn't change why we'd had to break up. Besides, I wasn't in a state to add any more stress to my life before the dance-a-thon. I clearly wasn't able to deal with everything on my plate as it was. Unless that plate had cheese fries.

But the truth was that I missed him, too. I could avoid seeing him. I could overplan my days and weekends. But at the end of the day, nothing could fill the void of not having him here with me.

"Ryan." I didn't know what I was going to say to him. I didn't know what I could possibly say to him to let him know everything I was feeling.

He moved over to the seat beside me, his blue eyes focused on mine the entire time. Unlike yesterday, when I'd felt so distant and removed from my surroundings, this time there was an excited buzz around me. My body tingled with him being so close, my awareness heightened. I kept trying to think of what to say to him, but I was completely at a loss. All I wanted to do was to take him in. I'd kept my distance this past month, but my body was reacting with him so close.

He pulled my hand that was wrapped in his closer to him. I instinctually reached for him, and before I could process what we were doing, his lips were on mine. He pulled me into him, and I put my arm around his neck. It was as if his kiss was the answer for what was truly ailing me.

I had no idea if we were kissing for seconds, minutes, or hours. All I knew was that I didn't want it to end. I didn't want to pull away and face the harsh reality of the price he'd be forced to pay for being with me. Then I heard the sound of the garage door opening. I silently cursed whoever was coming home.

"God, I missed that," Ryan said breathlessly, his hands still around my waist.

"Me, too," I admitted.

We quickly kissed one more time before pushing ourselves away from each other. I took a long drink of water, hoping I could swallow down everything I wanted to tell him.

The door opened from the garage. Mom stopped suddenly when she saw I had a visitor.

"Oh, hello, Ryan. I didn't realize you were here. I came by to check on Penny Lane." She gave me a quick smile that grew when she saw my face. "You look so much better — you've got the color back in your face." She came over and put the back of her hand against my cheek. "You're really hot. Let me take your temperature." She ran off to get the thermometer from her bathroom.

I couldn't meet Ryan's eyes. We both knew what was causing my temperature to soar. I quickly stole a glance and saw that his cheeks were ruddy. "You should probably go before she decides to take your temperature, too."

"It would be worth it." He looked back to make sure the coast was clear and planted another quick kiss on me. "I'll check in on you this weekend. Let me know if you need anything, okay?"

"Yes." I kissed him again before he got up to leave.

I heard him talking to Mom in the hallway before she came back and shoved the thermometer into my mouth. "That was nice for him to stop by. I thought things were . . ." She raised her eyebrow at me. I was grateful the thermometer prevented me from giving a response.

I had no idea where things were with us. All I did know was that I couldn't deny how much his kiss meant to me and how quickly I wanted to get another one.

Twenty-seven

I WAS FEELING SIGNIFICANTLY BETTER BY Friday night. It was most likely because of the countless numbers of hours I spent sleeping and the medicine I was taking, but all I could think of were those kisses with Ryan. He'd texted me throughout the day to see how I was doing. I kept telling him I needed more cheese fries.

Diane and Tracy came over under the watchful eye of my mom, who didn't want me "overdoing things." So I stayed planted on the couch in the basement while Tracy and Diane kept me updated on the Club's progress. I calmly listened to them, not once wanting to take over or become stressed.

"Everything seems to be going well." I pulled a blanket over me instead of reaching for the event binder that Diane had put within my reach. "Send everybody my love tomorrow. I'll be back to one hundred percent by school on Monday." I yawned. "Or at least ninety percent."

Diane handed me some water. "Do you want to pick a day to go Prom dress shopping when you're better? Or we could delay it?"

"No, that's okay." I took a sip of water to placate her. "I won't worry about the dress until after the dance-a-thon."

"That'll only give you a few days," Diane reminded me.

"Oh, well." I repeated my new mantra: "It'll work out."

"Of course it will — you can make anything look *hawt.*" Tracy raised her eyebrow salaciously. "We'll also take care of the carpooling for Prom. We've got some more people joining us."

The way Tracy said it made me believe she was hiding something. "Like who?" I pressed.

"I mean, I figured it would be rude to not let Bruce join us after he single-handedly saved your life." Tracy started flipping through a magazine.

"Oh, yes, obviously," I agreed. "It would be really uncouth to not take him to Prom."

She groaned. "What was I supposed to do?"

I thought about my conversation with Bruce, and how what he needed was a positive experience with a great girl.

But of course there was no way I could let Tracy know that.

"Oh, Tracy, the sacrifices you make for me," I teased. "Having to endure a hot Australian guy who is crazy about you at a dance? You should be up for sainthood."

Tracy looked at me with a serious expression. "Thank you for finally realizing that." She put her hand up to her heart. "I fear that I'm not appreciated in my time. It's nice to know that *someone* recognizes my hardships."

Diane and I burst into laughter at the same time. Tracy leaned back in her seat and did her best to ignore us. She failed miserably.

"You guys are the worst," she scolded. "I should tell him no."

"No!" I protested a bit too much. "Bruce should come. He's fun, you're fun. Add the two together and it would be an insanely good time. Plus, Tyson needs some company."

"And Glen," Diane added.

"Who's Glen?" I asked.

Diane and Tracy looked at each other in alarm.

"What am I missing?"

Diane started speaking very slowly to me. "Glen is the guy Hilary has started dating. She was talking to you about it when you passed out."

The memory was hazy, but it was there. "Oh, yeah, right. I remember something about that. That's cool. Any other guys joining the crew?"

"I think that's it. For now," Tracy said.

"What does that mean? Are you planning on breaking more hearts?"

Tracy grabbed a pillow and held it over her head. "You should be lucky that you're in such a delicate condition or I'd so knock you on the head for that. I was simply implying that we'd be open to other guys coming. You know, like Ryan."

Ryan.

I was about to come clean about what had happened yesterday, but something held me back.

I tried to play it off. "Well, I guess we'll see who he ends up going with."

Diane tried to match my aloofness. "Yeah — I mean, it

would be nice to have him. I don't think he's planning on taking anybody, you know, outside of the group. Whatever." She grabbed the remote and started flipping channels.

Diane was many things, but she wasn't a good liar. It was pretty clear that she and Ryan had already discussed Prom arrangements.

I decided to call her bluff. "Yeah, I guess we'll see. What to the evs."

"Hey!" Tracy cried. "Can people stop stealing my line? I've so got to look into getting a copyright on that."

The three of us spent the rest of the evening watching TV and making the occasional comment about music for the dance-a-thon. But there was, thankfully, no more discussion of Prom, dresses, or dates.

I had other things to think about.

Well, only one thing.

Make that one person.

It was something I'd never thought would happen, yet here it was.

Ryan and I were spending a Saturday night together.

Since I wasn't allowed to leave home until I was better, and the Club was meeting at Diane's for the evening, I had nothing to do but sit at home.

And Ryan always knew the best way to my heart was through my stomach.

"What will people think?" he joked as he set down the pizza he'd brought. "Penny Lane Bloom spending a Saturday night *with a boy!*"

"I know — don't get used to it," I fired back as I grabbed a slice. My appetite had come back with such ferocity, I was secretly hoping Ryan had already eaten so I could have the pizza all to myself.

"Oh, I won't. I know better." He grabbed one of the smaller slices.

We'd spent the last couple days sending clandestine texts and living in the bubble where I didn't have to worry about the reality that existed outside my home.

But now reality was visiting.

"So my mom has signed the family up for the dance-a-thon." He leaned back on the couch. "I hope you can save at least one dance for me."

"It depends on how much of that pizza you plan on eating." I started in on my second slice.

"Fine." He wiped his hands after he finished his piece. "Although without food, I'm bound to get really, really tired." He moved over so his head was on my shoulder. I slouched so I could put my head next to his. But then I needed to move to get more food.

"Sorry," I apologized as he was forced to sit up. Then I made a huge deal of giving him another slice. "You've got to keep your strength up. I wouldn't want you to get sick, too."

"Well, I think we're a little late on that one." He leaned over and kissed me. I pushed my plate away as we put our arms around each other.

Time once again melted away as we held each other and kissed. Our moment was interrupted by the rumbling of my stomach. I was planning to ignore it, but Ryan was shaking.

I pulled away. "Are you laughing?"

"Sorry. Clearly, you need to eat, so please." He handed me back my plate. "We've got all night."

The thought of that made me feel increasingly better. In an effort to keep up my strength for the remainder of the evening, I started eating again.

Ryan reached for a slice but then took his hand away.

"Seriously, you can have one more slice," I said. "I'm not that big of a pig." Plus, I wanted him to have enough carbs in him for another marathon make-out session.

"You're the boss," he said as he grabbed another slice.

"I'm glad you realize my role in this —" I took a huge bite before I let *relationship* slip out of my mouth. I wasn't ready to define what "this" was.

"Oh, I know." He took an obedient bite of pizza. "You're so bossy."

"I am not! Tracy's the bossy one," I protested with a full mouth.

Ryan relented. "Okay, maybe *bossy* isn't the right word."

"Thank you."

"More like *intimidating*."

"I'm so not intimidating," I argued.

His eyes got wide. "Of course not."

"Are you being sarcastic?" I nudged him. Ryan wasn't the sarcastic type. That role was usually left to me.

"Noooo." He winked at me.

"Okay, so is telling me how bossy and intimidating I am your attempt to woo me?"

He raised his eyebrow. "So you're willing to be wooed?"

"Not anymore." I crossed my arms and pretended to sulk.

"Oh, come here." He reached out and wrapped his arms around me. We both sank back into the cushions of the couch. "You're beautiful, funny, smart, and, yes, a little intimidating."

"Whatever," I replied, even though I was soaking in all the other things he said about me. Ryan still liked me. And I still liked him. The only problem was how I was going to make everything work. I had nothing but time now that I was under house arrest, but things would change once I got back to school. Plus, things were better for him. Would it all come crumbling down if we started dating again? The last thing I wanted to do was cause him any more harm.

He laughed. "Okay, you do realize the problem that Todd has with you is that he's so used to intimidating people and getting what he wants with only a look. You not only turned him down on a date, you clearly do not care one bit about him. It drives him nuts."

I sat back up. "So you and Todd are friends again?" Because

last I knew, they weren't really speaking. And I actually preferred it that way, since while I wasn't sure how good I was for Ryan, I knew that Todd was nothing but trouble. For Ryan or anybody else on the planet that required oxygen.

"Not really. I don't want any more problems, so I'm not giving him the cold shoulder, but things with us will never be the same. He's changed. I have other friends I'd rather spend time with." He shrugged his shoulders indifferently. "And this was my choice, Penny. It had nothing to do with you. It never did."

But it did. It wasn't that I thought the earth revolved around me, but Todd and Ryan had been inseparable until I'd come along with The Lonely Hearts Club.

Ryan could sense I wasn't ready to talk about it. He laughed. "I do love that the only thing that rattles him is a girl who has zero respect for him."

"Are there people who actually respect Todd?" I shuddered exaggeratedly. "I question humanity."

"Let's not talk about Todd." Ryan pulled me in.

"But whatever are we going to do?" I feigned innocence.

He didn't answer. Instead, he kissed me again. His lips were soft, but there was a sense of urgency behind the kiss. I closed my eyes and relished every minute of it, not knowing how many more minutes like this we'd have.

I was getting better and it wouldn't be long before I had to head back into the real world.

Twenty-eight

I HAD GOTTEN USED TO THE whispers that followed me around as I walked the hallways at school. At first it was as the "pathetic" and "lonely" girl who'd started The Lonely Hearts Club.

Now it seemed I was the girl who'd fainted.

Tracy had warned me that the rumors about what had happened to me ranged from me being drunk or anorexic to me being so devastated about my breakup with Ryan that I couldn't handle a task as simple as walking down the hallway.

If they only knew.

I ignored the stares as I walked into school. Ryan and I had texted all day Sunday, but we'd kept things light. And I wanted it to stay that way. My few days off had been nice, but I had to get back to the dance-a-thon. And the Club. And schoolwork.

But still . . .

There was this voice in my head that kept trying to convince me it could work again.

I shook the thoughts from my head as I went to my locker, realizing there was no reason to stay away from it any longer. Ryan wasn't there, so I didn't have to worry about any awkward encounters this morning.

And at the same time, I knew what I really wanted was to kiss him again.

If only a relationship could be as simple as a kiss.

There was an extra buzz of excitement before the first bell rang.

"Ugh," Tracy said as she sat next to me in Trig. "Why do people find this so exciting?"

"Find what so exciting?" I was clueless about what was going on.

"Prom court announcement." She gestured to the speaker in the front of the room as it buzzed to life.

"Shh!" Pam Schneider commanded the class. She tapped her foot impatiently as the vice principal went over the other announcements of the day.

"And now to the junior Prom court," his voice crackled over the speaker. Pam was on the edge of her chair. "For junior Prom king, your nominees in alphabetical order are: Ryan Bauer, Todd Chesney, Don Levitz, and Brian Reed." Pam shrieked loudly when her boyfriend Brian's name was called.

Tracy let out a little groan. "So predictable."

The announcement continued. "And your nominees for Prom queen, this time in reverse alphabetical order —"

"Oh!" Tracy pretended to be scandalized. "How crazy! *Reverse* alphabetical order."

Pam turned around to give her a dirty look.

"Audrey Werner, Pam Schneider" — *of course* — "Diane Monroe, and . . ."

Tracy collapsed on her chair as if she was dying from boredom.

"Penny Lane Bloom."

WHAT?!?!

Tracy jolted her head up from her desk so quickly she probably gave herself whiplash. "Well, well, well." She smirked at me. "This just got interesting."

Being nominated for Prom court wasn't the only thing that was confusing me. Ryan wasn't at his locker all morning. I started to get worried that he was mad at me again, since the last time *he'd* stayed away from his locker was when I'd hurt him last semester.

My mind started racing as I made my way to lunch.

Maybe you were nominated solely so someone could pour pig's blood on you.

Maybe you can work out things with Ryan. It's called compromise.

But that didn't work out for you last time, did it?

I was so lost in my thoughts, I didn't hear Tracy calling my name as I walked to lunch.

"PENNY!" she shouted next to my ear.

"Huh?"

Tracy's eyebrows were creased with worry. "Are you feeling okay? Or are you already figuring out your campaign for Prom queen?"

"What? I'm not campaigning." I would never do something like that. And besides, there was only one true contender for the crown — and that was Diane. "I was *thinking*."

"Oh-kaaaay." Tracy shook her head at me. "Hey, you really do look so much better. It seems like you got all the rest you needed this weekend. Among other things."

"Yeah, I'm feeling nearly one hundred percent." I plunked my lunch bag down on our table.

The sound of a hacking cough came from behind us. I looked over and was horrified to find Ryan at his table, sitting with a stack of tissues at his side. He looked horrible, with a red nose and watery eyes.

Guilt overwhelmed me as he continued to cough.

He'd gotten that from me.

Of course he did.

I was going to ask him how he was, and if there was anything I could do (*cheese fries?*), but first Diane and I had to field everybody's congratulations for being nominated for Prom queen. Meanwhile, a few members started excitedly passing around photos on their phones of the dresses they'd tried on that past weekend. I tried my best to let the conversation distract me from my contagion guilt.

That was until Amy showed up. "Wow, Ryan's super sick. He came into class late this morning and he's a hot mess." She gestured over to me. "He's like you were last week."

I took a big bite of my sandwich so I wouldn't be expected to comment. I sat there hoping nobody would put two and two together, but by the looks around the table, they were calculating it out quite nicely.

Tracy saved me. "So I think I found a hot little number for

Prom." She pulled up a picture of a long, dark purple dress with a deep V in the back.

"Yeah," Kara agreed. "But I think if you wear that, we'll need to have an ambulance at the ready for when Bruce sees you."

"Hey!" Tracy threw her hands up. "The guy wanted to come with us — he should know the risk of being around something this smokin' hot. Okaaay." She playfully snapped her fingers.

I patiently listened to all the Prom talk for the rest of the lunch break. I couldn't wait until it was over so I could check in on Ryan. As soon as people started to leave, I jumped up to go to my locker.

Tracy was right on my heels. "So do you want to go shopping sometime next week for your dress? I'm not one hundred percent sold on that purple number."

"Sure," I agreed quickly, then started walking faster.

"And do you want me to come over after school today to fill you in on the dance-a-thon?"

"That'd be great."

"And would you like to explain to me why Ryan's so sick?"

I kept my quick pace, trying to not show her that she had me. "I don't know. Must be something going around."

"All right," Tracy said. "But then can you explain what his car was doing parked outside your house on Saturday night?"

So. Busted.

Tracy stepped in front of me so I was forced to look right at her. "Pen, if you guys are back together, that's great. But why wouldn't you tell us? Or at least me?" She looked hurt. This wasn't the first time I'd purposely held the truth from her, although I really wanted it to be the last.

"We're not back together — I don't know what we are," I said truthfully. "He came over on Thursday and things happened. But this weekend was different. We were in our own little bubble. Nobody knows, so it wasn't like I'd be ruining his reputation at school again. It was only the two of us. I was just Penny. I didn't have anything to do. There was time for a boyfriend. But now I'm back and there's so much going on, I don't know anymore. It didn't work before, so why would it now? I can't risk it."

"Those sound like excuses."

"They're not excuses. It's the truth."

Tracy was quiet for a few moments. Then she sighed loudly. "You know I love you, Pen, but sometimes you can be such an idiot."

She walked away and left me standing there in the hallway to think about what she said. Tracy had never said one negative thing about me, so if she thought I was truly being an idiot, then maybe I was.

How do you properly apologize for making someone sick from the mere act of kissing you?

Luckily, I didn't have to worry about that until after school when we were finally at our lockers at the same time.

Ryan let out a little laugh as I approached.

"Well, I guess you learned your lesson," I joked, even though I felt truly awful about his current state.

"Completely worth it," he said right before he sneezed violently. "Although I do think it's best if you stay away from me. This could become a very vicious cycle."

Even though he was joking and meant that I should stay away from him *physically* until he was better, that nagging voice was back. I was painfully aware of how much I should've stayed away from Ryan.

After another sneeze, he said, "I'm going to stay home tomorrow. Maybe even longer. So I do believe my wooing will be delayed a week until I'm one hundred percent better."

"We're still using the word *wooing*?" I teased.

He looked at me expectantly with his bleary, red eyes. "So . . . do you think I could take you out later this week? You know, a proper *wooing*."

"The dance-a-thon is this weekend, so things are a little crazy. But I promise to save you a dance. So that should give you motivation to get better soon."

"It does." Ryan nodded. "Well, there's next week. And Prom. And since we're both on Prom court . . ."

I wasn't sure why I wasn't simply inviting him along with us. It wouldn't have been a big deal if Ryan had joined the group. But it would be to him. And to me as well. Everything was so up in the air — would it really be the best thing to use Prom as our second first date?

Ryan could sense my hesitation. He reached out and I took a step back.

"Is that because you don't want to get sick again or because you don't want to go to Prom with me?" His voice was strained from the cold, but probably also from my behavior.

He was laying it all on the line, and my only response was to stand there and stare at him. I didn't know what to say. If I said I wanted to go to Prom with him, I could end up hurting him by putting him second to the Club. If I said I didn't want to go with him, I'd still hurt him.

It was lose-lose.

I continued to stand there utterly dumbfounded.

Even Ryan Bauer had his limits.

"This again?" Ryan turned his back and closed his locker door. "You know, Penny, I'm exhausted. I'm sick and I'm not really in the mood to play any games right now. I guess I'll talk to you about this later."

"Wait." I pulled at his sleeve. "I feel so bad about how sick you are, and things are a little crazy right now. Get better and we'll figure it out." I hoped delaying the inevitable would give me time to figure out what to do. Ryan had helped me immensely while I was sick and I wanted nothing but to do the same for him. "Please let me know if there's anything I can do to make you feel better. I hear Gatorade, ice cream, and cheese fries help."

He looked off into the distance. I couldn't really tell what he was thinking. Then he finally spoke. "You know what would make me feel better?"

I shook my head.

"There's only one thing that I've ever wanted." He finally turned to look directly in my eyes. "And that's you."

I fumbled over what to say. How could I have possibly responded to such a wonderful confession? There were many things I could've said right then. That I wanted him, too. That I'd find a way to make things work. That I wouldn't hurt him again.

Instead, I stood there with my mouth open, grasping.

Ryan wasn't going to wait any longer. He turned his back and walked away.

Tracy was right.

I, Penny Lane Bloom, am a complete idiot.

Twenty-nine

THERE WAS BEING AN IDIOT, AND then there was being me. Just like there was being busy, and then there were the days leading up to the dance-a-thon.

It was mass chaos. Between school, homework, and all of the things we needed to do to get ready, there was little time for breathing, let alone trying to make a relationship work. Still, I did go over to Ryan's house to bring him some cheese fries after school one day. He was allegedly sleeping, according to his mom. He wasn't at school for the rest of the week.

Maybe he was giving me the space that I'd originally asked for. Maybe he was tired of my constant uncertainties. Or maybe I needed to make a decision already.

But there were already too many decisions to be made.

Tracy and I were finalizing the playlist on our way to lunch the Friday before the dance-a-thon.

"Will anybody our age even want to dance to the fifties and sixties music?" Tracy asked as we turned the corner to the cafeteria.

"Don't worry, I'll cover that for our team," I offered, knowing that Tracy, Diane, Morgan, and Kara would much rather dance later in the day. I was only worried that the start of the event wouldn't be the best time for me to be out on the dance floor. "You'll be able to get your groove on with that crazy music the kids are listening to these days."

"You know it," Tracy said. "My dance moves are more for the modern era. I've got some moves that are going to make the older people wish they could turn back time."

When we reached our table, Diane's attention was elsewhere.

"What's going on?" I asked her.

She motioned her head to the other side of the room. "That's what I'm trying to figure out."

Off to the side, Missy was in a deep discussion with Todd. The second I saw them leaning in, near the spot where he had admonished her over a month ago, I felt sick. There was no way this could be good.

Instead of fretting over possible conspiracy theories, I decided to walk over there. Maybe she needed backup. The fact that I was worried about Missy and going there to potentially rescue her was almost too alien to comprehend.

Todd was leaning against the wall, his hand on Missy's shoulder. He was talking softly and didn't notice that I was approaching.

"Is everything okay?" I asked Missy.

She nodded slowly, like she wasn't sure if it was true.

"Relax," Todd said with an angry curl of his lip. "I'm talking to Missy. You don't own her."

"I know that," I responded a bit too defensively. "But last

time I checked, you were being a Class A jerkwad, and for some reason I doubt that has changed."

"Baby." Todd began rubbing Missy's arm. "You know I said I'm sorry and I really mean it. So let's stop this nonsense and come join me. I miss you. We all miss you. You belong with us. You belong with me." He then wrapped his massive arms around Missy's tiny frame.

I'd never seen Todd's "magic" up close. I assumed he possessed some voodoo skills to get as many girlfriends as he'd had. He was saying all the right things. But saying was completely different from doing. He was writing checks he couldn't cash.

Missy bit her lip. She was falling for his lines, for his lies.

I tried to bring her back to reality. "Missy," I said, "it's up to you, but you know we'd love for you to join us."

She kept looking between the two tables, confusion lining her face. She finally looked at me. "I'm so sorry," she said in a small voice as she took Todd's hand and walked with him to her promised land.

I became angrier with every step I took back to our table. But what was weird was, it wasn't Missy I was mad at. I was furious at Todd for getting back together with her only to eventually dump her again.

Wait a second. Am I actually feeling bad for Missy?

We'd been planning on surprising her after the dance-a-thon and making her a full-fledged member. Her heart was in the right place and she'd worked her butt off for the dance-a-thon.

"What was *that*?" Tracy asked as Missy was greeted back at the popular table like a kidnap victim who was finally free of her captors.

I turned toward Michelle. "Please tell me that you can get the baskets she arranged for the dance-a-thon."

Michelle nodded solemnly. "I'll call them after school. I can't believe she . . ."

"I know."

I couldn't help but feel a little betrayed that Missy had gone back with Todd. Although I understood all too well how tempting it could be to be given a second chance.

But just because you're given one doesn't mean you should take it.

At nine sharp on Saturday morning, we were at the high school getting ready. Everybody had a task to do. The hallways and gymnasium were a flurry of activity.

Stations were being set up, Tyson's band was doing a sound check, I was running around with my head cut off — so everything was going according to plan. There was even a line outside the front doors.

After I did my last run-through with everybody, a familiar figure approached me with a large basket in her hands.

"There was one more that needed to be picked up," Missy said to me in an apologetic tone.

"Oh, thanks." I pointed toward the table overflowing with our raffle and silent auction items.

She set down the basket brimming with spa products. "Well, I guess I should . . ." She let the words hang in the air as if I was going to insist that she stay.

"Yes," I agreed. "But thank you for the basket."

Missy hesitated before turning around. "I know you probably regret giving me a chance, and I get it." Her voice began to quiver. "Did you forget what it was like to be a freshman? You probably didn't even care about where you stood in the popularity chain; it was beneath you. Yeah, well, it matters to me. So call me shallow, call me whatever you want. I feel better when I'm with someone. I need that. Maybe that makes me weak. But it makes me happy."

I didn't know what to say to that. But I didn't have to say anything. She left the gym before I could.

Diane came over. "What was that?"

"It wouldn't be a proper day in my life without some meltdowns," I joked, even though that was scarily becoming my reality.

"Don't let it get to you." Diane rubbed my back.

I gave her a look that made it clear I wasn't ever going to let Missy Winston get to me.

Diane checked her watch. "I guess we're ready, right?" A flicker of doubt flashed over her face briefly before she took a deep breath. "No, we're ready."

Everybody was in place. The music started with Elvis Presley's "Hound Dog" blasting. A few of the volunteers were already dancing, including Mom and Dad.

Tracy was at the front doors, getting ready to open them. Her face was serious and she intoned, "I hereby declare the dance-a-thon officially started. Get ready for twelve hours of insanity." She reached for the door handle. "As Sir Kevin Bacon once said in the classic motion picture *Footloose* . . . LET'S DANCE!"

Get Back

"Get back to where you once belonged."

Thirty

THE GYMNASIUM WAS PACKED WITH YOUNG and old, female and male, Parkview residents and people from neighboring towns, those who knew about The Lonely Hearts Club and those who were only now finding out about our fabulousness.

We all danced in shifts. Three hours in, as the sixties gave way to the disco sounds of the seventies, one of my shifts ended, and I turned the dancing over to Tracy. Bruce grabbed her hand and started twirling her around. She shimmied up closer to him, a mischievous grin on her face.

As much as Tracy protested Bruce's constant attention, she didn't seem to mind it as they took over the dance floor. And by the excited expression on Bruce's face, he seemed to be enjoying himself as well. I wondered if, when he'd taken that heartbroken, long plane ride to the States back in January, he'd imagined himself being able to be as happy as he was right now.

I plunked down next to Kara to help her at the information desk. She was busy calculating some figures out on her phone. "I think this is going to be big. With pledges and the raffle tickets, we're close to thirty."

"I'm sorry — do you mean that we'll be close to thirty *thousand* dollars?"

"Yep, insane, huh?"

Insane was an understatement.

And we still had nine hours to go.

I scanned the dance floor for Ryan. I'd spotted him earlier, dancing with his stepsister, grateful he felt well enough to come today. I'd been planning on asking him to dance with me for a bit, but then I'd had to help solve a raffle ticket problem.

Timing never seemed to be on our side.

"I'm going to get a soda. Want anything?" I offered to Kara before I exited to the concession stands outside the gym doors.

There was no sign of Ryan or Katie. Since I was in for a long night, I opted for the biggest cup of Cherry Coke I could buy. And a double chocolate chip cookie. I figured when tired and in doubt, best to go for caffeine *and* sugar.

As I turned to head back into the gym, I caught Principal Braddock's eye from across the hallway. He motioned for me to join him and I instantly felt sick. Everything had been going so well, but I should've known he would find something to pick apart.

"Hi," I greeted him as warmly as I could. "Thanks for coming."

He looked around the hallway, surveying the lines of people getting food and signing up for the silent auction. "It looks like everything's going well."

"Yes." I agreed and left out my desire to add *until you showed up*.

"As I've said, I'm still not on board with this little club of yours. I still feel that you're a bit too exclusive for my tastes."

I couldn't help myself. "Oh, so I can join the football team next year?"

He wisely ignored my comment. "However, I can't deny what you've done today. I think that you should present your scholarship at our awards night."

"Really?" I stood there with my mouth open. Awards night was when the school presented scholarships and academic awards. It was an official McKinley High School event. And Braddock wanted The Lonely Hearts Club to be part of it. "That would be amazing. Thank you."

He gave me a quick nod. "You've pulled off something truly impressive."

"Well, it really was a team effort. The Club is more than one person, and none of this would've happened without each and every member."

He chuckled. "Yes, that's your club's motto or something, isn't it? It's basically the same thing Miss Monroe said to me when she took her name off Prom court."

"WHAT?" I practically shouted in his ear.

"You didn't know?" Braddock's lips curled up into a smirk. "She came into my office and said that she didn't feel it was fair to be singled out among her fellow classmates. She won't be on the ballot for Prom queen."

It wasn't something I could fathom. I thought I knew Diane, and she'd basically been a Prom-queen-in-training since grade school. She was a shoo-in to win. Why would she withdraw — and not share that information with any of us?

I excused myself from Braddock and went in search of the Prom court deserter. And of course since I wasn't looking for Ryan, he appeared seemingly out of thin air.

"Hey!" I gave his arm a squeeze. "You made it! How are you feeling?"

"Good," he said, a little out of breath from dancing. "Congrats! Everything's going great."

"Thanks!" I kept looking around for Diane. "Listen, I want that dance I promised you, but I need to find Diane first. Have you seen her?"

He pointed to the far corner of the room. "Last time I saw her, she was guarding the requests table."

Before I left him, I felt I needed to do some damage control. "I really want to dance with you — it's a little crazy right now. But we've got . . . more than eight hours left."

If I couldn't make time within eight hours to have one dance with Ryan, he would have every right to never want me back.

Diane was taking down requests for the DJs (aka Tyson and Morgan) to do special shout-outs to groups, all for a dollar. It was amazing how many people wanted to either hear their names over a loudspeaker or embarrass someone in public. There was a lot of the latter.

She was counting a stack of ones when I approached her. "You dropped out of Prom court?"

She didn't even miss a beat as she continued to count the money. "I was going to tell you after today."

"But why?"

"It seemed pretty obvious."

"That you'd drop out?" I asked. Because it wasn't obvious to me.

"No." She looked around to make sure nobody could hear her. "It seemed obvious that I would win. That's what Diane Monroe does. She gets a sparkly crown. She smiles and does what she's supposed to. I'm not interested in being the version of what everybody expects me to be. I want to be me."

"But you are you," I reasoned with her. "You quit the cheerleading squad, you kicked ass in basketball. You don't need to be anybody but you because the real Diane Monroe is pretty freakin' special."

She tucked a strand of her short hair behind her ear. "I'm still figuring out who that person is. I always had a plan: be the girlfriend, be the cheerleader, be the straight-A student, but then I flipped everything over. Believe me when I say I'm so happy I did it. But I'm not done growing. All I want is to figure out what I want to do. Meanwhile, you know what would make me very happy?"

"What?"

"*You* winning Prom queen."

I laughed. "Oh, please — that would bring the social hierarchy of this school to its knees. It's never going to happen."

"You never know," Diane teased. "How much fun do you think I'm going to have watching Pam and Audrey scratch each other's eyes out since they'll now assume they're the front-runners?"

I didn't know what to find harder to believe: someone besides Diane being Prom queen or Diane getting joy out of disrupting the delicate balance of her former cheerleading besties.

Who knew Diane Monroe would be such a troublemaker?

Not me, but I wholeheartedly approved.

Tyson's band took the stage at eight o'clock. There were only four hours left to go.

Morgan happily took to the dance floor for this shift. The rest of our group sat on the bleachers, eating pizza. The band would be playing for an hour, switching between covers and originals — all upbeat to keep the momentum up.

Mom approached us, wiping the sweat off her forehead. She'd been out there dancing practically the entire time. "I'm going for a coffee run — can I get you girls anything?"

Usually, Mom would tsk if she saw me drinking coffee, always harping that it was going to stunt my growth, even though I was already four inches taller than her. But it was clear these were desperate times.

And desperate times called for caffeine.

I started writing down our sugary coffee orders when Tyson's band launched into a cover of "I Saw Her Standing There."

Morgan came dancing over, motioning us to join her. Mom looked suspiciously at her.

That woman never forgets anything.

We obliged Morgan and danced along to the song. It was nice to have these moments when we could fully enjoy ourselves and not worry about the next hour or what we had to do.

The audience applauded enthusiastically after the number ended. Morgan glowed as she cheered for Tyson. He, in turn, blew her a kiss.

They made it seem so easy. Morgan liked Tyson. Tyson liked Morgan. They go out. They make time for each other.

Why did I have to always complicate things?

Morgan pulled on my arm. "I was so freaked out to see your mom. I figured she would take one look at me and just *know*."

I started to nod before I realized I didn't quite understand what Morgan was referring to. She put her hand up to her mouth and started giggling. Like full-on girly-girl giggling, which was so not like Morgan.

"Wait." I looked around and tried to be as quiet as one could during a rock concert. "Have you guys . . ."

Morgan nodded. "It happened a couple weeks ago. I was going to tell you, but you were really sick and already had a lot to deal with."

"Oh my God!" I couldn't help but exclaim. "How was it?" I asked before I could really think about it. I was so curious, but also knew this was a private thing.

Morgan looked up at Tyson with a huge grin. "It was good. I mean, it hurt a little the first time. But now it feels right."

I was fully aware I was standing still, full-on staring at Morgan while everyone around us was focused on the concert and dancing around. I delicately placed my hand on her arm. "You okay?" While she seemed more than fine, I wished I could've been there for her while she figured out this life-changing decision.

"I'm fabulous." She was practically glowing.

"No regrets?"

"Let me tell you something, Penny." She started dancing around me. "Life is so much better if you live it without regrets."

No regrets.

I went in search, yet again, for Ryan, and found him eating with his mom and stepsister.

"Hey, guys," I said as I approached them. "Having fun?"

"Yes." Ryan's mom nodded. "Although I don't think Katie's going to last much longer."

Even with her head bobbing in a fight against sleep, Katie protested the idea of being sent home early with her dad.

"Well, I was hoping I could steal Ryan away for a dance," I said awkwardly, as if I needed his mom's permission.

Ryan set his cheeseburger down and took my hand. "I thought you'd never ask."

As we walked to the dance floor, my body tingled at his touch. Although it was familiar, it had been awhile since we'd shown any affection in public.

I hoped we could finally have that conversation we'd been avoiding. Well, I had been avoiding.

"Penny!" Kara shouted at me before we even had a chance to get on the dance floor. "We're out of flyers. Do you know where we have more?"

I shook my head. "Tracy should have them. Have you seen her?" I made a futile attempt to look around, knowing it was nearly impossible to spot anybody in the crowded gym.

"No, which is why I came to you."

I looked at Ryan apologetically. "Let me take care of this and I'll be right back."

He gave me a borderline-understanding smile before I rushed off again.

Kara and I went separate ways to locate Tracy. I sent her a text, hoping she'd make this easier on us. I walked up and down the gym, stopping occasionally to receive compliments about the dance-a-thon.

"Have you seen Tracy?" I asked Maria, who was dancing with her older brother.

She, thankfully, nodded. "Yeah, I saw her go backstage a few minutes ago."

I headed toward the side of the stage and weaved in between the cases from Tyson's band. They were nearly done with their set, which meant there were only three hours left. The backstage area was dark. Tracy wasn't anywhere stage left, so I walked behind the curtain to the other side.

There was movement in the corner behind the curtain, where we'd stored some of our bags and boxes. I automatically assumed it was Tracy or maybe even Kara finding more flyers.

"Tracy?" I called out, but was drowned out by the band playing "Shout."

I pulled the curtain open and froze at the sight of Tracy in full make-out mode with Bruce.

Oh. My. Sir Paul.

Tracy quickly pulled away from Bruce's passionate grasp, and smoothed out her hair and clothes. "Hey, Pen, what's up?"

Bruce was breathless, a contented look on his face. "Ah, maybe I should get back to . . ." He grinned broadly as he turned to Tracy. "So I'll catch up with you later?"

"We'll see," Tracy said with a flirtatious smirk.

I couldn't help but gape. I waited for a confession or some explanation of what was going on.

Bruce leaned in and did his best to whisper in my ear, "My faith in the female gender has been restored."

I stood there and continued to stare at Tracy for what felt like months.

When she finally spoke, it was to say, "You can't tell anybody."

"Tell anybody *what?*" I was pretty sure my eyes were out of their sockets. "I'm trying to understand what I saw, because it looked like you were macking hard on Bruce."

"Well, that's true . . ." Tracy laughed. "I mean, yeah, he's hot. And a good guy, so I felt like, you know, kissing him. Better get my practice in."

"Tracy!" I said excitedly. "You had your first kiss! And it was so secretive."

"And pretty hot," Tracy added. "But seriously, Pen, you can't tell anybody."

"Why not?" I couldn't understand why Tracy would want to keep this to herself. Not that I expected her to make an announcement over the PA system, but still.

"I don't want to ruin my reputation," she said in a serious tone.

"Tracy, making out with a guy isn't going to taint you as some harlot," I said incredulously.

"That's not what I mean." She looked around cautiously. "I like being the girl who isn't desperate to get a boyfriend. I like that I don't focus on guys anymore. And Bruce is sweet, but it still doesn't change the fact that he's headed back home in a month. I simply thought that I shouldn't wait until I'm in my twenties to finally kiss a guy. It seemed pretty innocent and it won't hurt anybody. Yeah, I know Bruce likes me — I mean the guy he has great taste, *obvs*. But we both know what this was. I don't think he has any complaints. He knows not to say anything."

I processed what she said. "Tracy, are you seriously telling me you made out with Bruce solely for practice?"

"I mean, it was nice, don't get me wrong." Tracy started playing with her bracelet. "But yeah, I did. I figure guys do it all the time." It was as if Tracy could sense my concern about Bruce. "And you should know Bruce told me all about the girl back home. He knows we're only having fun. So there's no need to look so worried."

"Okay, your awesome, sexy secret is safe with me." I'd almost forgotten why I was looking for her in the first place. "Do you have any more flyers?"

"Yeah, I'm on it." She ducked under the other curtain to grab more flyers, then headed in the direction opposite from the one Bruce had gone.

I stayed for a few seconds to collect my thoughts.

Was *everybody* keeping secrets from me?

"Penny?" Ryan's voice brought me back to the present. I turned around and found him looking furious, his hands wrapped tightly in fists.

"What's wrong?" I asked automatically.

He looked disgusted. "What's wrong? Are you *kidding me*? Like you don't know."

My stomach instantly dropped. I had no idea what he was talking about. "What? I don't, what are you . . . ?"

"I can't believe this." He looked so hurt. I took a step forward to try to comfort him, to try to figure out what was wrong. But he stepped back, his face curled in revulsion. He laughed bitterly. "I was looking for you, and Brian told me that he saw Bruce making out with some girl up here. Then Bruce comes out all flustered, but wouldn't say anything to me. And then I come back here to find you."

"What?" I tried to understand what he was accusing me of. "You think I was kissing Bruce? That wasn't what happened."

"Oh, so who was Bruce kissing, then, if it wasn't you? You're the only one back here." He made a dramatic show of looking around.

"He was with —" I stopped myself when I remembered the promise I'd made to Tracy. "I can't say — but you have to believe me. You know I'd never do that."

"I can't do this anymore, Penny." His voice was laced with sadness. "I kept thinking we'd find a way to work this out, but it's too much. I never know where I stand with you. One minute it seems that you want to get back together, then the next you give me the cold shoulder. I can't keep putting myself out there for you, only to be pushed aside. Nothing is ever going to change, is it?"

I reached out to touch his arm. "Ryan, please listen to me," I pleaded, my voice cracking.

He took a sharp step away from me, like I was poisonous. "I can't."

I could hardly breathe, wishing he'd listen to what I had to say.

He kept making his distance from me greater. "It's over." Then he paused for a second, his jaw clenched. "For good."

He rushed to the stairs, and I tried to call out to him, but it was too late.

I started typing furiously into my phone.

I need you. Backstage. Now.

Then I sat down on the floor, shaking and crying. Even if I hadn't been kissing Bruce, I felt Ryan was right. He had put up with a lot and all I'd done was push him aside. I was the one who treated him poorly.

I was his Nate.

"Pen?" Tracy ran up to me, Diane closely following her. She kneeled next to me and wrapped her arms around me. "What's wrong? What happened?"

"I've messed everything up," I confessed. "Ryan has had enough. He's given up on me. He thinks I was back here kissing Bruce — he thinks that little of me. But maybe I deserve that."

Diane kneeled on the other side of me and began rubbing my back. "I thought you and Ryan were . . ." She mercifully didn't say *through, finished, over.*

"We were, are . . ." I grabbed the tissue that Diane had out for me. "But . . ."

And then I told them everything. About the secretive hook-ups. About how I'd wanted to make it work. About how much I'd hurt him.

They were both quiet as I finished. Tracy had a determined look on her face. "I'll tell him the truth about Bruce."

Diane looked confused, but kept her mouth shut. She'd figure it out on her own. I couldn't believe that Ryan hadn't done the same.

"Thanks, but I don't think any of that would matter." It was truly a lost cause.

"Why did you keep playing it off like you were fine with the breakup?" Diane asked.

"Because I made a mistake!" I finally admitted. As soon as that confession left my mouth, I knew what a total disaster I had made of my relationship with Ryan. "I'm not perfect. In fact, I have been behaving like a complete idiot. But I don't know how to undo it all. Everything's a mess."

"Pen." Tracy looked at me intensely. "What do you want?"

My mind flashed back to being in the car with Ryan when we'd broken up. He'd asked me that same question. I'd lied to him then. But I wasn't going to hide the truth anymore. It was a simple answer.

"I want to be with Ryan," I stated with certainty. "But then I think about what you said, Tracy."

Tracy was perplexed. "What *I* said?"

"'What's the point?'"

Tracy studied me for a few seconds before laughing. "Oh. My. God. Seriously, Pen? You're going to take relationship advice from *me*? What on earth were you thinking? I've never been in a relationship. I have no *clue* what I'm talking about."

"But —"

Tracy waved her hand to silence me. "No *but*s, Pen. You used what Ryan was going through as an excuse to break up with him. You use the Club as an excuse for why you can't be with him. *Enough.* The Lonely Hearts Club is like a self-sustaining organism now. You don't need to feel the pressure to do everything or be everywhere or be everything to everyone. I think when it comes down to it, you keep coming up with excuses because you're scared of getting hurt again."

"Like you aren't scared of getting hurt," I fired back at her.

"What are you talking about?"

"Is the reason why you don't want to be with Bruce because you've seen how all my failed relationships led me to form The Lonely Hearts Club in the first place?"

"WHAT?" Tracy shook her head. "I can't believe you thought that. No, the reason I don't want to be with Bruce is because I don't want to be with anybody. I want to make out with him because he's gorgeous and a fun little fling. Something I've realized about myself this past year is that I'm actually pretty practical. I hate to break it to you, but *you're* the romantic one."

"Yeah," Diane agreed. "That makes sense, Penny. You always had your head on straight with guys, but when you really like someone, like you do with Ryan, you go all in. And you should. You should be with Ryan. No excuses."

"What's the point?" I asked.

"Stop saying that!" Tracy scolded.

"What I mean is that none of this matters. We can say what we want, but it doesn't change the fact that Ryan thinks I'm a lying, cheating wench. I've hurt him *yet again*. I can't do that to him anymore. So it doesn't matter what I want, does it?"

"But —" Diane tried to reason with me, but I held my hand up to silence her.

"I don't want to talk about it anymore. There *is* no point. The damage has been done and then some." I wiped away a tear forcefully. "Can we just go out there and pretend like none of this ever happened?"

I think the only way I was going to survive the rest of the school year was to pretend that Ryan and I never happened.

"If that's what you want." Diane relented.

"It is." Although it didn't really matter what I wanted anymore. Maybe I didn't deserve to have what I wanted.

"You're really okay going back out there?"

I nodded weakly.

Because we still had two hours of dancing to do.

After Diane helped me clean up my tear-stained face, the three of us locked arms and walked back out into the gymnasium where the party was still in full swing. There was no need to even look around — I knew I wouldn't find Ryan.

"Let's do this!" Tracy declared as she took me by the hand. Then she began to dance in a playful, faux-exotic manner. "This is why I need to stay single — nobody could handle all of this. Too much mystery, too much awesome, too much everything."

I forced a smile. "Too much bravado?"

"You know it." She spun me around. "Listen, don't worry about Ryan. He'll come around. Bruce and I will come clean to him. It's my fault he thinks you were cheating. Although you wouldn't have technically been cheating since you weren't officially together, but you know how boys can be." She shook her head in joking exasperation.

Amy came running toward us. "There's a camera crew here from Channel Five news."

Diane perked up and looked over at the corner where a woman in a smart blue suit was standing in front of lights. "They came? That's amazing. This is going to be huge for the Club."

"They want to interview Penny about the Club and the dance-a-thon." Amy studied my face with worry. Apparently, it was going to take more than a few tissues and tinted moisturizer to hide my misery.

I turned to Diane. "Can you please do it for me? I can't." Even those words took more energy than I had left.

"Of course," she replied. "I'll make sure they have everything they need. Do *not* worry about it." She took some lip gloss out of her jeans pocket and began applying it.

"Thanks. I owe you."

Diane stopped her primping and looked at me with such focus. "Penny, you don't owe me anything."

I gave her a look that made it clear that I owed her. A lot.

She kissed me on the cheek and whispered, "Oh, Penny, I don't think there's anybody who has benefited more than me from having you in my life. Take the help. You need balance, you need to delegate, remember?"

She was right. Diane was always right. "Yes."

"Everything's going to be okay," she said, with such confidence I desperately wanted to believe her. "Right?" She prodded me.

I closed my eyes and said, with as much certainty that I could muster, "Everything is going to be okay."

Thirty-one

THE WEEK AFTER THE DANCE-A-THON, I should've been happily skipping down the hallway. We'd exceeded our expectations by bringing in nearly thirty-two thousand dollars to split between PARC and our scholarship recipient.

And then there was the explosion of the Club online after Diane nailed her interview, which had gone viral. We were currently at thirty-five clubs with one hundred forty-four members in four countries.

I should've been riding high, but instead, the week leading up to Prom had become oddly familiar. I had the usual suspects openly mocking me, this time for the fact that I was in contention for Prom queen.

And then there was the coldness from Ryan.

I was also being distant with my friends. Anytime they brought up Ryan, I changed the subject. Tracy had confessed to him about Bruce. She said that he hadn't really given her much of a reaction. And he was still hanging out with Bruce, so it seemed that he knew the truth. Even Diane had tried to plead my case.

But it was too little, too late.

When both Tracy and Diane didn't even mention Ryan to me anymore, or try to get me to talk, I knew it was time to move forward. Even though I desperately wanted to gaze long-ingly in the rearview mirror, where misery was much closer to my heart than it appeared.

I did try to get my spirits up in time for Prom. I got the dress, did the whole manicure, pedicure, hairdo thing. I was playing the role, trying to keep up appearances.

I'd joined Diane, Tracy, Morgan, and Kara at Tracy's house to put the final touches on our outfits before the motorcade left for our pre-Prom dinner. As Diane, Morgan, and Kara went downstairs, I stared in the mirror at my floor-length white chiffon dress with sweetheart neckline and beaded cap sleeves. I studied the way my hair fell in loose waves, framing my bronzed and blushed face. Anybody looking at this person would think she was getting ready for the night of her life.

But I was miserable inside.

"Ready?" Tracy asked as she put her last earring in and twirled around in her flowing black skirt, which she'd paired with a sparkling silver spaghetti-strap top. Downstairs in Tracy's living room, our parents were waiting with cameras in hand. There'd be plenty documentation of my sorrow.

"Yes." I tried to sound excited. I knew we'd have fun, we'd dance, laugh . . . but there was something missing. *Someone* missing.

"Well, I guess we should head down," Tracy declared before partially shutting her bedroom door. "But I think we need to have a talk first."

"What's going on?" I asked.

"Penny Lane Bloom, this is an intervention."

"A *what*?"

Tracy put my hands in hers. "I'm worried about you. You can't keep hiding your feelings. You're in total denial. We need to talk about this."

"Can you please not do this right now?" I begged. My makeup wouldn't survive it. "Besides there's no reason to. Ryan hates me. I screwed up in so many ways. There's nothing I can do about it."

"You're my best friend, Pen. I need to understand what's going on. Let's start with the breakup."

"Why?" My voice cracked.

"I think it would make you feel better to get it all out in the open."

"Fine!" I was so mad at Tracy for doing this to me. "I ruined the guy's life. I'm the reason why his friends abandoned him, I put him behind everything else in my life, I caused him so much suffering. And yeah, I'm also terrified of being hurt again."

It actually did feel good to get this out of my system. My voice started to rise. "You saw what happened to me after Nate, and what it took for me to get back to normal. I like Ryan so much more than I ever liked Nate. I like Ryan more than I thought it was possible to like another person. I was so devastated after Valentine's Day even thinking we were breaking up, that maybe I broke up with him to protect myself."

I slumped down in defeat. "Believe me when I say that I've been going over and over all the stupid stuff I've done to try to make sense of it. But I can't. Because none of it makes sense. Because I want to be with Ryan. I'm ready. No more excuses. But I can't because *he* doesn't want to be with *me* anymore. And I don't blame him!"

My chin started to quiver and I knew that if I continued, all of the makeup artists in all of the land wouldn't be able to put Penny Lane Bloom back together again. "Can we please just go so we can get tonight over with?"

I stormed past Tracy, pulled the door open, and ran into the person standing right outside. I gasped when I saw him.

Ryan Bauer in a tux.

With Diane right by his side.

Of course it would all come down to Ryan and Diane going to Prom. It was practically their destiny since birth.

Ryan's eyes were wide. "Did you mean everything you said?" he asked.

He'd heard everything. EVERYTHING.

Tracy walked by and gave my arm a gentle squeeze as she and Diane went downstairs.

Ryan and I stared at each other. All I wanted for the past week was to be able to come clean to him. I didn't think he wanted to hear from me. I didn't think he even wanted to be in the same hemisphere as me, let alone the same room.

Yet here he was.

Maybe all was not lost.

It was now or never.

"Yes," I replied. "Every single word. I should've said all of that to you sooner. I should've done a lot of things, Ryan."

"Listen," he said as he wiped away a stray tear from my chin. "I need you to understand that everything that happened with Todd and my dad had nothing to do with you, especially Todd. And, yeah, it wasn't fun feeling like an afterthought, but I also know how much the Club means to you. I know you were trying. I'll admit that I was being stubborn, but I was also really hurt."

"I'm so sorry."

"Stop." He gently put a finger up to my lips. "You don't have to apologize anymore. I heard everything. That must've been really hard for you. But I'm glad I finally understand what you were going through."

"Okay, I'll stop apologizing."

He took a step forward. "And you really like me more than you thought it would be possible to like another person?" His lip started to curl into that crooked smile he did when he knew he had me.

I stammered over my words.

"Because" — he was trying to not laugh — "I could take that to mean that I am the single greatest guy you've ever met."

Oh, he was really enjoying this.

"I guess you're okay 'n' stuff," I said as I grabbed one of his hands.

"Uh-huh." He put his other arm around my waist. "And you're ready to make this work? No more excuses?"

"Yes." Because it really was that simple. "Are you willing to give me a second chance? Or is this the third chance?" At this point, it was hard to tell. All I did know was that if he took me back, I'd never sabotage us again.

I had learned my lesson. A very painful lesson.

He didn't respond. Instead he leaned in and kissed me.

It was the only answer I needed.

When we pulled away, I said what I should've said to him a long time ago. "Thank you. For everything. For understanding. For being you. For being here right now. For looking ridiculously good in a tux."

He adjusted his bowtie with a raised eyebrow. "So, do you like me in a tuxedo more than you thought it was possible to like someone in a tux?"

"Oh my God." I pulled my arm away. "You're never going to forget that, are you?"

"Are you kidding me?" He laughed. "There's no way I'm going to let you live that down. I like that more than I think it's possible to like something."

I groaned. But I also couldn't fight back the smile that was creeping onto my face. He deserved to hear the truth. I *did* like him more than I thought was possible. Plus, I also deserved as much grief as he could give for what I put him through.

"Although I have a confession to make as well." He leaned down so we were only inches away from each other. "I like you more than I thought it was possible to like another person." He held out his elbow for me. "Miss Penny Lane Bloom, would you do me the honor of being your escort to Prom?"

I put my arm around his as we walked to the staircase. I was expecting to see a throng of friends and parents taking pictures, but the only person downstairs was Tracy, looking quite smug with herself.

I whispered to Ryan, "I know I shouldn't ask because it doesn't matter, but how did Diane get you to come tonight?"

"Yeah." Ryan shook his head. "That club of yours is awfully persistent."

"WHAT?"

"So," Tracy said with a troublemaking grin as we made our way downstairs, "I have a confession to make. I guess I actually *am* a romantic. Who knew?"

"You mean . . ." My mind started to race. "You knew about this?" I pointed to Ryan. "You knew he was on the other side of the door, so that's why you wanted me to pour my heart out?"

"Oh, come on," Tracy said with a sigh. "You were both being so stubborn. You needed to tell him the truth and Ryan needed to listen to you. So we came up with this plan. I personally wanted to kidnap you both and bury you in a shallow grave, but I was voted down. You know I love the Club, but what a bunch of wusses."

"I'll have to disagree with you on the wusses part, Tracy." Ryan pretended to get chills down his spine. "They kept coming up to me before school, after school, during class, at

PARC, at home. Everywhere I turned, there was a Lonely Hearts Club member telling me that I had to hear you out. It was a little freaky. Then Diane made me swear I'd come here tonight or she'd leave me alone in a soundproof room with Tracy."

"I was so ready to come after you, Bauer." Tracy glared at him, before play hitting him on the shoulder. "Just kidding." Tracy then looked at me and mouthed, *I'm not kidding.*

"Oh, God." I should've been horrified, but I was so touched that the Club went through so much . . . *stalking* to get Ryan here.

Tracy placed her hands on her hips. "I probably should've let you know what our plan was, but you sort of had a week of wallowing coming to you. Now maybe you'll not screw this up again. I don't think anybody can take any more drama between you two."

"Especially me," I replied.

Ryan pulled me in even closer. "And me."

Tracy crossed her arms. "Fair warning, Pen: You go crazy again and the Club will haul you off to the loony bin and save us all some time." She turned toward the basement door. "It's safe to come out!"

I faced Ryan as everybody — Club members, dates, and parents — started reemerging from the basement. "Ryan, I don't think I can tell you again how —"

"Please, don't," he interrupted. "Let's start everything fresh. It's a new beginning. We can do this. Clean slate. Compromises." He tilted his chin toward me. "Copious amounts of PDA."

"I think that can be arranged." I kissed him again until I heard a voice clear itself loudly next to me.

Ryan could sense me tense and pull away. "Is everything —"

"Hello, Ryan," Mom cut him off. Her arms were folded tightly. "Good to see you."

"Yes, hello." He reached out to shake my parents' hands. "Good to see you."

I pulled him over to where everybody was getting pictures taken. I hoped to save him from the Bloom Inquisition.

"Come on." Tracy wrapped her leg around Bruce playfully. "Let's get some pictures so you can show all your friends back home the sexy American girl you took to Prom. Maybe The Lonely Hearts Club won't be the only thing to go global. But do we really feel the world is ready for Tracy Larson?"

We all stayed silent, since we knew better than to answer that question truthfully.

The pictures seemed to take forever. We had to get ones with the Club members, then the couples, then every other mixture we could think of, including one where all the girls surrounded Bruce. "Gotta make some memories," Tracy teased him.

We were all grabbing our wraps and purses, about to leave, when Mom asked to speak with me.

"You look beautiful, Penny Lane," she said, brushing a stray piece of hair out of my face. "Remember that you need to be home no later than midnight. And you need to check in when you get to Diane's after-party. Call us if anybody needs a ride home. And please remind Ryan that I know where he lives."

Yeah, like I was going to risk that.

I'd always been excited about the possibility of Prom.

I'd hung out in Lucy's and Rita's rooms as they got ready for their junior and senior Proms. I'd felt the excitement when the doorbell rang and their dates had come to pick them up. I'd admired their corsages and woke up early in the morning anticipating hearing every detail.

But as high school had approached, and the realities of being a high school girl set in, I became a little prejudiced against Prom. What if I didn't get asked? What if I went with the wrong person? What if the night was a complete disaster?

Once The Lonely Hearts Club started up, I knew I wouldn't have to fret about a date. We'd all agreed we'd go together as a big group.

But as I arrived at our junior Prom with the Club, and with Ryan on my arm, I realized that this Prom was going to be better than any I'd ever imagined.

I gave Ryan a squeeze as we waited in line for our official Prom photos. I kept touching him and looking at him, not fully believing he was there with me. If I had only one goal for the night, it was to live in the present, not thinking beyond tonight or high school.

There was no way anybody could predict the future. Instead

of always assuming it was going to end in heartbreak, I had to believe in my good fortune.

The auditorium was decorated with twinkling lights and silver stars hanging from the ceiling. After we found our table, I grabbed Ryan and danced with him.

"I realize I'm a week late on my promise," I said as we swayed to the music.

"Better late than never," Ryan whispered in my ear.

I held on to him tighter, even though the music had changed to a more upbeat song. I didn't want to let go.

"Come on!" Tracy nudged me. "I know you can bust a move better than that."

Ryan and I stopped our slow dance and began dancing with our group. Everybody was in high spirits, dancing along, enjoying ourselves.

No drama. No crossed signals. No hiding my feelings.

Simply the pure joy of being around the people I cared about.

This lasted until a burst of feedback came from the microphone. "Can I have your attention, please?" Principal Braddock's voice boomed throughout the gym. "Will the Prom court make its way to the stage for crowning."

A couple of girls gave me a thumbs-up, while I took that moment to glare at Diane. Ryan had to practically drag me to the stage.

I reluctantly lined up next to Pam and Audrey. They ignored me and kept preening each other. On the other side of the stage, Ryan, Todd, Brian, and Don stood in a group talking.

The spotlight blinded me, so I fortunately didn't have to look out at the entire class, who probably thought I was a huge hypocrite.

Pam and Audrey held hands excitedly while Braddock droned on about our theme, which was the oh-so-clever "Night Under the Stars." More like "Night Under a Tight Budget."

"And now the moment you've all been waiting for," he announced with great fanfare, even though I think the only two people who'd really been waiting for it all night were Pam and Audrey.

"The McKinley High junior Prom king is . . . Brian Reed."

Pam nearly fainted because she knew what it meant to have her boyfriend chosen. Prom King: Athletic Stud. Prom Queen: Said Stud's Cheerleader Girlfriend.

I glanced over at Ryan, who gave Brian a pat on the shoulder. I'd honestly thought it was going to be Ryan.

Brian pumped his fist as the crown was placed on his forehead. Pam was shaking next to me. "I can't believe it," she said under her breath.

Braddock returned to the microphone. "And your junior Prom queen is . . ." He opened the envelope as Pam took a step forward. "Penny Lane Bloom."

You've got to be kidding me.

I looked apologetically at Pam, who glared at me with disgust. So much for being a gracious runner-up. I tried to appear comfortable as a crown was placed on my head, and bobby pins were shoved painfully in to make sure it didn't fall off. I did my best to not roll my eyes at Ryan, who seemed to be enjoying this more than anybody.

Brian held out his arm to me so we could get our official picture taken. We both smiled for the cameras, but it felt so fake. And confusing.

Brian and I went down to the dance floor while some manufactured boy band sang a cheesy ballad about "lovin' you, girl." It was a typical clichéd song for an extremely non-clichéd couple. Brian put his arms awkwardly around my hips, while I placed my hands on his shoulders.

"So . . ." he said, and I realized that in heels I was taller than him. A bead of sweat was making its way down his cheek.

"So, this is . . ." I searched for the appropriate word.

"Awkward," he finished.

I couldn't help but laugh. "Yeah. I'm sorry that Pam didn't get picked."

He glanced over to the corner and winced. "Believe me, I'll be made to feel sorry, too." He exhaled deeply. "Actually, do you think you could talk to her sometime?"

I forgot that there were hundreds of eyes, not to mention cameras, on us. I stopped cold, trying to actually understand what Brian was asking me.

"Ah, Penny." He lightly squeezed his hand on my hip, which reminded me to move with the music.

"You want me to talk to Pam?" I asked. "About how not life-changing being Prom queen is?"

He leaned in close so the other couples now dancing couldn't hear him. "She can be a bit intense. And like, everything has to be a big deal. She wants to spend all this time together, and I want to see her, but I shouldn't feel guilty about wanting to hang with my friends, too. She puts too much attention on me. It's a lot of pressure. And you and your club seem to have your heads on right."

I was nodding along with him, but it seemed that he was finished. "I'm sorry," I said, "but you want Pam to join The Lonely Hearts Club?"

Were we really getting to the point where guys wanted their girlfriends to join?

He tensed up, and I could see Pam fuming in the corner, her hand wound tightly around a damp tissue. "Uh . . . I don't know. I just think — I really love the girl, but girls can be so dramatic, you know?"

Oh, I do know.

"I'll try," I said. "But I don't really think she'd listen to me. We aren't exactly friends."

"Come on, Penny." He laughed. "There's a reason you have that crown on your head. People respect you. I mean, yeah, I didn't get the Club at first, but I'm not going to deny what it's done for my little sister."

Brian's little sister was Michelle. He often dropped her and a few other girls off for our meetings. I guess he really did support the Club.

"And," he continued even though the song had finished and Pam was looking extremely impatient, "there's a reason I'm here with you. Everybody knows how you feel about Todd, and you and Ryan were broken up during the voting. So it was between me and Don — I guess I'm considered the lesser of two evils. I should probably be flattered."

"Yeah." I nodded in a daze. Did the majority of the class really see me that way?

"Anyways, I better . . ." Brian broke away as Pam bounded toward him.

I made my way back to my table. Once I got there, everyone applauded. "Oh, I'm sorry," I said, pointing at my crown. "You see this? Why aren't you bowing? Do you not realize this means I'm far superior to you mere mortals?"

Leave it to Tracy to put a quick end to my charade. "I think you're misusing the word *superior*. I believe you mean *sub par*."

She had me there.

I wrapped my arms around Ryan. "Hey." I leaned in and gave him a kiss.

"Well, hello to you," he replied, with a huge grin. "Does your crown ward off the fear of PDA? Because if it does, then I'll do all the bowing your highness requires."

"No," I said as I pressed myself against him. "I really wish it was you who'd been dancing with me. And I just have to say again how grateful I am that you've been able to forgive me."

"I think we need to move on." He placed a gentle kiss on my lips.

"Move forward," I replied while kissing him again.

"Move . . . upward," he grasped on to another response, although he didn't need one to justify another kiss.

A paper napkin came flying over and hit us on the side of our faces. "Get a room!" Tracy yelled from the table.

"Well, it *is* Prom night," Ryan stated with raised eyebrows, then quickly corrected himself. "But I'm only joking. Your mom knows where I live."

"Oh my God, did she tell you that?" I tensed from embarrassment.

"Um, no, she didn't have to. It's not that big a town," he replied, playfully poking me in my side. "Why? Should I be worried?"

I knew I'd promised myself I wouldn't keep things from Ryan. That I was going to be open and honest with him. But I figured I could get away with this one small white lie.

"Worried about my mom?" I laughed. "Not at all."

In My Life

"I'll never lose affection for people . . .
that went before."

Thirty-two

FOUR WEEKS.

I had been able to successfully be in The Lonely Hearts Club and date Ryan Bauer for four weeks.

There were no disasters, breakdowns, fights, school suspensions, or tears.

Pretty normal really. And wonderful.

It almost made me forget why we'd broken up in the first place. Almost.

And Tracy was right (as she liked to hear me repeat ad nauseam): The Lonely Hearts Club was its own self-contained thing. If anything that had now spread to over a dozen states and five countries (and counting) could be considered self-contained.

We were busy fielding requests from the new clubs, but the pressure wasn't all on me. It was a team effort. Because the Club always worked better when we stood together, not apart.

Every now and then, though, one of us would take the spotlight.

At the school's end-of-year awards night, it was Tracy's turn.

Minutes before, she was pacing nervously in the hallway. "You sure you want me to do this?" she asked with a nervous tinge in her voice.

"Yes," Diane and I said in unison.

Tracy nodded to herself, while Diane gave her a pep talk. "It's going to be super easy; we have all of this written down. Simply go up there with Mrs. Coles and announce the scholarship recipient."

After her fab television interview, we'd appointed Diane to be our head of communications. She was a natural in front of the camera.

"We'd better go inside," I said as the last few people filed into the auditorium.

Tracy and I sat with our parents, while Diane went over with the National Honor Society to sit next to Ryan.

I glanced at the program that listed the academic, artistic, and athletic awards being presented, followed by the scholarships that were being awarded. During the ceremony, I began checking off each award, one by one, until it was our turn.

Tracy headed off to the wings as Principal Braddock started his introduction. "The next scholarship being presented tonight isn't a club that's run by the school, but in its first year has become quite popular with the girls at McKinley. Some of you may remember the successful dance-a-thon they threw last month that raised funds for the Parkview Area Recreation Center as well as the scholarship they're about to present. Here to represent The Lonely Hearts Club is junior Tracy Larson and the faculty member who advised them on the scholarship, Mrs. Coles."

Tracy approached the podium with a steely determination. She was one of the toughest people I knew; there was no way she was going to let a little public speaking get to her.

"The Lonely Hearts Club is not about the school," she began. "It's about friendship and the family that you choose. As with a lot of great things in life, it started with heartbreak. The best way to heal a heart is through love. As the Beatles once sang, 'All you need is love.' For some, that love may come from a spouse, a sibling, or a friend. For The Lonely Hearts Club, it's about having a community to help find what will heal your heart. As we say good-bye to our amazing senior members, we wanted to present one of them a scholarship to help her on the next chapter of her life." Tracy paused to look up from her script. "And it's pretty much certain that many of them will start their own clubs post-McKinley, since I highly doubt that guys mature the second they get to college."

There was scattered laughter in the room.

"We, as a group, felt it was best to have outside advisors pick this year's winner. So on behalf of Penny Lane Bloom, Diane Monroe, and the entire Lonely Hearts Club, I'd like to thank Mrs. Coles, Ms. Griffin of PARC, and Mr. Larson, aka my dad, for helping us pick the winner. So without further ado, the winner of the first annual Lonely Hearts Club scholarship is . . ."

I felt my heartbeat speed up as Mrs. Coles handed Tracy the envelope with the recipient's name. None of us knew who it was.

Tracy opened up the envelope and hesitated for a second. Then she smiled. "This is awesome," she said. "Okay, so the advisory committee said that it was a wonderful group of girls, *obvs*, so there are two recipients. The first winner is Laura Jaworski, who will be attending Syracuse University this fall, majoring in political science. And the other winner is Margaret Ross, who will be attending Loyola of Chicago, majoring in English."

I'd never been so grateful that we had a group of grown-ups involved. Why do one scholarship if we could do two? Both Laura and Meg were certainly worthy. My mind was already racing with what we could do next year, but then I took a deep breath.

There was plenty of time to work on next year. It would be something we could do together as a group. It wasn't all on me.

It appeared that you *could* teach a stubborn girl new tricks.

The Lonely Hearts Club wasn't solely a group of fantastically fun girls. We were also wicked smart.

All six senior members received some kind of award or scholarship that evening, and that was in addition to eight members being inducted into the National Honor Society. Personality and smarts? Oh, how the boys were missing out on the majority of us *choosing* to remain single.

"Congratulations!" Morgan ran up and kissed Tyson, who'd been awarded a music boosters scholarship to help with his Juilliard tuition.

We were all gathered for a special little end-of-year celebration after the award ceremony at PARC. They wanted to
show us where all the funds were going. We got to tour the
new jungle gym, see the new instruments in the music room
(they even put a *Sgt. Pepper's Lonely Hearts Club Band* poster up
in honor of us), and the new developmental toys for the
younger kids.

Tracy placed her hand on my shoulder. "We done good,
Pen. We done good."

"We certainly have," I agreed. It was nice to see how much
had come together with all our hard work.

Ryan approached us with punch in both hands. "Ladies."

Tracy took a cup and nodded in approval. "I never realized
that having a guy around could be a good thing. He can fetch
us stuff. Hey, Bauer, those cream puffs aren't magically going
to appear in my belly." She tapped her foot impatiently.

Ryan gave a playful sigh before heading off to do Tracy's
bidding.

"You know," she said, "I've had years training little brats, so
I don't think I'll have any problems whenever I get a boyfriend. That lucky, lucky bastard."

Any guy *would* be lucky to have Tracy as a girlfriend.
They'd only need to have the patience of a saint. Or a martyr.

Diane came over and clapped her hands at us. "We've got
some pictures to take for the website and an e-mail blast I'm
going to send out to local media. Come on!" She began usher-
ing all of us into the main lobby.

"You've created a monster," Tracy teased. "Diane Monroe, publicist." She pretended to shudder.

"I look at it more as *Diane Monroe, girl in charge and loving it*," I said as Diane gleefully began directing everybody where to stand.

Ryan came over with a plate full of food. "Miss Larson," he said with an exaggerated bow.

Tracy nodded. "Yep." She took a bite of food. "This is going to work out juuuuust fine."

Yes, I thought. *Yes, it is.*

"Thanks," I said as I planted a quick kiss on his lips. For the first time, Ryan's back stiffened at my touch. I became worried that something was wrong, although that was how I'd reacted to him in public for so much at the beginning of our relationship. But he'd always been more open than I was.

Fortunately, Ryan didn't make me fret too much. He quickly shook his head when he saw my worried face. "Sorry, but your mom's right over there." He tilted his head over to the side of the room where my parents were congratulating Meg.

I took a small step back. "Good point. Well, we have the whole summer to hang out."

"Really?" Ryan's eyes lit up. "Are you actually committing to seeing me beyond this evening?"

I wanted to tease him, to tell him it all depended on my mood. But Ryan deserved the truth. "Yes, I am. And I think that since our lockers are near each other, it would only be convenient for us to stay together next year."

"Of course," he said, nodding slowly, "we really need to start thinking about the people in the lockers next to us. How much more drama can they really take?"

"I like drama," Tracy said with her mouth full. "It makes life more interesting."

"Well, then." I extended my arm out to Tracy like I was handing her something. "The torch is all yours. I plan on being boring and predictable for the remainder of my high school existence."

"You could never be boring," Ryan said.

"I second that." Tracy held her fist out for Ryan to bump it, which he gladly did.

"I don't know how much I like having you two gang up on me," I confessed. Of course, having your best friend and boyfriend get along could be a good thing. I knew that if Tracy took Ryan's side, I'd never get away with anything ever again.

"Well, get used to it." Tracy put her arm around me. "Bauer here is good for you. And for me." She handed him her empty glass. "You know what to do."

Ryan grimaced before going off again to be Tracy's errand boy.

Tracy leaned into my ear. "You know I'm only teasing him, but I give him mad props for putting up with me."

"Mad props?"

She threw her arms into the air dramatically. "I'm being real, okaaaay!"

Diane came over to us right as I was about to respond to Tracy. "Penny, please don't roll your eyes during the photos. I don't think you realize how much you do it and it's so unbecoming." She ushered me into the center with the director of PARC. We took a bunch of photos, and all the flashes reminded me of my birthday, Valentine's Day, Lucy's wedding, and Prom. This year already had so many memories I wanted to last . . . and it was only May.

After the photos were over, Diane had everybody stay where they were. There was one more speech that needed to be given that evening. While Tracy had done the honors at the awards ceremony, it was my turn now.

"I wanted to quickly say a few things," I began as I looked out at the many faces that had meant so much to me over the past school year. "Next week, McKinley High will be losing six of the finest females they've ever had. But I don't see The Lonely Hearts Club as ever losing Erin Fitzgerald, Laura Jaworski, Marisa Klein, Teresa Finer, Maria Gonzales, and Meg Ross." I looked over to see the six of them holding hands. "You will always be welcomed whenever you need us.

"And next year we'll have new members, and more of us will leave. Including me. But The Lonely Hearts Club will live on because we've made it a strong club, together." I felt my throat waver and turned to nod to Tyson, who came forward with his acoustic guitar in hand.

"Don't worry, I won't be singing," I alerted the crowd, to some laughter. "But when I think about what I wanted to say, it shouldn't come as a surprise that four lads from Liverpool said it best." I heard Mom sniffle in the corner, pretty sure she was only moved because of the Beatles reference. "I'm only seventeen years old, but it's amazing how many people have already come in and out of my life. And even though there are some new ones" — I looked over at the freshmen and sophomores of the group — "it doesn't mean you care any less for the people who have been in your life a long time." I nodded toward Tracy and Diane. "Because at the end of the day, I truly, deeply am appreciative for every single person in this room. And despite rumors about me, that includes you guys as well." I winked at Ryan.

"So this is my way to tell you everything that I'm feeling." I motioned for Tyson to begin. He started playing the opening notes of "In My Life."

As he began singing about places he's remembered, I reflected on everything that had happened. I knew that I didn't have everything figured out. But who ever did?

What I did know was that relationships, like life, are all about balance. And that the heart really is the strongest muscle. It would heal. All it would take was time and some awesome friends by your side.

Because in the end, all you really need is a support group of people who love you for you. People who will be in your corner no matter what. I knew that with The Lonely Hearts Club beside me, I'd always be able to work out any problems that would come my way.

And having a guy like Ryan? Well, that was icing on an already delicious cake.

I mean, really, what more could I have asked for?

I couldn't help but feel extremely fortunate to be in this place, and in this moment, with the people who mattered the most to me: the best group of friends, a supportive (and let's not forget hot) boyfriend, and even, yes, a great family (even with their crazy Beatles antics).

I intended for it to stay that way for a very long time.

Because in my life, I really did love them all.

The End

"The love you take is equal to the love you make."

With Love from Me to . . .

This sequel has been a dream of mine since I finished writing *The Lonely Hearts Club*. There are so many people who've helped turn that dream into reality. So, All Together Now:

Do You Want to Know a Secret? David Levithan is an awesome editor. Although, that's not really a secret. Thank you for being on this crazy ride with me through six books (say *wha?*). I appreciate your patience and wisdom so much that I *beam* (and occasionally *roll my eyes*). Oh, and I'm Happy Just to Dance (and karaoke) with You.

I get by With a Little Help from My Friends at Scholastic (okay, I DEPEND on A LOT of help): Erin Black, Sheila Marie Everett, Elizabeth Parisi, Kelly Ashton, Tracy van Straaten, Bess Braswell, Emily Morrow, Alan Smagler, Leslie Garych, Lizette Serrano, Emily Heddleson, Antonio Gonzalez, Joy Simpkins, Elizabeth Starr Baer, Sue Flynn, Roz Hilden, Nikki Mutch, and all the Scholastic sales reps.

Rosemary Stimola's persistence made this sequel possible. Thank You, Girl.

All My Loving to my family, who sadly are NOT crazy Beatles fanatics, but I appreciate them all the same.

There are so many people in my life who've Come Together to help with this book and my writing life: Kirk Benshoff, who takes such good care of my website; Natalie Thrasher, who read a rough draft and provided me with fabulous feedback; and, Markus Zusak, who answered my Aussie slang questions. You're *ace*! Oh, wait, no, er, *bottler*!

I'm so lucky to have such wonderful Paperback Writer friends I can go to when I need Help! Special thanks to Jen Calonita, Sarah Mlynowski, and Jennifer E. Smith, who helped me when all I wanted to do was Cry Baby Cry.

It blows my mind how much *The Lonely Hearts Club* has spread Across the Universe. Thanks so much to my foreign publishers around the world, especially Alfaguara.

And, of course, none of this would've been possible without John, Paul, George, and Ringo. P.S. I Love You.

Elizabeth Eulberg wishes that she would've thought of The Lonely Hearts Club when she was just seventeen (you know what we mean). Instead, she had to rely on her love of music to help her get through stupid boy shenanigans. She still has to listen to a lot of music. She also gets her strength (some would call it revenge) by writing books — many books (*The Lonely Hearts Club, Prom & Prejudice, Take a Bow, Revenge of the Girl with the Great Personality,* and *Better Off Friends*). You can find Elizabeth at Sir Paul and Ringo concerts, as well as online at www.elizabetheulberg.com and @ElizEulberg on Twitter.